D1373621

ALL THE BLUES COME THROUGH

HEIR TO A MYTH
Book One

ALL
THE
BLUES
COME
THROUGH

METRA FARRARI

ISBN 13: 978-1-63489-427-2

Library of Congress Catalog Number has been applied for.
Printed in the United States of America
First Printing: 2021

25 24 23 22 21   5 4 3 2 1

Cover design by Holly Ovenden
Interior design by Patrick Maloney

Wise Ink Creative Publishing
807 Broadway St NE
Suite 46
Minneapolis, MN, 55413

To the Love Dove

AS SHE MOSEYED TO WORK along the well-worn path, Ryan checked that her mask was secure over her nose; the perfume of the honeysuckles wafted over her like a fragrant rain, and she was afraid the CO_2 was making its way in too. But the mask snugly hugged the bottom half of her face, so tight that Ryan's cheeks would bear flattering indentations when she arrived at the laboratory.

As she wove around some gangly, orange fir trees, the nondescript white building came into view, overpowered by the crown jewels glittering behind it in the early morning sunlight: the greenhouses. *Her* greenhouses. A miraculous oasis set amidst a sea of man-made pollution, the atmosphere so toxic lungs were at risk of disintegration.

As the foliage around her transitioned from barren to vibrant, Ryan removed her sunglasses and earbuds so she could focus the rest of the way to work. She admired a family of foxes prancing over some fallen tree branches, carefully skirted around a porcupine investigating an interesting scent, and abruptly stopped to let a moose cross in front of her. Even months after first navigating through this unforeseen animal sanctuary, a scene that could very well have been ripped from *The Lion King*, Ryan couldn't believe all these animals congregated relatively peacefully, all in the name of clean air. Well, there was the mauled, headless bunny that had left her screaming all the way home, but the animals didn't need the news to tell them the atmosphere was harmful; they instinctively sought cleaner air themselves, albeit in a very tight radius around her workplace.

As the sun grew brighter, cutting through the dense smog, she was tempted to take off her mask and inhale a deep breath of clean air, now filtered through the forcefield of her miracle plants. But with governmental protocols in place, Ryan wanted to set a good example for her staff and, most importantly, Greta.

A squawk up ahead drew her attention. *For the love of Dunkin' Donuts*, she thought, *they're back.* A flock of Canada geese had conveniently congregated around the entrance to her lab. The aggressive, black-and-white-headed, winged devils seemed to have a special vendetta against Ryan, despite her being the reason their dumb goose lungs were clear.

She stomped her foot in annoyance as she surveyed the obstacle ahead. *Don't they know today could be the day?* A rush of anticipation flowed through her veins, filling her body with confidence.

"Shoo! I need to get through," she said, flapping her arms at the geese, who turned their heads loftily, as though they'd been expecting her. "This is a matter of public safety. Git!" Again, the geese eyed her intently, their garden-hose necks bobbing threateningly. Ryan did the only thing she could think of: head held high, shoulders back, with the regal air of a kickass female scientist single-handedly saving the world, she ran shrieking into the building, swiping her ID card like a ninja.

As she slipped through the door, thankfully goose free, she ripped off her mask to welcome a rush of crisp, wonderfully fresh air. Smiling, adrenaline propelling her feet directly to her office, she passed the normal hustle and bustle of people, a merry-go-round of names and faces in this twenty-four-seven operation. As she passed by, they greeted her with *hello*s and *good morning*s, but each person carefully avoided eye contact. Ryan's confidence waned. The tightness around their mouths confirmed the news she was dreading.

She set her things down in a jumble on her desk and burst into the control lab, rushing to the pots. Nothing. All ten of them, meticulously planted by a machine that mimicked the exact process that Ryan followed when planting her seeds, were barren. There should have been sprouts by this time.

Shoulders slumped, she heard the telltale signs of Greta shimmying over. A hand gently squeezed her shoulders, followed by a comforting, "I know."

"I got my hopes up again," Ryan said dejectedly. She rubbed her eyes, wariness filling her bones. The last two minutes' dramatic plummet from high anticipation to low hopelessness made her want to face the geese devils again so that she could crawl back into bed.

"Yeah. Hard not to. But we'll figure it out. Now, I made your coffee just the way you like it. Extra strong with almond milk. No rumbly tummies or accidental toots for this important scientist boss lady." Greta guided Ryan to her desk outside the lab doors, where a steaming cup of coffee beckoned her.

Wiggling her fingers over the touchpad to wake up her laptop, Ryan took a sip of coffee. Surreptitiously peeking through the windows behind her desk, she confirmed: there were still no buds. She twirled her chair back to the front, where Greta was fiddling with her *Golden Girls* calendar. "What time did you get here?"

"Oh, about an hour ago," Greta replied, scooting herself up to sit between the David Bowie figurine and the lava lamp on Ryan's desk. Even at seventy-two, Greta moved more gracefully than Ryan, who often tripped like a teenage boy who hadn't grown into his feet.

"You should have woken me up," Ryan grumbled.

"You were in the deepest sleep when I peeked in, a river of drool puddling on your pillow like the mighty Mississippi," Greta said with a sparkle in her eye. Ryan absently wiped her mouth. "Besides, you need your rest, Ryan. You're wearing yourself ragged! And we need to make sure those magical, invaluable green thumbs don't get worn raw." She slid a gossip magazine out from under a pile of files. "Did you know Taylor Swift insures her legs? I should look into insuring your thumbs . . ."

Ryan smiled at her landlord turned office manager. A fateful trip to the Shop 'n Save during the botanist's first week of residency in Grayville had set their trajectory of friendship in motion. Ryan had asked one of the grocery clerks where the wasabi was located. The unmistakably local boy had scratched his head, asked her to repeat the item's name, and then skulked over to his manager. He spoke just loudly enough for Ryan to hear him say, "Dat woman over dair is lookin' fer wersabbey."

Blood had rushed to Ryan's face as she heard a fellow customer's voice boom, "Oh, for God's sake, Toby, she asked for wuh-sah-bi. It's Japanese horseradish, which you do not carry, but if you're going to take over this grocery store from your father, I suggest you invest in carrying something other than nine types of white bread and an array of bologna so we're not forever stuck in the 1960s."

The older woman had then turned her attention to the scrawny, awkward stranger in front of her. "I'm sorry, hun, but the most Asian product you'll find in this store is microwavable white rice. I ordered some wasabi online for myself when I was on my sushi-making kick." She puffed out her chest, a grave expression on her face, and said, "I'll admit, I didn't quite know the strength of wasabi until it was too late, and I was crying my eyes out. But now I immensely enjoy the stuff . . . in moderation."

Her shock sliding into amusement at this grocery-shopping hurricane of a woman, Ryan had quietly replied, "I had a similar experience with its potency when I forgot to wash my hands before using the restroom." Greta had looked at her for a few seconds with a deadpan expression before breaking into a howl of laughter.

They'd soon discovered that Greta had a room for rent, and Ryan needed housing before starting her new job at the laboratory down the street. The grocery-shopping meet-cute had led to a bargain, and Greta and Ryan had been roommates and coworkers ever since. Despite the nearly fifty-year age difference, the older woman had become Ryan's closest friend (that didn't require photosynthesis).

Ryan pulled her long, brown hair into a knot on the top of her head, took one more slug of coffee, and said, "Shall we?"

Greta had attempted to tie her own topknot, which resembled a silver bee's nest atop her head. "Looking freaky fresh. Let's start our day."

As they walked by Greta's desk, adorned with pictures of Chadwick Boseman and Keanu Reeves, Ryan asked, "Did you wear your mask in?"

"You betcha," Greta replied.

"Where is it?" It was hard to miss Greta's mask, bedazzled with knockoff Swarovski crystals.

Greta bristled. "You step outside our doorstep and it's a haven of clean air."

"Greta, it's the rule. The path between our house and the lab could still have pockets of CO_2. The flowers only project a twenty-foot radius of clean air. Yes, the wind can waft it here and there, but you could be exposed."

"I'm healthy as a horse," Greta responded, doing a little one-person tango in celebration.

"The cancer could come back. I just don't want to lose you."

Mid-dip, Greta stopped and took Ryan's hand. "OK, my love."

Only a couple of months into their cohabitation, Greta had dropped a bomb: she'd been diagnosed with an aggressive form of cancer that had spread. Ryan had been defiant against the thought that her new friend could be ripped from her life like so many before. In the same vein, Greta, ever the fighter, had been doing experimental treatments to delay the inevitable. She had time, she'd been told, but not much. In the face of the bleak diagnosis, Ryan and Greta had spent most of their time together, Ryan religiously driving her to treatments.

A year ago, to the utter astonishment of her doctors, Greta had received the news that the cancer was inexplicably receding; the tumors were recoiling like a snake from her organs and lymph nodes. There was no explanation; the doctors had deemed the experimental therapy a failure after all the other patients had perished. All except Greta. Ryan had been flabbergasted, demanding answers from doctors who hadn't had any besides an incredible stroke of luck. Greta, however, had taken it in stride, as though she'd made a deal with Death himself.

They got to the largest of the four greenhouses, where there were rows upon rows of flowers in different stages of growth. A few employees gently watered the newly emerged baby sprouts, while another couple gingerly pruned deep green leaves off older ones a few rows over. At the far corner, the mature sapphire-blue blossoms regally stretched to three feet, watching over their floral kingdom.

When Ryan had accidentally created this species of the *Campanulaceae saphiria*, or Weeping Dianas, as the team informally called them, she hadn't expected the flower to blossom so beautifully. Depending on the angle, the bloom looked as though it were inexplicably hand sculpted from glass like a Tiffany lamp or expertly swathed in velvet by the hands of an award-winning costume designer. Minuscule hairs of brilliant sapphire blue, reminiscent of Princess Diana's striking engagement ring, coated each petal as though it were a living, breathing animal rather than a flower. The petals cascaded like gowns twirling in a royal court, revealing three tendril-like stamens, where the anther was a perfect little pearl. The whole flower wept, bowing its beautiful head from its deep-jade, almost-black stem.

"OK, what do I need to know about today? What's on the agenda?" Ryan asked, belatedly feeling the effects of a joyful surge of caffeine running through her veins.

"We've got an aggressive four hundred and twenty orders to fulfill. The truck drivers will be in and out all morning, so we'll have some peace and quiet this afternoon. Another five hundred buds are being prepped to go out tomorrow." Greta looked down at her tablet. "You'll need to plant . . . er, try for four hundred new pots today."

"Greta, how many do we really need? To keep up with orders?"

"It's unrealistic, Ryan," Greta said gently.

"How many? Governments, royalty, schools, normal folks are all waiting for these plants," Ryan said with urgency.

"We'd need you to plant one thousand to stay on track . . ."

Nodding, Ryan felt the color pale from her face as she did the math. She would have to work through lunch and dinner, but if she put on some good jams and maybe an audiobook, she could crank it out. *Don't forget the pee breaks*, she heard her bladder bellow from below.

Cracking her knuckles in anxiety, she said, "OK, please call Yale and let them know the machine didn't work to reproduce the Weeping Dianas. Another five million of funding down the drain.

Another avenue to get these flowers into the hands of millions at a time failed. And more fodder for the Weepy Willow people to use."

"Haters gonna hate, Ryan," Greta murmured, shaking her head.

What should have been Ryan's crowning achievement and lasting impact on the botany community, and the world in general, had become a giant thorn in her career path. She had originally set out to create a flower that nourished the dwindling butterfly population, but through hybridization and isolation breeding, she'd created a new species that absorbed CO_2 from the atmosphere. Where it took a forest of trees to absorb a ton of CO_2, a single flower of the Weeping Diana did the same. If every family on earth had access to one of the Weeping Dianas, Ryan's flowers could absorb more than two million tons of CO_2 a year. Scientists projected that people would no longer need to wear masks—asthma rates would go down and climate change–related mortality would drop drastically, for both humans and animals.

There was no doubt her flowers were effective; the doubt was how this was achieved, as no other botanist or scientist had been able to replicate her results. Maddeningly, Ryan was the only one who could get these plants to grow. She'd spent a year painstakingly recording the method that had repeatedly worked for her and enlisted scientists to work side by side with her. She'd watched them cross-pollinate, ensured their methods were identical; but still, hers grew and theirs didn't.

It had all come to a head a couple months ago, when a national news program invited Ryan for a live interview about her enormous scientific breakthrough. She'd been thrilled; not only would her miracle flowers get more publicity, but she hoped young girls and boys would be inspired by a female scientist set on saving the world. And just maybe someone watching would be the key in helping to explain why she could grow these plants when others had failed.

Ryan's interview did receive enormous publicity, but for all the wrong reasons. Instead of asking about her journey to creating the Weeping Diana, the reporter had subjected Ryan to a verbal assault, questioning her ethics, grilling her on whether she was hoarding the secrets to manufacture the flower for herself, insinuating she was pulling this stunt solely for monetary benefit.

Shocked by the direction the interview took, Ryan had helplessly denied and refuted these allegations, eventually breaking down into an ugly cry before the reporter was satisfied. Predictably, Ryan became Weepy Willow, an internet meme and a digital villain during what should have been her fifteen minutes of fame.

Despite licking her wounds in isolation, only getting out of the house to go to work, Ryan's drive remained intact. Head down from both embarrassment and determination, she diligently continued to spend each day obsessing over why the plants grew for her, working toward finding out how to share her green thumb.

"OK, and who do we have shadowing me today?" she asked as they made their way back to their desks.

Greta perked up. Taking a good look at her, Ryan asked, "Are you wearing *lipstick*?"

"Wait until you see him, Ryan. That is one son-of-a-sexy-botanist," Greta stage-whispered.

"Doesn't even make sense . . ." Ryan muttered, rolling her eyes.

"His name is Cyrus. He's a hunk and a half! He's from MIT. Doctoral program. His eyes, Ryan. Windex blue. You two . . . I see it happening," Greta babbled, nodding furiously.

Ryan blushed in spite of herself. "This is business, Greta. Trying to save the world here. No time for . . . that." She lazily flicked her hand as though swatting a fly.

"There is *always* time for . . . that," Greta retorted, wiggling her penciled-in brows up and down.

Ryan gave her an inquisitive look. "Did you have an Irish coffee this morning?"

"'Course not," Greta said loftily, walking back to her desk. And quietly added, "Just a nip of Baileys. Nothing to get your granny panties in a bunch over."

CYRUS WAS WAITING FOR HER in the break room. Greta was right; he was irrationally attractive, especially considering most of the folks in their small town of Grayville were unmistakably forgettable. The fluorescent tube lights, which made everyone else look ashen and drab, managed to beautifully reflect off his dark, onyx hair and warm, brown skin. His startling blue eyes locked on hers while his juicy, supple lips moved hypnotically . . . wait, why were they moving?

He's talking to you, you idiot.

"I'm sorry, what did you say?" Ryan asked sheepishly, her eyes hungrily scanning his right hand for signs of a commitment. It was ringless. *Yes!*

Cyrus stood up and stepped toward her, a paper cup of coffee sloshing haphazardly in his hands as he repeated, a little slower, "You're Miss Bell?"

"Yup, that's me!" Ryan reddened, her voice coming out an octave higher than normal. She was suddenly very aware of the moisture under her armpits. As she furiously thought back to whether she had swiped on some deodorant that morning, she continued, "Please, call me Ryan," extending a slightly shaking hand.

Clumsily switching the mug to his other hand, splashing coffee in the process, Cyrus hastily wiped his shirt and extended his damp hand to return the handshake. As she watched their hands clasp, Ryan silently reprimanded herself for peeling off half her gel manicure last night, anxiously watching an episode of *Dateline*.

When she motioned for him to sit back down, he nearly missed his chair. She was encouraged by his clumsiness; attractive guys of this magnitude usually measured in on the cocky end of the personality spectrum. But he was a scientist, so it was entirely possible that he simply didn't notice he was a babe.

"Thrilled to be your shadow for the day," Cyrus told her.

"Me too!" Ryan replied. "I mean, I'm not shadowing you shadowing me . . . well, you know what I mean."

There was an awkward silence as the two shared a sheepish grin.

"Let me show you the lab." They both got up, and Ryan pretended not to see him miss the garbage can after shooting his coffee cup like a basketball. After quickly picking it up and dunking it in, he caught up with her.

"Your work is truly fascinating. I've been following it since the first scientific journal covered it."

"Thank you. It's been a whirlwind. It's crazy how we've only been in production six months; every day feels like an eternity."

"Insane," he jovially agreed.

"Let's get suited up and into the lab." They put on protective scrubs, facemasks, and hairnets. Ryan realized too late that she probably looked like a conehead with the hair net over her topknot; she surreptitiously patted it down.

"I've never gotten suited up to plant flowers before. It's like we're going into surgery. Scalpel," Cyrus said, his hand outstretched.

Giggling, Ryan pretended to hand him a tool. "We do this to rule out cross-contamination. I'm willing to take all sorts of precautions when being shadowed, to give us the highest possible chance to get this right."

He saluted her. She bowed back to him, inwardly cringing as she led them into the laboratory, where there was a long table with several microscopes, vials, machines, and pieces of equipment.

"I'm assuming you read through the four-hundred-page instruction booklet that was sent ahead of time?"

Cyrus nodded in response.

"Great. So you'll just copy the exact movements and measurements I make."

She started the process, talking him through mixing the seed specimen and planting the first couple pots. His movements were disjointed, his arms moving mechanically; it quickly became clear that he wasn't overly familiar with the equipment like the other visiting botanists. After he accidentally elbowed a seed slide off the table, Ryan decided she needed to slow down, not only demonstrating her method but also showing him how to actually use the instruments.

This guy was either super nervous, so much so that he'd left all his knowhow outside with the Canada geese, or he was super unqualified to be here. Trying to be casual, she asked, "So what sort of position do you have at MIT? Any exciting, cutting-edge research?"

"Oh, well, I'm working through my PhD currently. I work as a research assistant in a lab," he responded.

She frowned as she went to adjust the microscope. *Vague.* The scientists she'd worked with previously absolutely loved bragging about their research ad nauseam.

"I know, you're probably used to working with scientists . . . of a more distinguished nature," he continued, as though sensing her hesitation.

"I will work with anyone to try to figure out this puzzle," she responded kindly.

"OK, good. I know I'm woefully inexperienced. My, er, boss wasn't super excited to send me here," he admitted.

She nodded. "Let me guess: your boss believes I'm sabotaging everyone so that I remain the sole producer of this flower?"

"Something like that."

With a rueful sigh, Ryan said, "I'll prove them all wrong someday." She took a big, calming breath. "OK, now that the seeds are prepped, we plant them. So *carefully*," she emphasized, having witnessed his lack of care already, "take the tweezers and gently lay it into the soil. Great. Now, a small trough of dirt to top it. Lastly, three squirts of this water bottle. Yes. And, presto! Two pots done." *Only nine hundred ninety-eight to go*, she thought numbly.

"That's it?" Cyrus asked, a deep frown on his chiseled face.

"Yep." She sensed his skepticism. "I know, it's crazy that it's a relatively simple process, yet I highly doubt yours will grow, unfortunately. Not a reflection on your lack of ability," she added quickly.

"Can I watch you do a few more?" he asked.

"Absolutely," she said, grateful that she could go at her normal, supersonic pace. She easily potted ten more in a matter of a couple minutes.

"That's literally all you do," he confirmed, dumbfounded.

"Yes. In seven to ten days, little sprouts will peek their beautiful heads out of the soil. In eight weeks, the heads will bud; in sixty to seventy days, they'll bloom and be ready to be sent to their new homes," she said, chest puffed out like a proud mama bear.

"Wow, seven days?" he said incredulously. "You wait a week for them to just get out of the soil and then eight weeks for them to be plants?"

"Yeah," she said, frowning. "It's pretty typical for a flower of this variety. Roughly the same timetable as a cornflower or nigella."

He nodded, still frowning. "Do you handle the flowers after planting them?"

"Not anymore. The employees handle their care after the seeding is done. It's the only part that I have to do on my own," she replied, deftly scratching her nose without leaving behind a smudge of dirt, the mark of a great botanist.

"Do you do any sort of, say, good-luck ritual or have some sort of lucky charm that you work with?"

She laughed at the absurdity of the question. "No, I'm not superstitious. I literally just do what I showed you." She shrugged. "It's science."

"Hmm," he said, studying her with intense curiosity.

Her cheeks burned red under his scrutiny. "Any other questions? We should keep going. Or else the boss lady will crack down on us."

"Aren't you the boss lady?"

"You'd think so . . ." she replied, her embarrassment breaking into a smile.

After he got the rhythm of it, they worked in silence. She was a little peeved that he wasn't doing his pots as tidily as she'd showed him, but she knew that they'd just try replanting the barren pots in two weeks with another visiting scientist when the plants didn't grow.

Suddenly, "Lady in Red" crooned over the speakers. Ryan looked behind her at the window out of the lab, where Greta was holding onto her phone.

Face strained, Ryan said loudly through the glass, "Um, Greta, something more upbeat, please?"

Greta looked down at her phone; a moment later, her face lit up as Whitney Houston's "I Will Always Love You" burst through the Bluetooth speakers.

Through her protective eyewear, Ryan widened her eyes

menacingly, mouthing silent threats. Cheeks just as flushed as Ryan's, Cyrus chuckled, then chivalrously bent over a flowerpot so as not to witness the argument play out between the two women.

Greta scrolled through her phone some more, then exaggeratedly mouthed, "My fav-or-ite" as Snoop Dogg played. She proceeded to perform a PG-13-rated dance behind the glass partition. As Ryan made a lunge to the door, the older woman hastily mimed, "OK, OK," and finally put on some Fleetwood Mac.

"Sorry," Ryan muttered, pulse easing as Stevie Nicks's melancholic crooning settled into the room. "Sometimes I think too much oxygen gets to her brain and she gets . . . frisky."

"Is she your grandma?" Cyrus asked.

"Ooh," Ryan cringed, whipping her head back to the door. "Don't let her hear you say that. She's convinced she's not old enough to be a grandma. But no, no relation."

"Because you're an orphan with no ties to your real family?"

Ryan's eyebrows nearly shot off her forehead. "Wow. Thanks for putting that so delicately."

A sheepish expression instantly formed on his face. "Sorry, that was crass."

"Greta and I aren't related by blood, but it doesn't matter—she's my family," replied Ryan a bit frostily. "Many relatives rolled into one."

"You really don't think that bloodlines matter? I'd have thought since your adoptive family turned out to be such a disaster, you'd be curious where you really came from," Cyrus said, watching her intently. "Have you ever searched for your real parents? Your biological link to this world?"

Ahhh, so he's been doing his research, Ryan thought. She studied him dubiously, wondering about his lack of social graces. The most likely explanation was that he was either a socially awkward academic or another goon who didn't particularly care who he offended. But the way he was watching her . . . it was as though he were *hoping* to get a reaction out of her.

"Again, that's a little harsh to say to someone who is . . . how did you so eloquently put it? 'An orphan with no family ties'?" she shot back at him. "I didn't exactly have a choice in the matter of which family I got—biological or adopted."

Seeing her deep scowl, he raised his hands in defeat. "I'm sorry. I'm not good at socializing with a—" He stopped himself. "You've just piqued my interest, is all. And we're very different, you and me. You probably think I'm an ignorant iris."

Her eyebrows rose an inch from their deep frown, and she gave him a begrudging pity snort. "More like a clueless calla lily."

He laughed. While she was still trying to figure out this guy in front of her, she appreciated that he could keep up with her when it came to a sense of humor.

"So do you have any idea where you're from?"

Looking at him, Ryan realized that as much as this guy wanted to delve into her personal life, she knew nothing about him. "Jeez, I feel like before we get into my familial ties, we should discuss lighter topics, like women's rights or gun control."

She could tell from his split-second freeze that this was not what Cyrus wanted to hear, but just as quickly, he gave her an easygoing grin and replied lightly, "I'd like that. Maybe I could take you out sometime. Over a hibiscus iced tea."

Ryan beamed—despite her disquiet at his prying, Cyrus's smile overpowered her hesitations. "Sounds good." She ducked her head, blushing fiercely into a pot of soil.

After a few more hours of small talk and seeding, Ryan used her elbow to turn the lab's television to the news channel and pushed mute.

"Do you mind? I like to turn on the news in the morning to make sure I'm up to date on what's going on. Did you see what happened yesterday? With the earthquake in Iceland? There's not even a fault line there! All those thousands of people . . . gone."

"Yeah," Cyrus said, head bent down.

"And last night, I saw that temperatures inexplicably dropped below freezing in India. They say it's going to kill their crops and cause a famine."

"Tragic," he replied, sounding bored.

Ryan frowned at him. He looked up. "Sorry! It's really sad," he said, his voice not conveying any sort of empathy.

Frown deepening, she told him, "These flowers won't cure that madness happening, but they have the potential to make a huge impact."

"Why do you want to save the world?"

What a very strange question. "Why wouldn't you want to save the world? If you had the power to?"

"Well, humans got themselves into this mess, with no fleeting thought about the effect industrialization would have on the environment, and they've been continuing to kill the earth for the past two hundred years. And now suddenly, everyone is all up in arms about saving the world?" He shook his head. "It's too late for humans."

"Says the man who's helping me plant the earth-saving flowers . . ."

"Whose doofus boss made him come . . ." He smirked at her.

Ryan rolled her eyes, unimpressed.

Cyrus's face grew serious, his eyes piercing into hers. "But, boy, am I extremely grateful she sent me . . ."

Ryan fidgeted with her hairnet in response. Then, clapping her hands together and sending a plume of soil into the air, she said, "OK, let's get you some lunch and then we'll keep at it this afternoon. I'm going to go at my normal speed—I need to whip out about seven hundred more of these bad boys before I can go home."

As they moved to exit the lab, Ryan pushed at the door only to find it stuck. Hastily, Greta popped up from behind the door, opening it for them to walk through.

"Dropped my pen. Cyrus, lunch is waiting in the breakroom. I'll join you shortly!" Greta said, smoothing her ruffled shirt.

When Cyrus was out of earshot, Ryan hissed, "Greta, I know full well you were listening to every single word behind the lab door."

Greta whipped around, all four feet eleven inches of her, and feigned surprise, then dismay. "Why, I never! I'm busting my hump here to make sure your lab stays afloat, and you have the gall to insinuate I was ear hustling?"

Ryan sighed. She didn't want to reward Greta's behavior, but of all people, she was the one the botanist wanted to squeal to and dish with. "On a scale of one to Matthew McConaughey, what'd you rate him?"

Smiling broadly, Greta strolled toward the breakroom. "Uff da! He was off the charts."

I T WAS CLOSE TO 8:00 p.m. by the time Ryan and Greta stumbled home, Greta wearing the mask Ryan had insisted she borrow. They were both giddily discussing Cyrus.

"He definitely has some quirks . . ."

"Such as?"

"He just seemed to move a little . . . robotically? Like he wasn't used to his body? And I know he wasn't the pick of the litter as far as coming out here to try to replicate, but he really, really didn't know his way around the lab. I mean, even you . . ." Ryan recognized the gravity of her misstep before she could stop her dumb mouth from going on.

Nostrils flaring, Greta pointed her finger at Ryan. "You know that I could give any one of those Harvard or MIT or TLC botanists a run for their money. I know the process and the science like the back of my hand." She looked at her hands in disgust. "Now if only I had the magic green thumbs," she grumbled.

"I'm sorry, G. I didn't mean to downplay the sacrifice and hard work you've put in through all this," Ryan said, wrapping her arm around Greta's petite frame.

Slowly, Greta's quaint little cottage came into view. Ryan loved their house. It was located on the outskirts of town, away from the prying eyes of the townies, and came with a fair amount of acreage in the backyard, giving them a pleasing sense of isolation. Green arms of ivy enveloped the exterior in a possessive hug, pleasantly hiding the crumbling brick façade that desperately needed a mason's adept attention. The roof sagged a little but didn't leak, the walls weren't fully wind resistant but had stayed sturdy, and the windows rattled like a horror movie but shouldn't need replacing for a few more years. Shackie Kennedy Onassis, as they'd christened Greta's manor, didn't believe in nips and tucks; she preferred to age gracefully, if not a bit dangerously.

As Ryan went to unlock the door, she was relieved to see there were still no reporters lurking in her hostas or camped out along their driveway. The journalists' unwelcome appearances had died down in the past month—after they'd failed to get new material to support the lifespan of her cringeworthy interview, they'd eventually begun moving on to another poor soul unwillingly thrust toward internet infamy.

When Ryan's laboratory had made the grand announcement about the miracle air-purifying qualities of her *Campanulaceae saphiria*, she had become a public figure overnight, mercilessly shoved into the spotlight. The fact that multibillion-dollar industries, high-profile companies, and powerful governments had all been racing to discover a way to remove the toxins in the air, only to be beat out by a no-name girl botanist, was fodder for a fantasy novel or a Hallmark movie. People couldn't get enough of Ryan Bell—some calling her Mother Nature incarnate—but the media had quickly become frustrated by two things. Ryan was notoriously shy and wary of the press and therefore didn't do interviews. And then there was the little hiccup of others—mainly the multibillion-dollar industries, high-profile companies, and powerful governments—being unable to replicate her results. Now, with a years-long waitlist for a *Campanulaceae saphiria*, the news cycle focused elsewhere, continuing its coverage of how every baby was now born with asthma, chronic lung disease had decreased the average lifespan to an all-time low, and particulate matter, ozone, and CO_2 continued to poison humanity.

"I could still kick you out," Greta stated.

Ryan shrugged. "I'd just become a squatter and refuse to leave."

"I'd fight you," Greta said, demonstrating a kung fu move she'd learned at her Silver Sneakers women's self-defense class. She kicked open the top of the mailbox and emptied it before following Ryan in.

"Oh! My *GQ* magazine came today! And . . . you got some mail." Chuckling under her breath, Greta handed the bulky envelope to Ryan.

The envelope was covered in stamps—not just American stamps, but stamps from all over the world. Ryan eyed postage from England, Greece, and Nigeria, to name a few.

"Wow. Either this was the first time they used the postal service or it's more international hate mail," she said, tossing the envelope on the couch. As she began to search for her fur baby, she heard Greta bellow from the kitchen.

"Lester, you fat sack of potatoes, get out of my way! I nearly stepped on him." In response, Lester streaked into the front room, lunged for the wall at an imaginary tease, and plopped down to give himself a bath.

"Hello, Mr. Lester the cat. How was your day?" Ryan asked lovingly, scooping up her big-boned kitty. The pair joined Greta in the kitchen, Lester yowling his melodious "feed me immediately" demand.

"Lester, you are pathetic! Your bowl is half full!" Ryan hollered at her sweet boy. He looked up at her with his apathetic, swampy-green eyes. "I guess you're a glass-half-empty kind of cat . . ."

He purred joyfully as she dutifully scooped him a large bowl of kibble.

Despite Greta's protestations and feigned cat allergy, Ryan had adopted Lester a couple years ago—or, more accurately, he'd adopted her. He'd been a feral cat wreaking all sorts of havoc on the neighbors down the road—they'd thought a coyote was shredding their laundry, terrorizing the sheep, and spooking the kids at night with his yowl. One day, Ryan had seen something in their backyard, struggling inside a gargantuan pair of tighty-whities. She'd assumed it was the coyote and tried to ignore its pitiful screech, but after fifteen minutes, she'd gone to investigate. Assessing the peculiar situation, she'd calmly told the coyote that she was going to use a rake as a device to remove the irksome undies.

The creature had calmed down while Ryan managed to de-pants it. To her utter astonishment, it was not a coyote but an exceptionally large cat. He'd rubbed up against her legs in thanks and strutted into the open patio door as though he owned the place. Named after *Dateline* host extraordinaire Lester Holt, the cat went to great lengths to live up to the prestige of his criminally investigative namesake, particularly when it came to guarding the refrigerator with the utmost ferocity.

"That creature belongs outdoors," Greta grumbled, sourly looking down at the cat; Lester scowled back, food crumbs spilling from his snaggle-toothed mouth.

"What can I say? I have a knack for domesticating feral things," Ryan replied with a smirk.

"Hardy har har. Very funny. What shall I toss into the oven?"

Ryan opened the freezer and peered in. "Veggie supreme. I feel like being healthy tonight."

Every Friday night was the same: frozen pizza and a fancy cocktail. All week, they'd scan social media, hunting for that week's drink of choice. Whether it be a sangria, a simple high-quality bourbon, or the cocktail all the celebrities were drinking at Cannes, Greta and Ryan considered themselves quite the mixologists. A few weekends ago, they'd purchased fourteen different ingredients to concoct an overly complicated cocktail they'd seen on Pinterest.

Of course, the experiments didn't always turn out drinkable. When this happened, it was dubbed a Pinterest Fail, the ingredients buried in the "boozeyard": a cabinet in the kitchen where all the booze went to die. Nearly full bottles of curaçao, essence of elderflower, and bitters were reminders of Friday nights past. Their drinks concocted and the pizza in the oven, they'd turn on HBO, Showtime, or Netflix and devour the latest series in their queue.

Ryan's phone dinged. Before she could stop herself, she shrieked, "HE TEXTED!"

"Cyrus? You didn't tell me you gave him your digits," Greta squealed right back.

"You didn't ask," Ryan teased, coyly hiding her phone against her chest.

Eyes aglow, Greta demanded, "Well, what did lover boy say?"

"A lady doesn't text and tell . . ." Ryan said, sashaying out of the kitchen.

"You little sh—"

"OK, OK! *Hey, Ryan—it was great meeting you today. I hope we can see each other soon.*" Ryan looked at Greta and asked, "What do you think he meant by that?"

After dissecting the text for ten minutes, looking for forensic clues hidden within his prose to withdraw his true feelings and intentions, they agreed upon the perfect semi-flirty, semi-formal response.

Message decoded, Ryan went to her room to change. Now wearing her Friday night uniform (a vintage Abercrombie sweatshirt from her middle school days and clean leggings), she walked out to the living room, where Greta was putting the finishing sprig of mint on top of crushed ice in their new copper mugs.

The living room was tidy enough; it was undeniable that the house was inhabited by a boring twenty-something woman and a vivacious seventy-something. There were scarves draped over antique doorknobs, a secondhand wine rack with an impressive collection of under-fifteen-dollar wine, and enough mismatching wine glasses to host a small wedding if they wanted to (but mostly so they could enjoy a glass of wine each night without having to wash the dishes for a week). The living room had a chaise lounge angled toward a weathered wood-burning stove and a big, comfy secondhand couch pointed toward an ample television. There were remotes strewn all over the coffee table—one for the DVR, one for the speakers, one for the Apple TV, one for the satellite—lovingly mixed in with the latest paged-through copies of *Us Weekly* and *Martha Stewart Living*.

"Did he text back?" Greta bubbled exuberantly, despite being a mere two feet away.

"Greta, it's been, like, ten minutes," Ryan replied, although she knew it'd been sixteen.

"Moscow Mule, milady?"

"Oui, oui," replied Ryan. They clinked cups and then moved to the couch, where Ryan sat on the previously abandoned envelope.

"Yowch, that wasn't fun to sit on. You should have asked for consent first," she admonished the piece of mail.

"Open it," Greta barked, clapping her hands. "It could be from a faraway prince who's obsessed with your flowers and wants your hand in marriage."

"We need to lay off the British historical dramas," the botanist muttered as she opened the odd bundle.

Out fell a photo, and Ryan gasped.

It was her flowers—hundreds of them, lined up in pots on what looked like a beach. Interspersed amongst the flowers were three people, who not only seemed very distinctly international but were also apparently not ready for the photo to be taken. Ryan's eyes were immediately drawn to a muscular guy faintly resembling Hercules, who was gesturing toward the photographer as though giving instructions.

"Greta, they look like my Weeping Dianas. Where is this from?" She studied the envelope carefully, reading each of the stamps for clues of its origin. "Do you think someone sent this as a thank-you for an order?"

"Usually those come straight to the lab . . . is there a letter?" Greta asked, examining the photograph through her magenta readers.

"Yeah." She read aloud:

Dear Ryan,

We are excited to announce that we have successfully cloned your flower!

We invite you to join us for a research symposium to compare our findings so we can work together to increase the flower's abundance.

Please use the electronic mail address below to send your response and press send on your personal computing device.

Sincerely,
Nicholas.

Mouths open, Greta and Ryan stared at each other, then back down at the photo.

Feeling lightheaded, Ryan stuttered, "They . . . they replicated it?"

"They look legit, Ryan," Greta breathed.

"They look identical. Look, the wind from wherever they took this photo is making the tiny hairs on the flower petals change colors, like crushed velvet . . ." Ryan said, her voice a crescendo of excitement.

Even though the people in the photo weren't picture ready, the flowers were really giving it to the photographer, their hallmark features bursting to life. Ryan noted that the shades of blue were a bit muted compared to their real-life counterparts, but the effect could have been from the exposure of the film.

"They do look like they're floating underwater," Greta agreed. She scratched a nail on the photo, hoping to reveal its validity. "I suppose they could have Photoshopped this," she murmured.

"Yes, that is true," Ryan replied, biting her cheek. She reached for the letter again. "But something tells me they're not very technically savvy. 'Electronic mail'? And these stamps all over the envelope. And their clothing . . . check them out, Greta."

All three of the humans looked like they came straight from a thrift shop. Their clothing was not only mismatched in color and pattern but seasonally inappropriate as well. Ryan pointed out a rather formal evening gown paired with galoshes on a breathtakingly beautiful woman. The Hercules look-alike donned a heavy parka along with ultra-short running shorts, which tantalizingly flirted with the tops of his golden thighs. Strange attire in general, but even stranger for supposed scientists or botanists.

"Maybe the climate is unpredictable?" Greta guessed, pointing to the beach-like backdrop of the photo. "Or they have a boss with excellent taste in uniforms? I wouldn't mind if we put Henry, the greenhouse manager, in one of those," she said as she pointed to the leather biker vest on the last male in the photo, who was also gorgeous.

Ryan sank back into the couch. "Wow, is this real life?"

"Are you going to go?"

"What? No. I can't go!" She launched herself from the couch to pick up Lester, then paced back and forth, cradling the hulking body of her cat. "I can't leave the greenhouses and the lab. The orders are piling up as it is." She kissed Lester's head and gently placed him back on the floor with a loud *thunk.* "I can't leave you and Lester."

Greta looked down at the letter. Gently, she said, "You've got to weigh the pros and cons, love. If these people are able to clone them, then we can figure out what we've been missing, and together, we can get these into the hands of more people."

Biting her nails, tasting the ever-present earthy remnants of soil, Ryan considered it. "Yeah."

"And you've been stressed about how we need more room in the greenhouses. We could use the time you're away to expand our production facilities. All our seeding would have to come to a halt during construction anyway, so what if we synchronized it to the weeks you were away?"

"Yeah, I guess that'd be a good opportunity to do it. I'll think about it." Ryan plopped down next to Greta again and took a large sip of her cocktail.

Greta patted Ryan's knee and got up to check on the pizza. "Lord, mercy, today brought us cloned flowers and a side piece. This has been one for the record books!"

* * *

Two days and many tedious conversations later, Ryan began the well-worn argument over again: "I'm not going."

Eyes to the sky, Greta murmured to herself, "For the love of Chris Hemsworth, please grant me the patience to deal with this child . . ." In a more clipped tone, she said to Ryan, "We've been over this."

Head down, Ryan sowed at a dizzying pace, hovering over a pot for a few seconds before shuffling to the next. "I know. But their correspondence is strange."

"Yes, I agree, the last"—Greta gestured air quotes—"*electronic mail* was odd. But they live halfway around the world. Maybe English isn't their first language. Maybe they don't have technology or Wi-Fi or, heaven forbid, the Tinders, like we do."

Ryan shook her head as she thought back to her last email with Nicholas. He'd said the group lived on a tiny island off the coast of Athens—so small, he noted, that it wasn't significant enough to make it onto maps. When she'd asked why their laboratory was based on this off-the-beaten-path island, he'd responded that their work was so technical and top secret that they needed to be quarantined away from the public. It made sense to Ryan, scientifically speaking. She was grateful her own laboratory was in a small town, a couple hours outside of Minneapolis.

But living in her small town, especially after the embarrassment of her viral interview, Ryan had become more of a homebody, or a house cat, as Greta said. She didn't aspire to travel afar or meet new people. *If I could just save the world from my living room couch, that'd be great*, she often thought. But these people were asking her to take an international flight and then meet them at a seaport, where she would board a ferry and reach her final destination a few hours later. It was such a leap of faith, and Ryan was clumsy on her feet.

"It's not a good time," she started without any conviction, knowing she'd lose this argument.

Fired up, Greta responded, "It'd be a terrible time to change your mind. Don't you see the pile of lumber and materials in the parking lot ready and waiting to be assembled? We have contractors and laborers lined up and ready to complete this in two weeks. We need more space to produce the Weeping Dianas, Ryan. We've gotten too big for our britches. Let's expand your workspace. That way when you get back and you've cracked the case on how these other scientists were able to clone it, more people can start producing your miracle flower."

Ryan protruded her lower lip, giving Greta her best puppy-dog eyes. "Come with me."

The older woman held up four fingers. "One, my passport is expired. Two, I'm pretty sure maritime law bars me from traveling in international waters after dating that pirate back in the seventies." She trailed off, then cleared her throat. "Three, I wasn't invited. And four, I need to be here to facilitate the construction."

Ryan nodded dejectedly. "And five, you have to take care of Lester."

"That's actually on my list of reasons *to* go," Greta muttered under her breath.

Ryan finished a line of pots, stretched her neck back and forth, and started on the opposite side. Rain lashed down melodically on the greenhouse panes above, a nice accompaniment to her rhythmic planting routine.

"Does Cyrus have anything to do with this?" Greta asked delicately.

Ryan shot back a quick "no," then scrunched her nose, knowing how defensive and unbelievable her response had come out. She looked up at Greta and giggled sheepishly. "No, he truly doesn't.

But it's not helping that he keeps asking all these probing questions about where I'm going and who I'm meeting, when I hardly know myself."

"He sounds protective," Greta said with approval.

Protective, Ryan thought, *but also a little nosy.* She immensely enjoyed returning to her phone during lunch break to see a bunch of texts from Cyrus waiting for her. But she'd noticed that he had a habit of skirting away from answering any questions about himself, and that they spent most of the time talking about her. From what she'd gleaned from her daily consumption of reality television, this sort of attention was novel and refreshing, as it sounded like most guys her age were self-involved narcissists. But still, she'd appreciate a little more information so she could stalk him more thoroughly on the interwebs.

Quietly, she admitted, "We have a date when I get back."

Greta whooped. "And you'll come back with a tan from the Mediterranean! Hair full of sun-bleached highlights, soft waves framing your face. You'll be date-ready!"

"Probably burned," Ryan muttered. "And wait, why would my hair be wavy?"

"Part of my fantasy," Greta responded.

Snickering, Ryan finished the last row of pots and gazed out at the thousands of newly sown pots in front of her. Each one a little bucket of hope.

"That's a new high score," Greta noted.

Ryan shook off her gloves and took a lavish bow, Greta erupting in applause. They laughed and took one last look at the greenhouse.

"OK, well, I guess that's it."

"Let's go home and finish packing," Greta said.

R YAN PANICKED AS SHE SCANNED the names held up by waiting chauffeurs outside the baggage claim, not seeing anyone waiting for her—it would be just her luck for a marathon of uneventful flights into Athens to end in disaster. Just as she was unzipping her carry-on to recheck her pickup instructions, she spied a man lazily leaning against a pillar, arms crossed and eyes glued to the escalator, entranced. Ryan recognized the leather biker vest from the photograph and sighed with relief. He was definitely not the sterile, laboratory-type scientist she was used to working with during her succession of visiting botanists; he had a carefree aura to him, like someone who worked out in the field. Timidly, juggling her carry-on and suitcase, she rolled over to introduce herself. He told her his name was Elias.

They pulled up to the seaport after a twenty-minute taxi ride, Ryan idly observing Elias white-knuckling the seat in front of him the entire way. To her utter dismay, a ferry was not waiting to transport them to the island; Elias led her to a tiny, insignificant dinghy that was apparently capable of transporting them across the wide-open ocean. There was barely enough room for the three of them: Ryan, Elias, and her ginormous suitcase, which Elias easily tossed in without a second thought.

As they set off, the reassuring solid land and Greek people growing smaller and smaller, the pair enjoyed small talk about her flight. Elias asked several questions about the airplane and how it stayed up in the air; Ryan answered his curiosity with vague babble about aerodynamics, focusing on the enormous waves and the tininess of their watercraft rather than why a scientist was asking about basic physics.

A few minutes later, when they were out on the open water, Elias told her that she could take off her mask; she wouldn't need it where they were going.

"Oh, OK. Are there not any protocols in place to protect the islanders where you live?" she asked.

Elias shook his head, his wavy mane, dark as espresso, glistening in the sunlight. "No. With the plants, our island is protected and safe."

Impressed, Ryan nodded, tucking away her mask into her carry-on. "How many people live here?"

Elias squinted his dark eyes into the distance, thinking. "I don't know the exact number, but definitely under a thousand. Several hundred?"

"Wow! And they're all scientists? Or botanists?" asked Ryan, picturing a mecca of people as passionate about plants as she was. Like Elias, the inhabitants of her fantasy were all oddly beautiful.

"Not exactly." As Elias turned the rudder to the left, Ryan noted that he used nothing to guide them toward their destination; how he could do so without a map or the help of landmarks, she had no idea. "About a third of us are . . . scientists. The rest are family and others who help keep the island running."

"Cool. So staff and family members. Are you guys contracted to work a couple weeks or months on the island and then go back home?"

"No, we live here full time," Elias responded.

"Wow," Ryan breathed. "Now that's dedication."

"But hopefully not for too much longer. Your arrival opens many doors for us."

Ryan nodded. "Yeah, if we're able to work together to figure out how to grow the Weeping Dianas in bulk, we'll need help with production and training out there." She pointed to the mainland, or the general vicinity of where she thought the mainland was.

Elias looked at her and smiled. "That's the plan." His tone was light, but as he looked into the distance, Ryan saw him bite the inside of his cheek. As they rode in silence, she did her best to unobtrusively study him. She guessed he was around ten years older than her, with tanned skin that hugged bulky muscles and sultry bedroom eyes.

Elias caught her staring at him, and a devilish smile broke on his face; Ryan's reddened in response. She was wary of his attractiveness; he was a heartbreaker, and both of them knew it.

He opened a satchel and handed her a smaller bag. "In case you're hungry." Inside was a hunk of feta and some pita bread. Ryan frowned, examining the bag. She couldn't figure out how the feta had stayed cool without an ice pack, and the pita bread was still warm without aluminum foil. She offered Elias a piece, but he declined.

Two hours later, as Ryan bemoaned her decision to polish off the proffered canteen of passion fruit juice, Elias turned to her and said, "We're almost there, but a bit of an ocean haze is coming up. See it?" he asked, pointing to a wall of mist so thick she couldn't see through to the other side. "We must pass through it to get to the island. It's just something that happens with the jet stream in the Aegean."

"Oh, strange. The Aegean's own Bermuda Triangle," she responded lightly, her innards clenching with anxiety.

As they approached the dense fog, Ryan praying their small boat wouldn't simply ricochet off, Elias started singing a strange song in a low, gravelly voice. The boat sailed through the barrier, and Ryan gasped as she felt an enormous bucket of water splash atop her head. Cold and sure she'd been drenched to the bone, she started wiping off her arms and face with her hands. *That's odd*, she thought, realizing she wasn't wet. Alarmed, her head shot back to inspect the misty wall, but it was gone.

"What the f—"

"There's the island," Elias interrupted, pointing ahead.

Emerging from the ocean was a great, hulking mountain, reaching far above the thin cloud line. Her mind still addled from the mysterious waterless rain wall they'd driven through, Ryan wordlessly stared at the sudden appearance of this island skyscraper. It didn't make sense; the mountain was so enormous, so striking, she should have seen it in the distance miles ago. She should have seen it from the seaport. She should have seen it from the airplane. It was *that* big. How could this Everest-sized peak in the middle of the ocean be omitted from maps?

* * *

Twenty minutes later, Ryan spied a long wooden dock stretching out into the water, where a statuesque woman and man paced back and forth. Even from a distance, their anticipation was palpable; Ryan watched as the two occasionally hung off a wooden post at the very edge of the dock, as though they couldn't get close enough to the approaching vessel. These people were excited to meet her, and their nerves weren't the only ones on edge.

"Ryan, welcome!"

The dazzling woman from the original photograph Nicholas had sent offered her hand, effortlessly pulling the botanist from the boat to the dock. Ryan promptly tipped over, her legs the consistency of jelly after sitting an exorbitant amount of time both in the air and on the sea.

"Oh my gods, are you OK?" the woman bellowed, dusting Ryan off after setting her upright like a sack of flour. "How was your trip?" she asked eagerly, adjusting the neckline of her khaki-colored robe. *Is she wearing a toga?* Ryan wondered.

"It was long!" Ryan responded. "I've never flown internationally. So that was an experience. And the boat, well, that was interesting too." Ryan was rambling, nervous to have finally reached her destination and feeling a bit underdressed in her comfy travel outfit.

"We've never flown internationally either. I'm Kosta," said the majestic, Herculean guy from the photo, extending a hand. As she shook his soft, masculine hand, a jolt ran up her arm and down her chest, instructing her stomach to release a hurricane of butterflies.

Kosta also wore a matching khaki toga, a very island-y laboratory uniform, Ryan surmised. A strap of leather tied around his head kept his chin-length hair out of his eyes. His luxurious locks flopped adorably over the band, ultimately gathering behind his ears to form a loose, short ponytail. It was so shiny, straight out of an expensive shampoo commercial. She'd never had hair envy with a guy before. *Totally one of those people who has the scent of freshly washed hair linger in their wake*, she thought. *I could nuzzle into those soft locks and hibernate the winter away.*

She flushed as she realized she was daydreaming in front of all these people. *What has jet lag done to me?* She hastily looked away from Kosta and tucked her own hair behind her ear, annoyed to note its greasiness.

"No domestic flights either, for that matter," Elias added jovially.

36

The group all laughed, including Ryan, who didn't understand the joke but was relieved by the good nature of their company.

Elias added, "This is Melina." The woman who'd greeted her first gave her a warm smile and little wave.

"And I am Nicholas," said an older man who had just joined them on the dock. He flicked his great, long beard over his shoulder as he clasped Ryan's hands in both of his. "Welcome. We corresponded on the electronic mail. We are so glad you are here," he said, his piercing ice-blue eyes gazing compassionately into hers. She couldn't help feeling like he was looking at her in an overly familiar manner; more an intimate look a father would give a daughter than that of a stranger.

Her four hosts all looked at her expectantly, like she was supposed to perform or something. Ryan smiled and sort of bobbed her head, waiting for them to say something or take charge. "Yes, I'm eager to see the specimen!"

Nicholas clasped his hands together. "Yes, yes! Would you like to rest for a bit and then begin?" He gestured toward the beach with his hand, and they began to walk off the dock.

"Actually, I was able to sleep on the flight, so I'm rested. I loaded a bunch of *Barefoot Contessa* episodes onto my iPad; Ina's voice always makes me drowsy. Pair that with some melatonin and a few too many Chardonnays . . ." She giggled to herself, only to look up and see a bunch of blank looks and polite smiles. Continuing, she added, "So yeah, after a quick bathroom break, I'd be happy to get right to work."

"Great! This way," Melina said.

As they started for the beach, Nicholas dropped back and asked Elias, "How was the trip?"

"Nothing of note. Nothing out of the ordinary," Elias responded.

"Except that weird mist phenomenon!" Ryan called back. "I felt like we walked through a bunch of dementors! Minus the whole inner turmoil stuff."

"Yes, that is a weird anomaly that happens with the ocean current," Kosta responded.

"I thought you said it was the jet stream, Elias," Ryan said, frowning.

There was a pause; then Melina said, "Let's just say atmospheric sciences aren't the men's strong suit." She giggled, making Ryan smile. "The bathroom's right this way."

Melina guided her to an archaic-looking hut with a thatched roof and bamboo walls. Looking left, Ryan saw tropical vegetation stretch behind a sandy beach, reminding her of every deserted island date from *The Bachelor*. It curved out of sight, the ocean rhythmically lapping the coastline. Turning her head to the right, her neck craned to gaze at the massive mountain, which jutted ominously out of the water. Her eyes followed the mountain upward, noting little overhangs, openings, and impressive cliffs. The peak gradually narrowed, its pinnacle indiscernible as it continued above the cloud line. Its sheer magnitude engulfed her.

Ducking out of the tropical loo, Ryan said, "This is an absurdly beautiful island. Are your houses and building located behind this mountain? On the other side? Where does everyone live?"

Melina squinted at the mountain as though seeing it for the first time. After a beat, she nodded quickly. "Yes, there are mansions and condo-liniums just out of view. With sparkly chandeliers and refrigerators and everything."

Stifling a giggle, Ryan smiled encouragingly at Melina. *She must be just as nervous as me, with her misspeaking and random ramblings.*

Following Melina away from the sandy beach, toward the rocky mountain, Ryan spied a makeshift open-air tent resembling an over-sized cabana. Three canvas sheets stretched twelve feet into the air and were rigged at various areas against the mountain, which created rippling walls in the breeze. Kosta had dragged her suitcase and carry-on bag and placed them on a round table with a view of the sea, a perfect vantage point to watch the sun continue its journey to the horizon for the evening.

As Ryan smiled at the waiting figures of Elias, Nicholas, and Kosta, a hint of sapphire blue peeped into her peripheral vision. Behind the table were her flowers.

"Oh my god! Here they are!"

She ran over, bestowing a smile upon the blossoms like long-lost friends. As she inhaled the familiar floral fragrance and gently stroked a velvety petal in greeting, her chest decompressed, her shoulders relaxed, and tension released from her body like steam from a boiling teapot. *Finally, someone else can do it too*, she thought numbly, tears escaping her eyes as she gratefully gazed up at each of the four people in front of her. She was so touched that these strangers had made it their goal to help *her*, an intimate action that was so foreign to her, what with her own family doing far less.

Dabbing her eyes and wiping her dripping nose with her sleeve in as ladylike a manner as she could, Ryan walked back over to the group, croaking, "This is a miracle. I am so, so happy you guys did it!" She giggled with glee and then hiccupped. Covering her mouth with her hand, Ryan caught the eye of Kosta, whose own eyes mirrored the joy of this monumental moment.

Tearing her eyes away, she said to the group, "I can't wait to see how you grew them!"

"I guarantee we've been waiting longer," Elias said in a singsong voice, making Melina and Kosta chortle in response.

"We are just as anxious to compare methods. Would you like to show us your process first?" Nicholas asked, his eyes bright with curiosity.

"Oh, sure, yes. Let's do it! Shall we go to your lab?" Ryan asked, moving toward her luggage.

The four of them looked at one another. "Our lab?" Melina asked, eyes squinted in concentration.

"Yes, to demonstrate how I create the seedlings and then sow them?" Ryan responded.

"Oh, we have these," Nicholas said helpfully, pointing to a bunch of pots of dirt. "Do you need more than this?"

Her laugh stopped abruptly when they didn't join in. Slower this time, Ryan said, "I need the same equipment you guys used to create the seeds."

An awkward silence followed. Elias shot Nicholas a knowing look, as though silently confirming something. Kosta rubbed his jaw repeatedly while Melina bit her lip. Clearly, Ryan had unwittingly caused some sort of turmoil; hoping to quickly defuse the tension from the perplexed people in front of her, she lightly said, "I have my equipment with me . . . too bad they don't make travel-sized microscopes, am I right?" She smiled, keeping her tone casual and upbeat. "Let's make use of these pots of dirt." She regarded the table that was set up; clearly, their intention was to work here alongside the beach. "And this table will work just fine."

She could sense relief as they moved to help her arrange her things. As Ryan set up her microscope, she stole glances at the four. These scientists didn't look very *scientist-y*. She gazed at the full-grown flowers as her hands went on autopilot, organizing the petri dishes and slides; the Weeping Dianas were the real deal, and her confidence grew again as the sapphire-blue blossom waved back at her in the wind. The reactions and behavior of these scientists were strange, but perhaps their process was completely different than hers—that was OK. It was all a part of the mystery Ryan would finally unravel.

"OK, I'm all set up," she began.

"You use all this when you make your flowers?" Kosta asked, confusion flooding his intoxicating caramel eyes.

"Well, this is a stripped-down version of it. I have a lot more equipment in my lab and greenhouses, but for our purposes, this will work. This is the island way to do this. All I'm missing now is my piña colada."

In response, Kosta opened Ryan's carry-on bag, peeked inside, and then handed it to her. "I'm sorry, I don't know what that looks like."

Ryan scrunched up her face and shoulders. "That was a joke. A poor one, might I add. Let's get started, shall we?"

Now in her element, Ryan narrated the spiel she'd gone through endless times with all the visiting botanists to her own laboratory. Nicholas, Melina, and Kosta hunched over, closely watching her every move, while Elias leaned against the table and regarded the process from afar. Never had she imagined enjoying a soft, tropical island breeze while prepping the specimen—and with such luscious company, she thought, glancing at Kosta's pouty lips, his head bent close to hers as he examined the seeds.

Ten minutes later, the group raptly watched as she put the seed into the pot and tucked it in its bed of soil. Brushing the excess dirt off her hands, she finished by saying, "And then, in approximately seven days, a sprout will pop up!"

"You have to wait that long?" Nicholas said agog, peering into the pot.

"Well, yes. I guess it is a bit longer than, say, grass, but in the grand scheme of things, it's short. As soon as the bud sprouts through, it starts cleaning the air. When they're juvenile plants, before they blossom, they're at forty percent CO_2 cleaning. When they bloom, they're at one hundred percent. From then on, it's just maintaining them, pruning them, and keeping them in optimal conditions. Well, you know that," she said, gesturing at their flowers.

Taking off her gloves, she looked up at her audience. She wasn't expecting a standing ovation, but she also hadn't expected their reaction. *Why do they look crestfallen?* she wondered.

"And you don't do . . . anything else?" Kosta asked, probing deeply into her eyes, as though searching for something.

She looked down at the pot. "Well, a little serenade of 'Baby Got Back' never hurt anyone."

Suddenly, the others perked up. "She sings to them!" Melina uttered.

"Brilliant," Nicholas said, smiling and nodding his head boisterously.

"Go on, sing to them," Kosta urged, his enormous hands grasping her arms, gently pushing her toward the pots.

Ryan laughed, looking down at her arms, wondering if Kosta could feel the pinpricks of goosebumps erupting on her skin. "Um . . . I don't think so. One of my and Greta's life rules: no karaoke."

"But that's the key!" Melina bellowed, her face full of enthusiasm.

"What? No. You guys are hysterical! I don't always sing to them. That was a joke," she said, watching Kosta's hands slide off her arms, the fourteen-year-old girl in her vowing to never wash them again. "So can I see how you guys do it now?"

They looked around at one another wordlessly. Nicholas glanced into the pot of dirt before saying, "Why don't we have dinner first? I bet you're starved. And I can tell you're getting a little tired."

As though on cue, Ryan stifled a yawn. She couldn't deny it; her journey was catching up to her. A full tummy would be the ticket to lasting another few hours before she needed to conk out. "I think that's a great idea."

They helped Ryan move her equipment back into her suitcase, then sat around the table, Ryan facing the ocean, watching the sun hover over the cloudless horizon. She heard people shuffling behind the back of the tent set against the rocky mountain wall. She realized there must have been catering staff back there preparing their food.

A couple waiters in black togas emerged from the curtain. As one poured water, another set warm, freshly baked pita bread, kalamata olives, and a delicious salad in front of her.

Another waiter brushed up against her arm and whispered, "Red wine or white, ma'am?"

"Oh, um, red, please," Ryan responded.

As she looked up to say her thanks, she saw a very hairy, ape-like man looking back at her.

RYAN CATAPULTED OUT OF HER chair and backpedaled toward the back of the tent, tripping on a long, brown, furry vine.

"Oww! She stepped on my tail!" the small monkey man screeched.

Two other ape-like creatures burst through the tent walls, ran past Ryan, and went to console the third, who was tenderly nursing his trampled tail. "You all right, brother?"

"Basilius! What are you doing?" hissed Nicholas, his face a mask of fury.

"I'm sorry! Yorgos got sick and they needed a backup server," the ape-man replied, his eyes darting between Ryan's and Nicholas's.

"And they chose *you*?" Kosta asked, walking toward Ryan, who had remained frozen throughout this exchange.

"I volunteered. And this is my thanks," wailed Basilius, clutching his tail.

There was a commotion behind Ryan—she quickly skittered away as the back-canvas wall fell in a large heap, revealing not the catering prep area she had envisioned but an entrance into an enormous cave.

She swiveled on her knees to get a better view of what looked to be a bustling city set inside the hollowed-out mountain. Rows of levels hugged the walls of the cave, stretching cylindrically so far up that Ryan had to squint to spy the tiny humans walking around toward the top. In the center of the open-air atrium was a white marble structure with a stream running lazily around the edges. Hundreds of people, who must have been milling about their business moments before, stood frozen in place, reflecting the wide-eyed shock on Ryan's face. *Is that a horse . . . or a person? A Centaur?!* she thought wildly.

Aloud, she breathlessly stammered, "What . . . what is this place?"

"Calm down," Kosta said, hands up, approaching her.

She vigorously rubbed her eyes. The people, Centaurs, and secret hollowed-out volcano hideaway were still there.

Ryan shot up and lunged to the table. She grabbed a butter knife, whipping it back and forth between Kosta and Nicholas, a giant chunk of feta bouncing off Kosta's forehead.

"Get away from me! I need to go home. NOW!" she yelled, brandishing the knife at each person in her vicinity. People had started congregating at the opening of the cave. Melina was scolding them to get back inside, while Elias shooed the monkey men farther into its mouth. Ryan walked backward toward the dock, the dull knife still pointing threateningly at Kosta and Nicholas.

"Yes, we can go now," Nicholas responded, gently nodding his head, his hands up in submission.

"Don't you want the flowers?" Kosta asked.

Ryan paused, her knife-wielding hand dropping a few inches. "I can take them with me?" she asked, trying to keep her voice from trembling.

"Yes, of course," Kosta responded, genuine tenderness in his answer.

Quickly Nicholas added, "All we ask is for you to listen to us. Give us five minutes. That's all."

Ryan glanced at the fully grown flowers, then back at the tiny boat she had arrived in. They'd never fit. But if she was able to take even a few back with her, they'd cover a bit of the work she had missed by traveling here. To this crazy island.

Fidgeting with the knife, she hatched a vague plan. She would get in contact with Greta once she reached the mainland and tell her that a partnership with these people was impossible (she'd have to iron out the details on why, but she'd spare her friend a description of the Centaurs). She'd say that as an act of goodwill, the scientists had let her keep the plants. Glancing at the collection of Weeping Dianas, she estimated there were roughly a few hundred. Ryan could ship them from Athens to fill existing orders in Europe and Asia.

Ryan exhaled and pushed her shoulders back. Warily, she said, "OK, I'll listen. But once you take me back, you must return to load the remaining plants and deliver them to me at the port. I'm taking them all back with me, no matter how many trips it takes."

"Yes, fair, brilliant," Kosta said, a relieved smile on his face.

"Please, sit, Ryan. I promise you're in no danger," Nicholas said, gesturing toward her knocked-over chair. Kosta ran over to it, tipped it upright, and dusted the sand off.

Ryan slowly strode toward it, then re-angled it in the sand so she could keep an eye on the mountain. *I don't want anyone or anything sneaking up on me*, she thought to herself. Melina and Elias walked back to the table with plates of food, the cave dwellers out of sight. Heavenly aromas swirled in the ocean breeze, but like her grasp on reality, Ryan's appetite was lost.

"What is this place?" she asked as everyone sat down at the table. "You're not scientists . . ."

"No, Ryan. We are descendants of the Olympians," Nicholas responded resolutely. "We represent what is left of their bloodline."

Ryan stared wide-eyed at Nicholas, fighting to restrain her jaw from dropping and releasing a bubble of nervous laughter. She politely managed to choke out, "The Olympians . . . like, the Greek gods? Zeus and Athena and . . . oh my god." *Are they a cult? Some sort of religious group that worships gods of the past? Have they all been brainwashed? But the Centaurs, and those hairy ape things . . .*

Nicholas continued, "Well, 'oh my gods' is more accurate. There are twelve—Zeus, Hera, Poseidon, Demeter, Athena, Apollo, Ares, Aphrodite, Hephaestus, Hermes, Dionysus, and Artemis.

"We currently live in the confines of the lower half of Mount Olympus. The mountain itself is on a tiny, untraceable island in the middle of the Aegean Sea. There are no other inhabitants of this island except the people of this colony, descendants of the deities.

"And up there"—he pointed to the top of the mountain—"are the trapped gods."

Ryan craned her head up to the cloud-hidden peak and snorted. By now, she had guessed that she'd have trouble locating a souvenir shop for Greta on the island. She'd accepted that there wasn't a convention center or a budget-friendly hotel or even a super-secret governmental laboratory lair down yonder. But that the gods were gallivanting on the top of this random, albeit grand, mountain—it was absurd. The whole thing was absurd.

But in an effort to be considerate and hold up her end of the bargain, she decided to humor them and play along. Or at least play devil's advocate. "I'm fairly sure Zeus is supposed to be, like, all-powerful. What's stopping him from using his lightning bolts to, I dunno, craft some sort of escalator down here?"

They glanced amongst themselves, puzzled. Looking at Ryan for confirmation, Melina said, "I think she's referring to a moving staircase."

Kosta smiled at Ryan. "Oh, I'm sure he's tried your elsa-kater idea, but Gaea—you know her as Mother Nature—used an ancient curse that's not only trapped the gods but has forbidden them to use their powers on earth."

Ryan nodded her head once and muttered under her breath, "Ah. Mother Nature is somehow woven into this story . . ."

"Allow me to start from the beginning." Nicholas cleared his throat and settled deeper into his chair. "Thousands of years ago, before the Ottoman Empire, the gods were present in everyday life. Greeks worshipped and feared the gods, and both mortals and immortals lived harmoniously.

"While the mortals worshipped the gods, the gods worshipped Gaea. Like Kosta said, Gaea is also known as Mother Nature. As well as being the mother of all earthly things, Gaea is also the mother of Zeus and the Titans."

Elias must have seen Ryan's eyes beginning to glaze over—he interrupted, "Now's not the time for long-winded explanations, Nicholas." Turning to the botanist, he said, "Look, it's convoluted. But basically, Gaea was pissed at Zeus for not freeing her Titan sons, and in an act of revenge, she lured the gods to their palace atop Mount Olympus and locked them up for good."

Ryan shot Elias a grateful smile for the pared-down mythological recap. "OK, gods are real, Mother Nature is real, they're enemies. Got it. And what does this have to do with you guys? You're worshippers of these long-forgotten gods, and this island is kind of a church for your congregation?"

Nicholas chuckled. "As the only direct lineage of the gods, it has been our duty for the past twenty-seven hundred years to free our forebearers from exile."

"And to think, you guys don't look a day over 2K," Ryan said, surveying each of them with a mischievous twinkle in her eyes.

Melina shrugged. "It's true: we've been very unsuccessful as a people in trying to overthrow Gaea and release the gods. Each generation lives and dies in hopes of conceiving various strategies and plans to do just that."

"But"—Nicholas paused dramatically, his eyes boring into Ryan's—"we are the generation to conquer this grave injustice. We've made a pivotal discovery: we are an incomplete set. Until we're all reunited, our powers are not strong enough to break the curse."

"Powers," repeated Ryan flatly. "Gods are real, Mother Nature is real, *and* you have powers." Despite her promise to listen, the more fantastical this story got, the more antsy she became. And she saw one glaring missing piece: what in the world did this have to do with her?

Nicholas nodded. "Incomplete powers, until now.

"We believe that you, Ryan Bell, are our missing link to finally overpower Gaea."

"Jesus!" she bellowed. The exclamation slid into an exasperated laugh at the humor in uttering the messiah's name to *this* group of people. "You guys . . ." she said helplessly, looking around in a half-serious attempt to spot the crew of a hidden-camera TV show. *It would totally be something Greta would sign me up for*, she thought to herself.

"I know it sounds crazy," Melina said gently.

Ryan snorted in disbelief, then snuck a peek at the mouth of the cave. Its inhabitants stood still, watching.

"Ryan, you're a descendant of the deities and the missing link to helping us save the Olympians."

"We think," Elias said under his breath.

"Come on!" Ryan cried. "What makes you think I'm a relative of a Greek god? I'm a botanist, from a little town in Minnesota. I'm

Norwegian and French, for god's sake!" *You don't know that,* said an inconvenient little voice in her head. With an exasperated sigh, she conceded, "Well, I'm adopted, but I can assure you I'm nowhere near anything as exotic as having roots from the Mediterranean."

"A botanist?" Kosta asked. "Try a demigod."

"A powerful one at that," Nicholas added, Melina nodding with him. Elias leaned back in his chair, watching the conversation intently.

"Tell us about your flowers," Kosta urged.

"My . . . you think I'm, like, a god because of the flowers?" Ryan pointed to the newly planted pot of dirt. "I literally just showed you how I produce them. It's science." It hit her that they had been asking those weird questions about what she did after planting the seeds because they believed she did some sort of hocus-pocus, some voodoo magic to make the plants grow. A fuzzy memory of Cyrus questioning her in a similar fashion made her neck prickle; she buried it below the surface, concentrating on those in front of her.

"How?" Nicholas asked simply.

She kept her face blank, hoping her eyes didn't betray the fact that she still struggled with the mystery of her discovery. "I voraciously studied up on creating a species of plant to nourish butterflies to help with the extinction problem. Instead, I accidentally created the *Campanulaceae saphiria.*"

As though talking to a four-year-old, Kosta slowly asked, "And has anyone else been able to replicate your process with your exact criteria? Are people around the world growing the *Campanulaceae saphiria?*"

"Well, no, not yet," Ryan said resignedly. "Chalk it up to another wonderful mystery of *science.*" She crossed her arms with an air of finality. Seeing the looks of skepticism on the faces that surrounded her, she added, "Lately, I've thought maybe it's my pheromones. My musk." Even as she spoke, she caught a whiff of herself—the line of questioning was making her sweaty.

"Ryan, you've got underlying powers just seeping out of you. Whether you realized it or not, you brought them to life because you are someone special. The blood of the gods runs through your veins," Nicholas said vehemently, his deep voice thundering against the rocky mountain.

Searching their faces, Ryan saw that these people believed every word they'd just said. And the intensity of their belief was frightening.

Glancing upward, Ryan vaguely wondered if she were dreaming. Was she asleep on the plane, crammed into her economy seat, drooling on her neighbor while her brain created a fantastical storyline about her future journey? Or was she still in her bed, having never received a strange invitation to this island in the first place? Aware that everyone was watching her every movement, she slowly crept her non-butter-knife-wielding hand beside her and pinched the flesh of her hip as hard as she could. *Mother trucker,* she thought in response to the very real pain that arose.

She thought back to what she'd consumed in the past twenty-four hours; she'd eaten the feta, pita, and passion fruit juice from Elias. She studied him; he'd definitely been less interested in her than the other three.

Noticing her examination, Elias squinted his eyes and then burst out laughing. "Let me guess: you think I drugged the feta."

"It was irrationally delicious," Ryan replied defensively.

"Ryan, we would never ever do you any harm," Nicholas protested. "We aren't savages."

"And you're not dreaming," Kosta said, pointing to her newly pinched love handle.

She stammered, frustrated that they could read her mind. "There are certainly some"—Ryan searched for the right word—"*anomalies* on this island that I'm sure scientists would champ at the bit to study. But the gods are myths. I learned about them in my high school mythology class. They weren't real. They were fiction . . . stories, like mermaids and unicorns. And Centaurs . . ." She trailed off, glancing back inside the cave. A few of the horselike creatures stood near the foreground, idly stamping their feet.

Kosta's eyes grew wide, a big belly laugh thundering the air. "Unicorns?! Unicorns don't exist, Ryan!" He slapped his knee as the others joined in, clearly amused at the depths of her imagination.

Despite the absurdity of the situation, Ryan watched the handsome man, caught up in a fleeting moment of wanting to make him laugh like that over and over again. She shook her head as he regained composure.

"Yes, shortly a unicorn is going to ride down the elsa-kater," Melina said, wiping her eyes. "But in all seriousness, you did get a crash course on some of our resident mythical creatures."

"Let's not overwhelm her," Elias said in a singsong voice.

"Ryan," Nicholas said gently. "The gods are very real indeed. As real as the flowers you created sitting in front of you." Ryan didn't make any sign of compliance; she simply stared at him, suddenly exhausted from the overstimulation of her trip and accusations of being a mythical goddess.

"Ryan, if you are indeed a Descendant, you are our missing link. The gods will at last be fully represented through our Olympian bloodline, so we can fight and overpower Gaea. We will free the gods so they can rule again," Kosta said excitedly, as though his statement would inspire her to believe. He could shout the words, whisper them, broadcast them in pig Latin while doing a little jig for all she cared. It wouldn't help his cause.

"OK, well, I'd love to help you with your plight, but this has nothing to do with me. I am a scientist. These plants are made with science." She looked at the plants the Descendants had made. "Well, at least the plants *I* make are made with science." She sighed. Melina and Kosta looked at each other, while Nicholas continued to gaze at her hard. Elias rocked back and forth on his chair, amusement on his face.

Ryan continued, standing up from her chair, "I think this has been a huge misunderstanding. I really do hope you find your last link to overthrow Geja or whoever that is, but I'm sorry. I listened, and now I've got to go."

Elias hopped up and grabbed her suitcase. "OK, let's load up," he said enthusiastically, charging toward the dock.

Wordlessly, Kosta guided Ryan toward the flowers, where they both picked up an armful of pots. Together, they followed Elias to the dock.

"Will it be safe to travel by boat at night?" Ryan asked fretfully, looking out into the black waves and moonless night.

"Yes, Elias traces his roots back to Poseidon, so he is excellent in water. He'll get you back to the port safely." Kosta lined the pots next to her suitcase and then stood up.

"Sorry about throwing feta in your face," Ryan said, awkwardly rubbing her arms. A chill that had nothing to do with the temperature ran amok through her body.

"No worries. I'd probably do the same if I saw an automobile for the first time," Kosta said, running his hands through his wavy brown hair.

Until now, Ryan hadn't reacted to the gravity of the fact that these people had apparently never left this island. "You've seriously never left here?"

"Born and raised."

"Wow. It's beautiful, though." She scanned down the mountain to look at Kosta. "So there's that. But never been in a car?"

"Nope."

"Or eaten a Happy Meal? Or been to a Target?"

He gave her a puzzled grin and shrugged.

"What about snow? We have a lot of that where I come from."

Another shrug. "I can make snow. With my *powers*," he added, mimicking her intonation. *Is he flirting?*

Kosta continued, "It was a big risk leaving the island to obtain a boat and fetch you."

"Why?"

"Gaea is on a merciless hunt to slaughter us."

"You didn't have to do that . . . risk it," she said a little defensively. "Seems a bit irresponsible if you ask me, plucking me out of obscurity and pinning some ancient Greek ancestry on me. If you guys truly are in danger."

A muscle in his jaw clenched. "I may not know about things out there, but I know about things here, and I am certain you are the key to our redemption."

"How can you say that? You don't even know me, Kosta," Ryan replied quietly, studying his eyes for something solid she could hold on to.

"Ryan, you've created something completely new, completely original. No one has ever done that before. Mortals before you, who have done incredible, astounding things—everything they've done has been a reflection of something Mother Nature created in the first place. But not you and your flowers.

"And what really blows me away" —Kosta was fired up again, spewing this monologue out into the sea as though Ryan weren't even there—"is that the thing that you created from your powers is a weapon in itself against Mother Nature, a direct assault to counter what she's been doing out there, a defense mechanism to save humanity." He shook his head in amazement, looking down at Ryan with awe. "How could you not be one of us?"

Ryan's face, she was sure, was a silent mix of lust and confusion.

He sighed. "I know it's a lot. And there's so much more. But I guess what I really want to say is that I don't regret orchestrating this. And although you don't believe it, this is very real to us. I saw you balk at our people staying on this island for twenty-seven hundred years and judge me for never having left—"

"Kosta, I didn't mean to offend—" Ryan cut in.

"—but it's a small sacrifice to pay for the greater good. We didn't take this risk lightly, and while I do appreciate you listening to us, I wish we could have presented it differently. I wish you could believe us."

Ryan watched in silence as Nicholas, Elias, and Melina lined the dock with the flowers to load onto the boat. Looking up at the forlorn Kosta, Ryan realized she'd never gotten to the bottom of how they'd made her flowers. Nicholas had mentioned powers, but . . . those weren't real, right? A few hours ago, she would have been able to definitively say so, but now, after all this? She wasn't so sure.

Ryan looked at the flowers and started doing the math. If they could somehow work together, both producing the flowers in their own, er, nontraditional, unique ways, the effects of the plants could have a greater reach. If she could get these . . . *Descendants* to agree to make more of them, Ryan wondered if she could say she'd obtained them from other scientists. Prove she wasn't a heartless, greedy jerk. *Well, can't exactly go on TV with the monkey-man creature stumbling out during a live interview.* But maybe she could have them manufacture for her and she could distribute? She'd need to gain their trust.

But can I trust them*?*

This opportunity could be life changing for so many.

What would Greta do? she wondered. *Follow your passion and instincts, Ryan. And heavens to Betsy, follow that man!*

"OK—would it help if I stayed and proved I'm not 'the one'?" she asked quietly.

Kosta's eyes grew wide. Excitedly, he replied, "Yes! We could test you and put you through some training to get your magic to come out."

Ryan closed her eyes, willing herself not to even begin thinking about the absurdity of what lay ahead if she were put through this *testing.* "And how long would that take?"

Scrunching his eyebrows in thought, Kosta said, "Well, you were already planning on staying here a couple weeks."

"And in that time, could you guys produce more of these flowers for me to take home, if I stay a little bit longer?"

"Absolutely!"

Ryan studied him, still trying to figure out how he supposedly *did* magic. He certainly excelled at making her heart twist and flip against her innards. *A Descendant of Aphrodite,* she considered with a half-suppressed smirk. More likely, she was experiencing hallucinations due to premature heart failure.

Tentatively, she asked, "And I'm not in any real danger? With all the other—what did you call them—mythicals?"

"I wouldn't go stepping on any more harpy tails or follow the Sirens' song off a cliff, but everyone else is nice," Kosta responded with a lopsided grin.

Nicholas and Elias came walking up with the last of the flowers, Melina following with a bag of what looked like more boat fare.

Ryan studied Nicholas as he approached them. He was a host of juxtapositions. His hair and beard were streaked with shocking gradients of gray, but the skin over his face and body was taut and devoid of wrinkles, save for crow's feet around his eyes. He was slightly hunched over and shorter than the others, but his movements were deft and agile, oddly reminiscent of a teenager's quick reflexes. His low and gravelly voice was certainly grandfatherly, yet his speech and intellect were razor sharp. His resemblance to Moses from those cheesy biblical made-for-TV movies was uncanny. Yet his face—it was a trustworthy and kind face, and although she didn't know how she'd earned it, he looked at Ryan as though he actually cared for her well-being. It was the same look that Greta gave her, the look that had utterly perplexed Ryan when they'd first started hanging out. Both looked at her as though she had value in this world. Inexplicably, Ryan felt like she'd miss Nicholas, someone she'd just met a couple hours ago, if she left now.

As the three strode up to her and Kosta, Ryan confidently said, "I'm staying."

"What?" Elias, Melina, and Nicholas asked in unified disbelief.

"You can test me, so that I can prove to you that I do *not* possess any magic."

"Yes, OK, wonderful!" Melina cheered, amiably slapping Kosta on the arm.

Nicholas beamed as well—but was she mistaken, or did she see a little hint of annoyance in Elias's face? Maybe it was because he'd have to unload all the flowers again.

"And I've agreed that we'll make her more plants in the meantime," Kosta told them.

"Yes, of course!" Melina gushed. She picked up Ryan's suitcase with ease; as she started back toward the end of the dock, she said, "We had planned to hide our true lifestyle until we saw your powers

in person. But seeing as our elaborate ruse was single-handedly ruined by a harpy desperate for attention, we have a very cozy room for
you set up inside the mountain."

"Would you like me to take you there now?" Nicholas asked.

Ryan nodded. Even as they turned back toward the formidable
mountain, she was second-guessing her decision to stay. She shivered
as she gave one last glance up to the top, wondering if the gods were
looking down on them now.

LIKE A BABY DUCKLING, RYAN followed Nicholas through the cavernous opening, all the while peeking over his shoulder at her new surroundings. Rocky, angular walls gave off a prehistoric feel, yet the faint aroma of earthiness, oregano, and citrus felt as though she were entering an expensive boutique.

The passageway spilled out into a giant open atrium, dwarfing Ryan and her guide. Speechless, she gazed at the hidden refuge set inside a hollowed-out volcano, spanning such a large area that it could easily swallow a couple football stadiums. The top of the summit ceiling rose so tall that it was hidden in shadow, but a large crevice set into the ledge of the mountain worked like an enormous natural skylight, revealing the starless night sky. Another opening near the ridge exposed the outdoors, creating an eerie echo of thunderous waves.

The most striking feature of the atrium sat directly in the center: a life-sized replica of the Parthenon. Ryan had seen pictures of the crumbling artifact in Athens, but the monument in front of her was what it must have looked like when it was first constructed. The marble columns seemed to sparkle in the dim cave lighting. Decorative stonework on the exterior pediments boasted rich colors, details so minute they looked like a tapestry. *Well, I can cross visiting the Parthenon off my bucket list.*

The enormity of the space itself took her breath away, but what kept her glued motionless to her spot was the existence of an entire bustling village housed within the mountain. Along the rocky walls were distinct levels that wrapped around, each fifty feet above the next. On each floor were a variety of buildings built into the mountain walls. Ryan could make out patios and porches with doorways that likely led to houses of the island inhabitants, each decorated spectacularly. Flags fluttered in a nonexistent wind and wildflowers swayed rhythmically to a lyre playing in the distance; a trick of the eye, Ryan thought. She couldn't be certain, but she thought she saw a donkey taking a siesta in a hammock in front of one abode.

Storefronts of all varieties dotted the levels as well. The lettering was all in Greek, but as Ryan's eyes swept from one business to the next, she made out a bakery with steaming pita in the window, a clothing store with breathtaking fabrics draped over moving mannequins, and what appeared to be a grocery store with bountiful produce in big bins out front.

There were doorways leading farther into the mountain, each framed with sparkling white columns. Instead of lava, Ryan's eyes followed a babbling brook zigzagging through the rotunda; upon it, a gondola-like raft slowly drifted by, stacked high with wheat or hay. Curiously, it seemed to guide itself along the waterway—there was no steersman visible to the botanist.

Nicholas watched with amusement and a hint of pride as Ryan took it all in. When she had swept over the breathtaking panorama in front of her one last time, they wordlessly agreed to move on. Although few people were out and about during the pre-bedtime hour, Ryan still followed Nicholas absurdly close—so close that when he stopped, she faceplanted into his surprisingly solid back. She peeked over his shoulder to see what had caught his attention and saw a group of Descendant teenagers closely huddled around someone, unaware they had visitors. Ryan was grateful to openly study the younger Descendant specimens.

Clothed in traditional toga-like robes in a range of vibrant jewel-tone colors, the Descendants as a group had physical features more dramatic and distinct than anyone else Ryan had ever seen. Although these teenagers were hunched over, it was evident they were statu-esquely tall, their builds ranging from athletic to lithe. Squinting, the botanist picked out eyes of green, blue, and brown, but their hues were slightly different, somehow otherworldly and enchanted. Their skin tones ranged across the board, from crystalline to olive to onyx, a dewy sheen highlighting their flesh. Both boys and girls had hair that seemed to sprout threads of gold, silver, and copper along-side its normal tresses, making them glow and radiate as though each were under a personal spotlight. Some sported traditional olive-leaf crowns, while others wore tiara-like headbands that sparkled like LED fireflies. They were stunningly beautiful, just like Kosta, Melina, and Elias; these Descendants were certainly a circus of wonder.

Ryan glanced up at Nicholas, wondering why he was so fixated on the teens. She could tell by the frown plastered on his face that he hadn't stopped to introduce her. Examining the group more closely, she realized they were trying their hardest to hide something; stand-ing on her tiptoes, she spied a moving picture on the ground of the cave and realized she could hear the familiar warble of a kooky blonde singing about a smelly cat. Ryan couldn't see it, but the per-son in the middle must have been aiming a projector at the ground so that the group could watch a TV show.

"Sandrine," snapped Nicholas.

The person at the center of the group jumped up in surprise, as did the teens huddled around her. Ryan couldn't see where Sandrine had tucked the projector, but judging from Nicholas's tone and the guilty look on her face, she had broken some sort of rule.

"I will be reporting this to Samir," Nicholas growled to the group, who managed to look sheepish. Without another word or an explanation of their transgression, Nicholas walked away.

With the departure of her godly shield, Ryan froze like a deer in headlights. The group of teens reflected her muted shock, each party stunned to suddenly be within each other's company.

Turning on her heel and bolting after Nicholas, Ryan heard a male Descendant mutter, "Gods, he's such a Monica."

After another five minutes through winding, twisty tunnels, at last Nicholas stopped in front of a door built into the rock wall. "Here we are. I'll swing by tomorrow morning to see if you're awake, and we'll grab breakfast together. Otherwise, if you're up and hungry before I arrive, you can head to the bakery and I'll meet you there." Pointing toward the direction they'd come from, he said, "It's down this hall, past the Centaur aerobics studio, a left at the Furies' torture room, and a right at the Sirens' wall of fame. If you hit the Muses' steam room, you've gone too far."

Aaaaaand those instructions are definitely giving me nightmares, Ryan thought to herself as she gave Nicholas a final wave.

Easing the door open, she walked into a cozy room with a small fireplace at one end and a bed at the other. Sheer fabric in gold and maroon cascaded dramatically over its canopy frame. An adorable window seat with overstuffed pillows overlooked the ocean, and a harvest moon shone brightly, bathing the room in relaxing celestial hues. She peeked into a small yet adequate bathro—

Wait a second, she thought. She turned toward the window again. She had just left the outdoors, where it was a moonless, starless night.

Shaking her head, she glanced at the fireplace, where gorgeous flames crackled amiably yet weren't emitting any oppressive heat into the small room. Knees tucked under her, she sat on the window seat and gazed out. *No,* she thought as she shook her head. *We're in the middle of the mountain right now. There's no way we could even be close to the outdoors. Besides, the moon is too perfect.* She sat there, watching the stars twinkle unnaturally yet pleasantly, deciding this was much more palatable than drifting on a boat in the pitch black with a gorgeous yet moody man.

There wasn't a Nespresso machine, and a Wi-Fi passcode wasn't given at check-in, but Ryan was grateful she had a little space to herself to process and have some "mortal me-time." She unpacked, washed her face, and changed into her soft nightshirt and shorts, absently wondering if she were perhaps neighbors with a certain handsome demigod. Feeling more like herself than she had in twenty-four hours, Ryan turned on her phone for the first time since landing in Athens to send Greta a quick "A-OK" message.

As expected, Greta had blown up her texts, Snapchat, Twitter, and Facebook with messages. Scrolling through the jungle of alerts, she was delighted to see that Cyrus had also texted a few times.

Leaning against the headboard and sipping a glass of red wine that had been left for her, Ryan FaceTimed Greta. It was eight hours behind at home; Greta answered from the office after two rings.

"She's alive! Good grief, I've been worried sick!" bellowed Greta.

"Greta, it's been six hours since I checked in that I was OK!" Ryan retorted with a laugh.

"And then you sent a photo of the minuscule boat you were taking to an uncharted island that even the Googles can't locate!" she cried indignantly. "But let's get to the most important matter . . ." She swung around on her desk chair and hunched over. Whispering, she asked, "The guy on the boat. Single?"

Ryan giggled and rolled her eyes. "Priorities, woman!"

"I'll take that as a no. But seriously, how are things?" Greta asked, her green eyes raking worriedly over Ryan through the screen.

Ryan kept her face and tone as carefree as possible, not wanting to give Greta any reason to suspect something was amiss. She'd been going back and forth on whether to tell the older woman about her monumental day, but she knew it would sound unbelievable. Ryan also knew how Greta operated; one wrong move and she would alert the Grecian SWAT team to track the botanist down. Ryan was going to keep this close to the cuff for as long as possible. At least until she herself could grasp who and what she was dealing with.

"It's different than I expected . . ."

"Well, if all those islander scientists look like the babes in that photo, I may be inquiring about a timeshare. Were the flowers true *Campanulaceae saphiria*?"

"Yes!" squealed Ryan.

"Oh, hallelujah! Oops!" There was a big clatter as Greta dropped the phone during her celebration dance. Hair disheveled, she came back on. "Did you already figure out the discrepancy on why others haven't been able to clone it? What's the secret?"

"Well, their process is a little . . . unorthodox. But we're going to explore more of it tomorrow."

"Oh, great! I hope everything is discovered."

Eyes stinging, Ryan swallowed a big lump in her throat. She was touched by how her cause had unquestionably become Greta's; the other woman radiated pure joy at the thought that Ryan's mission was a success. "Me too!" she croaked.

"Has everyone been nice?"

"Yes, there's an older man named Nicholas, around your age—"

"Did you show him my picture?"

Ryan laughed. "Not yet."

"Who'd play him in a movie?"

Ryan squinted her eyes in thought. "Let's say, if Robert De Niro and Robert Redford had a son . . ."

Greta drew in a sharp breath. "Ohhhhhhh."

"He's incredibly wise and has these trustworthy eyes. And there's Melina, who has total potential to become my new BFF—"

She heard Greta angrily huff in response.

"My new *island* best friend, that is. I get a good vibe from her, like bookish but chic about it. And she has these purplish eyes, but I don't think she's wearing contacts. I'll have to ask her.

"And Elias is the guy who drove me on the boat. I'm having a hard time reading him. He seems well liked by the others, but I get a feeling like he maybe wasn't 100 percent sure about me coming here."

Frowning, Greta responded, "That's odd."

"I dunno, maybe he's a Scorpio."

Greta nodded brusquely. "That would explain it."

Taking a sip of wine, Ryan swallowed and added, "And then the last guy from the photo is named Kosta."

Greta peered into the camera with anticipation. After a few seconds, she drawled, "Annnnnnnd?"

"And what?"

"You nearly gave me height, weight, and astrological details on the other three, but nothing about Kosta?"

"Oh, well, he's tall and built . . . nicely. And handsome. Totally out of my league. But kind."

"No one is out of your league, honey. Kosta. Kosta." Greta practiced it a bit off screen. "Love that name. It's untraditional, like Cyrus. Speaking of, have you heard . . ."

"Yes, he texted." Ryan grinned, raising her eyebrows mischievously.

Greta squealed. "I knew it! Sounds like he has a little competition with Kosta."

Rolling her eyes, Ryan leaned her head back on the headboard. "I knew you'd be like this, Greta! Kosta doesn't like me. It's purely professional. Although I guess I'm the one being unprofessional by saying he's nice to look at. Whoops. Anywho, how are things at work?"

Greta's face fell. "I suppose you haven't really been on your phone to check the news." Greta proceeded to tell Ryan in harrowing detail about the eight sinkholes that had inexplicably opened around the United States.

"They're the size of Hawaii, Ryan, and they all sank simultaneously. Millions of people. Gone"—Greta snapped her fingers—"in an instant. Luckily, we didn't have one in Minnesota, but who knows if or when the next one will strike."

"Oh my god, Greta," Ryan breathed. "That's really scary. What are they saying caused them?"

"Not sure. They're assuming they're another side effect of climate change, but they can't find any way to link them because the holes were so random. Everyone is shaken up—construction of the greenhouses has been put on hold."

Ryan sighed. Not the news she had hoped to get. Reports of these random disasters were becoming more commonplace—glacier-sized icebergs slamming into coastal towns, hurricanes ping-ponging from continent to continent at unprecedented speeds, rogue tornadoes appearing without any warning. The fact that Greta hadn't even opened up their conversation with this news showed how desensitized they'd become to these huge natural catastrophes. Part of her was ashamed that her first emotion was frustration for the time lost expanding her greenhouses, not grief for the people who'd perished. But it was the way of the world these days, with deaths growing exponentially from the toxic air or these seemingly human-influenced climate change incidents.

Ryan's flowers would decrease the death toll on one front. She reminded herself that at least she would come home with a ton of Weeping Dianas if all went to plan.

"I'm glad you're safe," she said, forcing herself out of her reverie. "How's Lester? Did he sleep on my pillow last night? He's always there when I come in after brushing my teeth, but I gotta lug him to the foot of the bed when it's lights out." Her heart gave a little pang knowing she wouldn't get to drag his dead weight down the bed while she was here.

Greta huffed. "That cat. He kept me up all night long, Ryan."

"Why?"

"Well, I went into your room to drop off your clean clothes . . ."

Ryan frowned. "I put them away before I left . . ."

Greta pursed her lips. "OK. I *may* have been trying on that tie-dye crop top you never wear."

Ryan giggled. "He totally busted you!"

"Yes, and he would not let me forget it. Every time I was about to fall asleep, he'd shoot out of *my* closet like a rocket, leaving behind a trail of clothes. Every single time, Ryan. What should I do?"

"Maybe keep your paws off my stuff," Ryan joked. She squinted at the screen. "Wait a second, Greta. Are you wearing the crop top right now?"

"What's that? The connection is cutting in and out. Better let you get some sleep. Talk to you tomorrow! Snap me a pic of Nicholas and get the lowdown on his relationship history."

Ryan giggled. "You got it."

After hanging up, she worked on the rest of her wine while scrolling through Cyrus's texts.

Hope you made it!

How was the flight?

Who picked you up? Did you find out the name of the island and why it's off the grid?

Dashing off a response, she typed: *Hey! Arrived in one piece and am definitely having an interesting time lol. Can't wait to tell you about this random adventure when we see each other next. It may or may not have something to do with Centaurs. But making progress with the flowers, which is why I came. Greta told me about the sinkholes—crazy stuff. Stay safe!*

As soon as she hit send, Ryan squinted over her phone, biting her nails as she critiqued her response with the dexterity of an acclaimed book editor. *Doh! Why did I mention Centaurs? I'm trying to keep things secret. And now he's going to question my sanity,* she thought miserably. *I am quite sufficient at questioning it myself, thank you very much.*

Sighing, she powered down her phone to make sure she wasn't going to get charged crazy international rates, snuggled deeply into her comfy bed, and drifted off to thoughts of Kosta and Cyrus.

RYAN STIRRED IN HER LAST moments of sleep, slowly creeping her right leg over to where she expected to feel a warm lump. As she stretched her leg to the end of its reach, she realized with a longing ache that Lester would not be at the foot of her bed.

Reluctantly prying her eyes open, the botanist looked up at the cave ceiling. The fire had died in the middle of the night, replaced by a perplexing yet comforting blue glow. Curtains she hadn't noticed before had been drawn over the magical window. Some rays of sunshine peeked through the cracks—she had no idea whether they truly reflected the weather outside the cave or if a storm ravaged outdoors.

Deeply comfortable and slightly afraid to face the day, she wondered how long she could play possum and stay in bed before she was undoubtedly summoned. On cue, a soft knock sounded at her door; groaning, Ryan burrowed her face back into her pillow.

"*Kaliméra*! Good morning, Ryan!" Nicholas greeted her from behind the door.

Ryan launched out of her bed, tripping over yesterday's clothes. "Ah, good morning, Nicholas," she called, stammering as she caught herself from falling in the heap. "I'm sorry, I didn't have an alarm clock and couldn't tell what time it was. I'll be right out!"

After plunging into her suitcase and tossing out the dress pants and blazers she'd thought she'd wear in an established laboratory setting with established scientists, she retrieved the travel outfit she'd intended to wear on the way back to Minnesota: a pair of high-waisted leggings, a faded sports bra, a vintage *Purple Rain* concert tee, and the "Save the Winos" rhino sweatshirt Greta had given her for Galentine's Day.

Pulling her hair up, hair binder between her teeth, she opened the door to Nicholas, who looked back at her with amusement. Ryan could tell he got a kick out of her behavior. It made her feel oddly precious to unintentionally bring joy to this near stranger. *Joy, and allegedly the resolution to a mystery spanning two millennia,* she thought as she grinned at him.

"You slept well?" he inquired.

"Yes, very comfy accommodations. Much better than the Four Seasons," she noted.

Eyes twinkling in response, he gestured for her to follow him down the path they had trekked last night.

A few minutes later, they were back in the atrium, the morning sun casting the cave with hues of peach and clementine through the skylight. Ryan craned her head toward the top tier of the cave, spying something too dark for her to have seen last night: twelve enormous figures stared back at her. Jutting out of the rocky wall, not unlike Mount Rushmore, were men and women sitting atop thrones, spaced out like hours on a clock overlooking the inhabitants. They surveyed with austere, powerful expressions, and although they were carved directly from the mountain, they were pristine and shiny ivory, as though the sculptor had struck marble. It was obvious which one was Zeus. The depictions in history and pop culture were pretty much spot on: strong, powerful body; long, flowing hair and beard; piercing, austere eyes. Ryan scanned each of the other eleven Olympians, absently wondering which of the intimidating gods was supposedly her kin.

As they neared the middle of the rotunda, there were hundreds of people milling around, clearly following their normal routine and paying no heed to Ryan's presence. She and Nicholas walked past what looked to be an all-women's choir practicing a heart-wrenching tune. Mesmerized by the notes, Ryan started slowly walking toward the opening of the cave—until Nicholas's hand firmly grabbed her arm. Immediately, the feeling dissipated. She looked up at Nicholas with curiosity, but he just smiled back at her.

Looking on, she spotted school-aged girls wearing togas in every color of the rainbow, dancing a little jig along the stream. Before her eyes, it looked as though the lily pads and flowers around the girls began to grow and bloom. She shook her head and looked away.

As she followed Nicholas at a leisurely pace, she confirmed that these Descendants seemed very content. There was a buzz in the room as people greeted one another, and a boom of laughter erupted often. Whatever was running through that stream, she wanted to bottle and distribute it.

After allowing Ryan to take in her surroundings uninterrupted, Nicholas finally spoke. "This is the foyer to our home. The entrance is just beyond that way. You will get a tour of the beach, the forest, and the rest of the island later."

He led her up to the third level, toward one of the storefronts she hadn't noticed. It appeared to be a restaurant with a patio overlooking the rotunda, little circular tables for two lined up in rows. She turned around and scrutinized how high they were; it was a gorgeous view looking down on the top of the Parthenon.

"Let's get you something to eat. I bet you're starving. Do you read Greek?" asked Nicholas.

"Just *un poco de français*, Nicholas," Ryan replied, looking up at the foreign-looking sign over the restaurant.

"This reads *Maria's*. Best calamari on the island. And only calamari on the island, for that matter."

"I'm guessing you guys don't have a Starbucks in this place . . ." Ryan turned around for one last look at the magnificent atrium.

Nicholas chuckled. "I'm afraid not. While we do have a few modern-day conveniences, we've been relatively untouched by the outside world. We're completely self-sufficient. We grow our own food. We ranch our own cattle and catch our own fish. We make our own wine, our own olive oil, our own clothes. We build anything we need with tools we've made ourselves."

"Wow," Ryan breathed. "So no one goes to the outside world for supplies?"

"Very rarely. Every time we leave the island, we risk detection from Gaea, who wants to eradicate our presence. When we leave the safety of our forcefield, Gaea can sense the effervescence of the genes she did not create—the godly genes. So we've built a life here ourselves."

Ryan glanced up at the imposing figures that seemed to watch her every move. "So you think I'm related to one of them?" She pointed meekly, irrationally not wanting the inanimate objects to catch her gesture.

"Yes: Artemis," he said, gesturing toward one of the ivory figures.

Of course, Ryan thought glumly. He'd pointed to the one figure Ryan had hoped *wasn't* her kin. All the other women looked intimidating yet regal, pulling off the whole godly royalty thing magnificently. Artemis, on the other hand, looked cold and forlorn. Greta would have taken one look at her and deemed her a dingy deity.

Even carved out of stone, her hair looked unkempt, her toga wrinkled, her bow tucked possessively under her athletic arm. If there was any resemblance between Artemis and herself, it was that they shared similar RBFs: Resting Bitch Faces.

"How are you certain it's Artemis that has this forgotten bloodline?"

"Of the twelve Olympians, only eleven procreated. Artemis never had any offspring."

Ryan snorted and pointed at herself. "Um, Nicholas? Do you see the problem here?"

Chuckling, he nodded, glancing up at the circle of god carvings. "For thousands of years, we, along with the gods, have believed that Artemis's lineage ended with her. There was no evidence to counter this belief. Artemis is a self-proclaimed spinster and proud of it. She made her father, Zeus, promise that she wouldn't have to marry. He kept his word."

"Right on, sister. Topple the patriarchy!" Ryan said, pumping her fist into the air. Under her breath, she muttered, "Real or mythological . . ."

Nicholas ignored her quip. "However, long, long ago, there was a colossal quarrel between Artemis and her twin brother, Apollo."

He pointed to the god next to Artemis. *Definitely fraternal twins,* Ryan thought, noting the physical differences between the two. Apollo's appearance was pristine—every hair in place, his robe meticulously draped for dramatic effect, his expression pensive with a hint of aggression beneath.

Nicholas continued, "Like most close siblings, they argued and squabbled, but after a few minutes, they'd be best friends again."

At the mention of best friends, Ryan remembered that she was supposed to snap a photo of Nicholas for hers.

"But there was one fight that was different. Neither would give way. Zeus had to get involved."

"What was the argument about?"

A saddened tone came over Nicholas's voice. "Apollo killed one of Artemis's hunting partners. Artemis got along amicably with Orion, the mortal who was an avid huntsman himself. But very suddenly, Apollo killed Orion in cold blood. Back then, we all assumed that Apollo was jealous of the time Artemis and Orion were spending together hunting.

"But time has given us the benefit of investigating the brutal execution under a different lens. What if Apollo suspected there was more to Artemis and Orion's friendship? What if he found out they had actually fallen in love? I don't know if he knew Artemis was pregnant at this point, but regardless, I think it's possible Apollo killed Orion to uphold the honor of his sister. Or he may have thought he was protecting his sister from the wrath of their father, Zeus, who'd be livid if he found out his daughter had made a fool of him."

Eyes squinted in concentration, Ryan said, "That's a lot of what-ifs, Nicholas . . ." *No wonder Elias is suspicious of my arrival on this island*, she thought. "There could have been countless reasons for Apollo to kill Orion. Wasn't it common for arguments to end up in death back then?"

"What's curious is what Apollo did to appease Artemis," he continued. "It was a grand gesture, which leads me to believe there were feelings involved."

Ryan spent a few moments silently digesting Nicholas's hypothesis. Then comprehension dawned on her. "Orion. The constellation."

Nicholas gave her an enormous smile. "Yes, you bright woman. Apollo sent Orion to the sky to watch over her. Apollo essentially made him immortal, like Artemis, through his constellation in the stars." He shook his head. "Why would he go to those lengths? To quell Artemis's fury, but also to mend a broken heart. As you mentioned, we're a violent bunch. Back when the Olympians roamed the earth, mortals were killed all the time. The death of Orion was treated differently. Yet it was subtle enough for none of us to think twice about it."

Ryan rubbed her face. She liked how it fit together; it was a romantic story. But it was a myth. "It's still such a leap of faith, Nicholas. I'm guessing you think Artemis gave up her secret baby? Left it to live with us mortals?"

Nicholas nodded. "It fits with her personality. If she made a bad decision or a mistake with a perceived unfavorable outcome, she would most likely have hidden it. She's always been keen to come off as free spirited. If anything happened to threaten that perception, I think she would defuse or counter the threat. She pleaded publicly with Zeus to allow her to be single for eternity. And then she got pregnant, which completely contradicted the lifestyle for which she had fought."

Ryan stared unseeingly out into the distance. She didn't respect Artemis's reason for abandoning her bloodline. Glancing up, she studied Zeus. *On the other hand, who wouldn't be afraid of the consequences when that guy is your father? Still, if this is all true, Artemis was a coward.* She shot a dirty look toward the inanimate object that was the goddess.

Nicholas watched, meeting her eyes. "It's incredible to think there's been a secret bloodline of the deities living amongst mortals for thousands of years!" he breathed. Ryan smiled at his confident face; it was clear that he believed 100 percent in this story. And that he believed 100 percent in her.

With one last glance upward, the botanist followed Nicholas

inside the restaurant and was immediately enveloped by the most delicious aromas. Along one side of the wall, huge fireplaces with enormous vats bubbled and steamed, emitting glorious smells that made Ryan's mouth water. Around each fireplace were comfy-looking armchairs and low tables where people could dine by the fire. Long wooden tables and benches stretched out in the middle of the room, littered with small groups of people enjoying their breakfast. The room's lighting mimicked a warm, sunny afternoon; looking up, Ryan saw chandelier-like candelabras hanging from the ceiling and noticed curiously that the flames were all different shades of yellow and orange. *Must be a different kind of wax or wick,* Ryan thought to herself. Opposite the fireplaces sat a long bar, where all sorts of strange bottles, pots, and barrels were stacked across the wall. The room stretched back farther than Ryan had anticipated, and toward the end, she saw an opening that led outside to some greenery.

The staff must have been expecting her. The moment they arrived, two women approached Ryan and hugged her. Taken aback, the botanist could do little more than perform a mechanical pat-pat-pat on the backs of these beautiful strangers, but she felt warmth from their embraces. The two quickly shuffled Ryan off toward a table. She climbed over the bench and sat down in front of the most delectable-looking yogurt parfait with plump berries; a piece of sticky, sweet honeycomb dripped lazily toward crusty bread still warm from the oven. Without further ado, she dug right in.

"Hello, Ryan."

She looked up, lips smeared with honey and breadcrumbs, straight into the caramel eyes of Kosta. She hastily swallowed the food in her mouth, choked, reached for her water, took a swig, cleared her throat, wiped tears from her eyes, and smiled. He peered down at her, returning her toothy grin.

"Hi, Kosta," she croaked. Glancing at his companion, she added, "Morning, Melina."

"Can we join you? We just got done with our early morning chores and we're starved," Melina said, stretching out her arms and wiping her sweaty forehead with the back of her hand. "Oh, those are the berries I just picked," she added, swiping a raspberry from Ryan's parfait.

"Of course. Pull up a bench," the botanist said, her voice a little louder and higher than she had anticipated. Kosta sat directly across from her.

"Enjoy your breakfast, Ryan. These two will be showing you around," Nicholas said, patting Melina and Kosta's shoulders.

Food was swiftly placed in front of the rest of the group, so Ryan continued to dig in.

"I can't get over how beautiful you are, Ryan," said Melina, squinting hard to take in the details of her face.

"*I* am?" Ryan asked in complete surprise, her spoon clumsily twirling out of her hand. "No way. You guys are, like, gods." Ducking to grab her fallen utensil, she immediately realized that this was probably not the right thing to say. "I'm sorry," she said quickly. "I don't know if that's sacrilegious."

"It's OK!" Kosta reassured her just as quickly.

"I'm just a normal woman. You guys are, like, extraordinary . . . like a good Instagram filter is constantly following you."

Her observation was more about stating an obvious fact than harboring feelings of jealousy for the gorgeous gang in front of her. Ryan had long ago come to terms with the fact that she was average looking—not homely in the least, but not a ten either. It wasn't that she necessarily had low self-esteem—she was just realistic in how she viewed her outward appearance. She lacked the wherewithal to operate a hot hair tool of any kind, so her not-quite-straight, not-quite-curly hair was more often than not in a messy bun atop her head. Her deep brown eyes matched her hair and were framed with bountiful eyebrows that needed to be tamed with a whip and tweezers daily. Her nose was a little too large for her face, her lips were pretty decent, and she had a secret dimple on her left cheek that only revealed itself when she was thoroughly amused. She possessed a darker complexion, but the name Ryan Bell didn't exactly scream which ethnicity her people originated from. She considered herself to have an athletic build without being remotely active; she had freakishly strong arms, curvy hips, a doughy belly, and thighs big enough to squash any hint of a "thigh gap."

"I don't know what an 'inster gramphilter' is, but you are the first outsider we've ever seen in person," Kosta explained.

"Yeah, sometimes we'll get the occasional contraband with photos or video of people outside the island, but it's strictly prohibited by the council, so it's hard to come by. It's amazing to meet someone who didn't come from this island. I never thought I'd see the day," Melina said around the spoon of yogurt in her mouth, leaning back to study Ryan intently.

Ryan flicked her gaze downward but studied Melina right back beneath her eyelashes. Her intricately braided hair was laced with what looked like beads of obsidian and pulled into a tight bun on top of her head. A maze of black ink ran up her arms to her shoulders, the intricate tattoos barely visible on her radiant umber skin.

Ryan put down her spoon and self-consciously tucked her hair behind her ear. "It's equally amazing to meet you guys, after you've been kept on this hidden island your whole lives."

"More like trapped," Elias said as he collapsed in a heap next to

Melina. He stole a ripe strawberry from her plate and was rewarded with a spoon smack.

"Poor guy. Has it so tough," Kosta said, rolling his eyes.

Elias flexed his arm muscles, patted them at Kosta, and said, "Tough is right," then tucked into the food in front of him.

"Yeah, what's that like?" asked Ryan. She supposed they weren't unlike anyone who'd been born and raised in the same town their whole life, but this island was a far cry from, say, Cleveland.

"You tell us. We can only dream what lies across this sea." Melina got a faraway look in her eyes. "New people. Technology. Junky food. Music. Starbuck. A whole world."

Ryan hid a grin, secretly getting a kick out of these vernacular mistakes. "I guess it's pretty isolating for you all."

"Don't get me wrong, we have plenty to do around here to stay busy," Melina said, suddenly businesslike. As she tore off a piece of bread, she continued, "But there's so much out there. And such freedom. No monotony, no responsibilities. So much adventure to seek, so many people to meet. How could anyone ever get bored out there?"

Ryan, Kosta, and Elias amusedly watched Melina spurt out this soliloquy with a dreamy look, honey slowly dripping down her wrist. *She's having a real* Little Mermaid *moment,* Ryan observed. She didn't have a grasp on the role Melina played on the island, but she had a feeling that the Descendant was a free spirit despite her obligations.

Melina snapped out of it suddenly, sheepishly grinning at them while attempting to lick the rogue honey from her hand. Ryan gave her a reassuring smile back.

"It is great out there, yes," the botanist told her, "but it's no utopia in the real world. It's complicated. Since you guys live . . . off the beaten path, shall we say, it doesn't seem like you're plagued with the effects of climate change like we are. The fact that you're still able to grow all this food"—she looked down in wonder, inspecting the beautiful blueberry in front of her—"we don't get produce like this anymore. The berries from our farms look sickly and aren't as flavorful as they used to be. The air is toxic, the water contaminated. People from different nations point fingers at one another; nobody agrees on a solution toward a brighter future. Or even a livable future, for that matter."

"It can get complicated in here too," Elias countered haughtily.

"Don't snap at her," Kosta bit back.

"I didn't!" Elias said, frowning at him. He tilted his head and moodily cracked his neck.

Ryan studied Elias quizzically, then said, "I didn't mean to downplay the experiences you guys have had here. The grass is always greener. But there are a lot of people out in the real world—different people of all shapes, colors, and sizes—with different ideals and beliefs and opinions. Conflict is an unfortunate product of individuality.

"Not to mention the unexplained natural atrocities occurring more frequently, which you also seem to be removed from . . ."

Melina pushed her plate away and stretched her beautifully toned arms above her head. "I promised Pavlos I would direct the honeybees to pollinate the almonds, cranberries, and blueberries this morning. Let's take a walk."

Ryan nodded, excited to get some fresh air and see their beehives.

Elias sighed, sulkily grabbing as much food as his giant hands could handle before trudging past her toward the exit; Kosta and Melina followed in tow. Ryan watched after him curiously; he sure could be cantankerous, but everyone seemed to accept him as he was, even to like him. She wondered if he got off easier because he was so darn good looking.

Standing, Ryan glanced at Nicholas, who hovered over a steaming bowl at the bar. She was slightly anxious about separating from him but longed to explore a different vantage point of the island.

As the three of them followed Elias out of the second exit opposite the rotunda, a sprightly breeze whipped Ryan's baby hairs all over her forehead; they were higher above the ocean than the last time she'd been outside. To the right, she could see the rocky exterior of the mountain, and spotted the opening that she had seen in the atrium. The natural doorway opened to a large, flat slab of rock that stood a few feet above the water line. The ocean was rougher and more unsettled than yesterday; it reminded her of what had gone on in her tummy when they had mentioned testing her later that week. Waves were crashing up the mountain, sending droplets at least twenty feet into the air.

"Elias, do you want me to take care of the fish—" Kosta began.

"I'll do it," Elias cut in.

Kosta huffed impatiently. "If you're going to be moodier than a harpy with a toothache—"

"I said, I'll do it," said Elias with a sneer.

Kosta took a calming breath and slowly said, "Your attitude sucks lately."

"I'm tired," the other Descendant grumbled, glancing behind him at the ocean.

"We're all tired," Kosta replied through his teeth.

"Cool it, you guys," Melina warned.

Kosta's eyes darted behind Elias, twinkling with sudden mischief. "She's right. You need to cool off."

And with that, he lifted Elias over his head and, to Ryan's absolute horror, tossed him off the cliff.

As if in slow motion, she watched Elias plunge into the raging water below. Ryan sank to her knees as she searched for a bobbing head in vain.

"Oh my god, Kosta! You killed him!" she shrieked.

8

RYAN HEARD MELINA GIGGLE BEHIND her. "I can't get enough of Ryan saying, 'Oh my god,'" she told Kosta. "Oh *my* god. Oh my *god*," she said to herself, mimicking the botanist with different inflections.

Ryan looked back in horror. Who were these people? Not only had Kosta committed a cold-blooded murder, but he and Melina were laughing as though nothing had happened. She looked back at the ocean, her nose starting to sting as tears streamed down her face. She hadn't been particularly fond of the guy, but she certainly hadn't wanted to see him dead.

Suddenly, right before her eyes, Elias came shooting out of the water like a champagne cork from a bottle. They had to have been a hundred feet up the mountain, but he rose straight into the air and hovered a few feet off the ledge where they were standing. Cheeks puffed out, Elias proceeded to squirt water like a possessed fire hydrant at Kosta, who stumbled a couple feet backward from the barrage of water.

Once Elias had finished spraying an inconceivable amount of water, he doubled over laughing, still hovering, standing on nothing at all.

"I deserved that," Kosta said, joining in with a deep belly laugh that echoed against the mountain.

Melina rolled her eyes and mumbled under her breath; Ryan caught the words "juvenile" and "backwash."

The botanist's mouth hung wide open. She looked meekly toward the ocean, her finger pointing down, slowly tracing Elias's flight path from the water to where he now stood in front of her. There weren't any wires or ropes attached to him, she thought, her brain numbly trying to make sense of what she'd witnessed with her own two eyes. He had plunged into the sea and then come back up of his own volition. How? She looked back at the group, who had moved to the topic of weather, looks of concern on their faces.

"Um, excuse me," she said weakly, an amalgamation of awe and bewilderment infiltrating her voice. The group stopped talking to look at her as though they'd completely forgotten she was there. Her pale face and shaky exterior snapped them back to reality.

"Oh, sorry, Ryan!" cried Melina, who grabbed her hand and patted it kindly. "We forgot . . . that must have been quite the shock."

"Wait, how?" Eyes wide as saucers, Ryan stuttered, "Is . . . did he do . . ."

"Yes, he used his powers," Kosta finished quietly.

"You guys," Ryan stammered, grasping Melina's hand hard. "I can't do that! Believe me, I cannot do that!" she repeated emphatically, pointing at the ocean.

"Elias has been a demigod since he was a toddler," Melina began.

"And he won't let any of us forget it," Kosta said under his breath.

Snorting, Melina continued, "His powers are incredibly strong, as he's had a lot of time to practice. We don't expect you to do that just yet." She gently pulled Ryan's body into a standing position, gave her arms a quick squeeze, and then turned toward the path.

Ryan stubbornly shook her head. "Y'all are in for a rude awakening."

"Ryan, I'm touched you cared so much about my well-being," Elias said with a smirk, holding his hands to his heart. Kosta looked from him to Ryan, a muscle in his jaw twitching.

"Time to fish," Elias said in a sarcastically excited tone—with that, he backflipped through the air, spinning faster and faster until he was nearly inches from the water. Instead of splashing in, he parted the water around him so that he gently landed on the sandy ocean floor.

Melina, Ryan, and Kosta watched as Elias lifted his left leg and stomped his foot into the ground with such force, water rapidly receded away from him. He repeated the mega leg stomp with his right leg so that the rest of the water flowed fifty feet away from the mountain, mysteriously held in place as if by a glass wall.

Now that the limestone ocean floor was exposed, Elias surveyed the frenzy of flapping sea creatures. Whistling, he strolled about the sea floor, collecting a pile of slender fish with prominent stripes, kicking an errant eel out of the way, happily navigating along the rocky Aegean seafloor like it was a themed underwater playground. After a few minutes, his hands on his hips, Elias seemed satisfied with his flailing haul of fish, enough to fill a small semitruck. Walking over, he began throwing each fish toward the rock slab, where five huge baskets were arranged in a line. His speed grew faster and faster, the edges of his body becoming blurry with motion, the flight of fish reminiscent of a machine gun spewing bullets neatly into the baskets. The melodic thwacks of fish on fish soon died down as Elias reached the last few.

He glanced up at Melina, Kosta, and Ryan, winked at them as though he knew they were impressed, and chucked the last catch up toward them, the fish slicing through the air more like a torpedo than a frisbee. Kosta lazily caught it. "I guess it's mackerel for lunch," he said, using his hands to make the fish swim toward Melina and kiss her on the cheek.

Smacking it away, Melina griped, "Asshole. He knows I prefer pike."

With a final look at the ocean, Elias lazily flicked his finger as though motioning "come here." The raging waves rushed back to their rightful place, the roar so deafening that Ryan covered her ears. The relief was palpable as the water surged over the suffocating sea creatures, a feeling Ryan compared to breathing pure, cleansed air from a Weeping Diana.

Who are these people? wondered Ryan. *And if they do possess powers, does that mean . . . ?*

She looked up to the indiscernible peak of Mount Olympus, squinting her eyes to see if she could make out the shadows of the gods behind the screen of clouds. Every few hours, facts that she'd believed were plain as day found themselves turned upside down, inside out, and backward. Mythical creatures had been fantasy two days ago, but yesterday they'd been proven real. Yesterday, powers had been fiction, but today they were concrete fact.

Looking out at the vastness of the ocean and replaying the scenes she'd just witnessed, Ryan thought: *What else am I wrong about?*

She turned and followed the group up a steep, grassy, well-worn footpath that hugged the mountainside. As she caught up with them at the peak of the path, she was gifted with a spectacular view: this entire side of the island was used as terraced farmland. Row upon row of vegetables, grains, legumes, fruit trees, and vines snaked around enormous hills. It reminded her of pictures she'd seen of rice fields in Vietnam, but these were in the middle of the Aegean Sea. She could see people interspersed within the rows, heads down, tending to the different plants.

The three of them continued walking down the path that ended at one of the terraced rows. Ryan saw that the perfectly manicured trees held enormous, meaty, purple kalamata olives. Plump figs decorated the row above, and Ryan saw walnuts strewn upon the ground in the row below. "Wow, Nicholas wasn't kidding about being a self-sufficient island."

Kosta turned around to behold the rows from Ryan's perspective. "I guess it's pretty impressive," he said, a hint of doubt in his voice. "Don't you guys have farms in Minnesota?"

"Yes, but . . . is that coffee I see in the distance? How does that even grow in this climate? Crops don't grow side by side like this. They all have different soil and climate needs." Ryan marveled at the abundance of crops; it was like walking through a farmer's market where all the produce was ripe on the vine.

Kosta nodded. "It takes a lot of effort. Those of us with powers must ensure that our food grows by communicating with the plants, keeping their needs catered to, adjusting the rows to specific atmospheric needs, and so on."

"Looks like Pavlos is ready for me," Melina said. "Kaliméra, Pavlos!" she shouted, her voice booming unnaturally loud, reaching the ears of a man who had to be half a mile away.

The man took off his straw hat and waved it in their direction. "Hello, Melina!" they saw him shout back, though it was barely audible.

"Ready for the bees?" she boomed again.

He gestured a thumbs-up.

"Where are the hives?" Ryan asked, looking around.

Melina smiled, raised her eyebrows mischievously, and turned her back toward Ryan. Facing the rows below them, she raised both arms to eye level like a conductor before an orchestra. Ryan's heart rate increased, knowing that what she was about to see was going to blow her mind again.

Melina lifted her arms over her head, as if to initiate the beginning of a song; then, to Ryan's astonishment, bees rose up a couple feet from the trees in unison. The most wonderful buzzing sound accompanied the sight, a hum Ryan felt deep in her chest.

"Let's get you guys into three groups," Melina murmured to herself. Arms still raised, she motioned her left hand to one side, waving a third of the bees toward one end. She repeated the motion with her right hand, the bees roughly separated into three masses.

"I need good listeners today," she reminded the bees sternly. As Melina used her hands to cup the air in front of her, Ryan watched the bees squish themselves into more defined groupings.

"Very good." Melina appraised their surroundings. "You guys go to the almonds," she said, pointing to a row of trees toward the top of the hill. The bees obediently followed her instructions and lined up like rows of soldiers ready for a pollination battle.

"You guys to the cranberries," she coaxed, pointing another group to a row of plants below them.

"And you guys, blueberries," she finished. The last group obediently took their places.

"Well, what are you waiting for?" Melina asked impatiently. As the bees began their journeys to their final destinations, she did a little flick with her fingers; to Ryan's amusement, the bees did a few loop-the-loops in the air, their buzzing a pleasing melody.

"Show-off," muttered Kosta. Melina smiled smugly.

Eyes wide, head shaking in wonder, Ryan clapped hard. Melina did a little curtsey, a rosy sheen spreading over her grinning brown cheeks.

"That was incredible," Ryan breathed.

"Thank you!" She stopped suddenly, head tilting as though listening to something in the distance. "Ooh! The corn is begging for a drink. It's so needy. I'll be right back," Melina said over her shoulder, jogging in the direction of the stalks of corn.

Wordlessly, Kosta led Ryan back toward a bench that had been carved into the mountain, overlooking the ocean below.

"So I gather that not everyone on the island has powers? I can't be the only one who doesn't hear the little kernels of corn pleading for water," Ryan said, her mouth curving upward as she plopped down.

"No. Once the gods were banished, Gaea and her crew began an all-out genocide on all demigods and creatures associated with the gods, to stamp out any reminder that they ever existed. So they all banded together here, creating a civilization to fight this injustice. Defiantly, we procreated, keeping the population of deity Descendants strong and powerful."

"Wow," Ryan said softly. "This godly gene must be very strong to withstand all the generations removed from actually being a direct relation to the gods."

"Well, it was. Typically, whenever a demigod had a child with another demigod, the genes would battle it out and the baby would eventually show characteristics of one of the parents' gods. But a couple generations ago, we noticed something alarming: a Descendant was not guaranteed. The bloodlines somehow started dying out. So although my mother, who was a Descendant of Athena, had three children with my father, a Descendant of Hephaestus, I was the only one who developed powers."

"Ahh." Ryan nodded slowly. "So the population of Descendant deities has decreased."

"Yes, substantially. There's only a hundred and twenty-six of us demigods out of nearly a thousand islanders. And within those, there are four Descendants of Zeus left. We're afraid that once we no longer represent all the gods, any hope of freeing them is lost."

"And this whole time, you think that you've been unable to do so because . . ."

"Artemis's line has been absent."

"A line you guys didn't know existed . . ." Ryan said slowly, scrutinizing Kosta.

"Until recently," Kosta replied, not meeting Ryan's eyes.

"And this has been your generation's response to fighting Gaea. To hunt for a long-lost relative and band together for the first time. And somehow, rallying everyone together will be enough to unlock the cloudy vault to free the gods."

"One of the responses," he muttered under his breath. Seeing Ryan's confusion, he cleared his throat and said, "Yes, all while the clock ticks down on our very existence."

"You guys are in quite a pickle," Ryan said grimly, making Kosta laugh.

"Yes. Indeed." He shifted his weight, the hem of his robe revealing a glimmer of golden, muscular thigh. Ryan tried to avert her curious eyes as Kosta said, "I guess you have the same weight on your shoulders. The weight of the world rests on your flowers."

She smiled ruefully. They did have a lot in common: the constant worry that their own worlds were going to end. With powers or without. "Well, I guess we are kind of in the same boat. Except mine is a ferry and yours is a yacht propelled by Elias's thunderous thighs."

"Seeing and hearing all this"—he gestured toward the terraced farmland and ocean—"is there any part of you that has awakened?" His forearm gently grazed hers as he sat down next to her. Her body exploded with goosebumps, sending the hairs on her arms reaching straight into the air, as though beckoning Kosta to move closer. Ryan stroked them down, trying to draw attention away from her hairy arms.

"Honestly? If I'm not hallucinating from some head injury and you are looking for someone who has magical powers, you've got the wrong girl. I think this is just a sad, twisted case of mistaken identity." Unexpectedly, Ryan felt her eyes start to sting as a breeze whipped her hair back and forth. "But I feel really sad to let you people down," she whispered.

"The only way you'd let us down is by not trying. I can't even imagine the shock and disbelief you're going through right now. I wouldn't survive if I were plucked unwillingly into your world, with the underground snake vehicles and the fireless boxes that warm up food. And then to be asked to do a task that you had previously thought was unthinkable?" Kosta shook his head in bewilderment, a flush creeping along his neck and chiseled jaw. "I get it. But I don't want you to feel like you're alone—we believe in you."

Before she could stop herself, she patted Kosta's thigh next to her. He immediately twitched it away. Mortified, she tried to play it off by wiping her hands of an imaginary bug and stood up.

"Thanks, Kosta," Ryan said, her back toward him. As she heard Melina run up to meet them, she added, "And you'd eventually get the hang of subway trains and microwaves."

"All right, they're satiated," Melina said, hands on her knees, catching her breath. "Those suckers can sure drink."

"I hope you carded them," Ryan joked. "Wouldn't want the corn to pickle."

Melina gave her a questioning look and then glanced at Kosta, who shrugged. *Apparently my humor does not transcend time zones,* the botanist surmised.

Awkward moments aside, Ryan enjoyed the remainder of the

day, tagging along with Melina and Kosta on their typical deity duties. Their focus was giving Ryan an introduction to their powers and what they were capable of. To her relief, they didn't ask her to participate yet, but Melina did "tag" Ryan and then shimmy up an enormous Ionic column, hoping she would take the bait and follow her right up like Spider-Man. And Kosta did offer to let her hold up the enormous marble pediment the two were repairing, though that could have just been chivalry.

Ryan also got to meet some other residents of the island. They ate a picnic lunch beside an idyllic waterfall with a group called the Graces. Ryan was so entranced by her Zen surroundings and the tranquil way the sunlight hit the droplets of spritzing water, she fell into a fugue-like state of serenity. Only after Melina repeatedly snapped her fingers in front of Ryan's face and implored the Graces to tone down the relaxation vibes was the botanist able to grasp that this group exuded different emotions or mental states into the atmosphere. Assuming Ryan would be anxious from her morning activities, the Graces had apparently piped too much Greek god Xanax into the air.

They also had a run-in with the kobaloi, who were congregated under a shady tree near a small temple in the forest. Resembling evil little Care Bears, they looked perturbed to be interrupted by Ryan, Melina, and Kosta. However, once Ryan jokingly mentioned how the temple could pass for a gift shop at a theme park, the kobaloi emptied the pockets of their robes, attempting to pawn off their treasures: amethyst diadems, emerald arm bands, and pearl pendants. After oohing and aahing, Ryan glanced toward Kosta, who shook his head imperceptibly. Melina shrewdly glared at one of the kobaloi, her palm out; guiltily, the creature placed a jade ring in it. The

Descendant huffily pushed it back on her finger and guided Ryan out of the temple and away from the naughty bears.

For dinner, they sat on the same bench with Elias at Maria's. As she helped herself to moussaka—some sort of casserole with beef, eggplant, and cinnamon—Ryan couldn't reconcile the earlier parfait-eating version of herself to the woman she was now: knee deep in this fantastical world where myth and reality collided.

As the sun began to set on Ryan's second day on the island, Melina slung her arm over the botanist's shoulder, smiled at her, and said, "Believe it or not, that was the most fun I've had in a while."

Ryan smiled back warmly. "My first full day was unreal."

"More to come tomorrow. For now, Kosta and I need to head down to a council meeting."

Ryan stood up. "Oh, OK. Can't I come with you?" she asked.

Melina looked at Kosta, who looked down at the ground. "It's only for the chosen representatives of each god. Maybe you can join another time," he suggested.

Ryan shrugged. "OK! Enjoy your meeting."

After Melina guided her back to her room before heading to the council meeting, Ryan rapidly tapped out a response to Greta's most recent text message: *Don't you dare, Greta. I know you're bored without me, but Lester does not need a lion haircut. If this suggestion is in retaliation to him shredding your favorite pair of Uggs, I will buy you a new pair. Lester is only acting out because he misses his mother. It also sounds like YOU'RE acting out because you miss your bestie. Which I can respect. Still, NO HAIRCUT.*

Exasperated, she swiped to Cyrus's latest text.

Hope you slept well! I am a grumpy gerbera today. The boss lady is pushing a pointless project, so I'm having a hard time staying motivated. Too distracted by the thought of a hibiscus iced tea with a certain lady.

Tell me more about this island to further distract me. How long was the boat ride?

Reading his texts, she almost felt guilty, like she was two-timing Cyrus with Kosta. It had been ages since she'd had a crush, and—BAM—she now had *two*. One was a fellow scientist—the other a demigod. These were ridiculously hard waters to navigate. She knew it was just physical attraction between her and Kosta; she hardly knew him. But her heart felt weirdly . . . attached to him. Like, instantly intimate. Was this part of the territory? she wondered. Had Hercules been a man-whore?

You're getting ahead of yourself, Ryan chastised herself. *This island, along with Kosta, will be a distant memory in a few days, and then my text repartee with Cyrus will fizzle out, the date will never come into fruition, and at last, I'll be back in my safe, comfortable zone of having exactly zero potential love interests.*

Ryan tapped back:

Sorry your boss is on your booty today! My morning has been a bit overwhelming, so the thought of a refreshing beverage sounds tantalizing. Oh gosh, my tummy doesn't want to think back to the rocky boat ride to this island—had to be a few hours? Not looking forward to the ride back. There is this breathtaking, enormous mountain here—can't even see its peak. Too bad I didn't bring my hiking boots!

Seeing her text go through, she cringed, woefully unsatisfied with her response. Booty? Tantalizing? Tummy? Hiking boots? She needed Greta in these situations.

As she was about to put down her phone, she saw that her text had been read by Cyrus. She eagerly waited a few seconds to see if he'd respond, but her phone pinged with a different alert: Cyrus had requested access to Ryan's location through her phone.

Odd, she thought. Greta didn't even allow them to share locations;

she was convinced the phone would somehow announce how often she visited the bathroom. Hottie or not, it was a bit forward and, quite frankly, weird for him to ask to virtually stalk her location. She neither declined nor accepted the invitation.

T HE NEXT MORNING WAS A flurry of activity. Melina bounded in, tutted at Ryan's "training" outfit, and threw open a drawer full of gorgeous white fabric. Picking one up, the Descendant studied Ryan for a few seconds and then swished the fabric, as if to air it out. It turned a magnificent shade of rose gold, causing the botanist to squee in delight.

After Melina showed Ryan multiple techniques for wearing the chiton (Melina had emphatically corrected her that togas were Roman, not Greek), she chose one of the more conservative styles. Ryan did some ninja moves and a few high kicks (immediately wishing she'd stretched first) and confirmed that nothing was exposed. After pulling her hair into her go-to high bun on top of her head, she examined her appearance in the full-length mirror. *Well, I'm ready,* she thought anxiously. *For what? I'm not sure. Either prom, a costume party, or superhero training.*

As they journeyed out of the mountain toward the training arena, the two women chitchatted about completely ordinary topics, like other mythicals of the island (including a half woman, half spider called an arachne who wove silk used in the very chiton robe Ryan was wearing), the Fates (a trio of sisters who lived on the island, determining each person's destiny on earth), and the Muses (nine sisters whose collective knowledge spanned to the beginning of time).

Twenty minutes later, a slightly out-of-breath Ryan complained, "We've been walking for ages!" Keeping up with Melina's brisk stride had proved to be a bit of a challenge for her. The well-beaten path dipped and rose like a roller-coaster track, the terrain becoming rocky and mountainous yet still thick with trees. As she smoothed the frizz from her face, she irritably noticed Melina's beautiful braids were undisturbed by the humidity.

"We need to keep the operation a safe distance from our living area. Things can get a little rowdy here," Melina explained.

As they picked through a particularly thick knot of enormous trees at the top of a steep hill, the dense foliage suddenly parted like a curtain, exposing Melina and Ryan to a deeply clouded sky. Ryan gasped at the scene below.

"Welcome to training camp, Ryan," Melina said, grinning proudly.

The opening looked down into a massive valley that was surrounded by mountainous peaks. The expanse of grass stretched out like carpet, where groups of people, a couple hundred of them at least, were congregated. Shiny, ivory Greek columns surrounded the valley like a barrier, transforming the space into a natural, open-air stadium.

Even from their vantage point a half mile away, she could already make out things that proved seeing was believing. To the right side of the field, a group stood spectating a burning mountainside. One Descendant was waving his hands in the air, and Ryan realized he was conducting the fire in front of him—making it leap here and there, pirouette ten feet in the air, and then plummet to the ground in gusto. The effect was a fanciful synchronized amber dance.

Ryan saw another Descendant completely engulfed in flames. The human fireball paused after spreading a path of fire behind them, seemingly experimenting with the size of blaze emanating from their body. Ryan watched as the person's arms transformed into big fire limbs, stretching twenty feet long. They waved them around like two big lassos, fiery ashes lightly raining down like fluffy gray snowflakes.

Despite the infernal chaos wreaking havoc across the mountainside, the fire was contained enough that Descendants training nearby didn't even glance in its direction. Ryan realized that the Descendant whom she'd thought was simply spectating was anything but; as she surveyed the pyro people with intensity, a watery orb followed her gaze, gracefully bouncing every few feet like a playful squirrel, extinguishing errant flames here and there to ensure the fire didn't spread. A minute later, the fire conductor stopped, stretching out his arms as if they were tired, and the watery orb shot at the fireball human like a water balloon, revealing a smoking yet smiling man. With a jolt, Ryan recognized a very charred-looking Kosta. *Literally* and *figuratively too hot to handle*, she thought in awe.

Another orb had appeared, slowly expanding in the air until it grew to the size of a watery hot air balloon. Ryan watched as its owner walked up to the balloon and poked her pointer finger to pop it. A peal of laughter reverberated off the hills as she quickly retreated from the enormous splash to extinguish all the fire on the mountainside. A fourth Descendant, a woman with a long, flowing pink robe, walked to the middle of the charred mountainside and started slowly spinning like Julie Andrews in *The Sound of Music*. From her dress came big blossoms that spread over the burnt, crunchy ground, transforming it into a carpet of wildflowers in peak bloom.

Just as Ryan was about to study another brightly colored group toward the center of the field, a huge black owl with hazel eyes landed on the rock right in front of them.

"Ahh, I see we've been spotted." Melina gave the owl a little tickle under the wing, which made it undeniably giggle with hoots.

"Is this your pet owl?" Ryan watched as the bird tenderly brushed one of its wings across Melina's face, then flew away just as quickly as it had appeared.

"No, that was my cousin, Alexandros," she said nonchalantly. Melina scrutinized Ryan, raw curiosity on her face. "Have you started to feel it?"

Ryan was quiet. She surveyed the action taking place between two enormous columns in front of her. She saw a woman and man in hand-to-hand combat, performing moves that made the Marvel superheroes look like toddlers fighting. On the other side of the pitch, she saw a man doing the backstroke in midair, his hair and chiton robe mesmerizingly floating as though truly immersed in water. Another group of younger boys and girls slowly disappeared before Ryan's eyes until they were completely invisible, reappearing a few feet away. She saw a sheep sitting on its rump, looking bored as it filed its nails. Another Descendant meandered over and started conversing with the sheep. *I must be dreaming*, Ryan thought incredulously.

Melina watched her mull things over in her head and evidently decided a non-response was more promising than a negative one.

"So how am I supposed to . . . 'do' magic?" Ryan cautiously asked.

"Well, to be completely honest, we're not sure."

Ryan rolled her eyes. "Just the pep talk and vote of confidence I need."

Melina laughed. "When our abilities begin to creep out, it's obvious which god's powers we're developing. I started showing signs of Zeus when I was four. Kosta showed telltale signs of pyromancy when he was a bit older at six, and Elias was just two years old when he disappeared one day, having swum all the way to the edge of our forcefield."

Ryan nodded, suddenly feeling unaccomplished at twenty-eight years old.

"But for you, since you're part—"

"Allegedly," Ryan interjected.

"—of a lost line of Descendants of Artemis," Melina said, her voice loud to drown out Ryan's interruption, "your powers should reflect hers."

"And Artemis is . . ."

"The Goddess of the Hunt," replied Melina, a mischievous look in her eyes.

Ryan stopped in her tracks, grabbing Melina's arm. "Well, see, this proves it! I'm not a hunter, nor do I have any sort of special ability to strategize when it comes to tracking and scavenging. In fact, I once got lost in an Ikea and had to call the store to assist me to an exit."

"Just because you don't possess an affinity for hunting doesn't mean you aren't a Descendant," Melina said patiently.

"Melina, hunting couldn't be further from my wheelhouse. I don't even hunt for a good sale! I buy full price." Emphatically, she repeated, "Full price."

Ryan continued, eyebrows drawn together in concentration, "In fact, creating life to ultimately save life—like the Weeping Diana does—seems like the very opposite of hunting."

Melina gave a noncommittal shrug. "Artemis is the goddess of many things, but hunting is the main one, and it's a good place for us to start."

Ryan sighed. "Sounds like the signs of Kosta and Elias's powers post-infancy were direct reflections of their gods."

"Listen, you're a scientist, right? This is our hypothesis. Let's test it and come to a conclusion." Melina turned toward Ryan, waiting patiently as the botanist stubbornly tried to avoid eye contact. "Ryan, what you've done with your plants is extraordinary, even in the eyes of us Descendants who have our own magical abilities. All I'm asking is for you to have an open mind and to release any qualms you have going into this day."

Letting out a deep breath, Ryan said, "I'm not trying to be difficult, but what you're asking me to do is easier said than done. I'm afraid it's not going to be the stress that is detrimental to the development of my powers but the fact that I just don't possess any. Kind of hard to develop something that truly isn't there."

Melina paused, absently rubbing a knot out of her shoulder, then said, "Ryan, when you are in your greenhouse, I'm assuming it's your happy place. I imagine that all the stress, all the negativity, all the pain melts away when you are in your little haven. That calm demeanor? That's where you are able to work your magic. We need to get you to that place so that you can explore your capabilities."

It was true—her greenhouse was her happy place. She'd always felt at home in the humid, fragrant, transparent structure, protected from both the elements and outside judgment. Ryan was doubtful that she could completely replicate the serenity from home, seeing as she'd been lured under false circumstances to an unplottable island full of magical ancient Greeks, but she didn't argue the point.

"Melina, say that I am able to, I dunno, create new species of plants. Unless I'm able to build a giant Gaea-eating plant, I don't exactly know how I'd help you fight her. As far as superheroes go, I don't see where a nerdy botanist fits in."

Melina laughed, a pleasant wind chime to Ryan's ears. "Ryan, while you may have unknowingly started to utilize one of your powers, a host of more powerful, extraordinary abilities have yet to be uncovered. With no training whatsoever, you already possess strong magic. And worse comes to worst, you can always give Gaea a nasty rash. Or mess with her allergies."

Ryan snorted. "Poison ivy is no laughing matter."

Melina snickered.

Ryan had to agree that creating the Weeping Dianas was a marvelous feat indeed. But had she really magicked them to life as Melina was insinuating? She had poured her blood, sweat, and tears into those flowers. *It wasn't magic that produced them,* thought Ryan, *it was me.* That little velvety green sprout peeking through the aromatic, earthy soil meant so much to her. It was both her crowning achievement and her biggest pitfall. If magic was involved, she didn't know if it would change the way she felt about her discovery.

"So who am I going to train with? You? Nicholas? Kosta?" she asked casually, not-so-casually whipping her head left and right to look for the latter.

"You'll be meeting with a few other Descendants of various godly backgrounds who have brainstormed ways to test you, based on ways Artemis's talent for hunting may translate through you."

Ryan pictured them barking impossible task after impossible task while the whole camp of Descendants looked on and laughed. Oddly enough, in this daydream she was also in her underwear. "I swear to god, if you give me a shotgun and expect me to track some sort of varmint . . ."

"Give us a little more credit, Ryan. We've been doing this for the past several millennia," responded Melina with a playful grin.

"I need whatever face cream you're using . . ." Ryan retorted, searching for even one wrinkle on Melina's smooth face.

As another one of her jokes went over Melina's head, she realized that they were walking toward what looked to be a greenhouse.

Nicholas stepped out of the structure as Ryan hungrily studied it. "Wow, it looks fully operational! Did you guys just build this?"

"We've been working on it since you arrived," said Nicholas, delighted with her praise. "Why don't you take a look inside?"

While the greenhouse's interior was laid out differently than her own, it looked authentic. The familiar atmosphere greeted her like an old friend; the air was heavy with condensation, and the damp aroma of earth filled her nose. Then she saw them: rows and rows of Weeping Dianas, all in different stages of development, including the still-barren pots she'd planted a couple evenings before.

"Ryan, this is Agalia, Descendant of Demeter," said Melina. Ryan shook the hand of the woman who looked like she could play a zesty, quick-witted aunt on a TV sitcom, the kind who would nonchalantly bring up your nonexistent love life or thickening midsection at a family dinner. The older woman immediately grasped Ryan's face and kissed both cheeks, causing the botanist to tactfully spit out a mouthful of her new acquaintance's salt-and-pepper hair. As though she'd known Ryan all her life, Agalia cradled Ryan's hand in hers while Nicholas continued.

"Agalia's powers are terrifying in warfare—"

Agalia bounced her shoulders in response, a pleased look on her face.

"—but in our day-to-day life, she is one of the Descendants who works to make sure our crops and food supply are bountiful."

"It is so nice to meet you, Ryan," Agalia crooned. She frowned and tugged the neckline on the botanist's chiton. "A little loose in the chest area, yes?" This woman was one step away from wiping dirt off Ryan's face with her own spit.

"Great to meet you too," Ryan responded, smoothing her hands over the front of her chiton as she walked over to examine the

Weeping Dianas. As she gingerly rubbed the familiar velvety petals, she noted that the blue hues were infinitesimally duller than the specimens produced in her lab, but she reasoned that a slight variation in color was logical when grown in an unknown environment. "They look very healthy and happy. Well done."

"Thank you." Agalia swooped down to dramatically bow, and then joined Ryan at the Weeping Dianas. "Really, they are a magnificent species you created." Clapping her hands together, she added, "Before we go, let me show you around, get you acquainted with some of my little flora friends." She opened her arms wide, presenting the plants before her, and gave another flourishing bow. Ryan giggled at her theatrics.

"Now this, *moro mou*, is—" Agalia began.

"—bay laurel," Ryan finished, fingering the leafy bush in front of her.

"Well done! Yes, laurel indeed. I have to keep a pretty big supply on hand for our Olympic games. We crown the champions with wreaths of laurels."

"Yes, they do that at toga parties too," Ryan said.

Agalia nodded enthusiastically as though she knew what these were. "Also," she said, leaning in conspiratorially, "it's said if two lovers break off a stick of laurel and each keep a piece, they will remain faithful to each other forever." She wriggled her eyebrows up and down animatedly. "I've given out tons of laurel sticks!"

Ryan burst out laughing. This woman's energy and spirit were contagious. "I think you and my friend Greta would get along swimmingly."

Agalia shimmied to another row of plants. "And this, what do you suppose this is?"

Ryan rose to the challenge. She recognized the plant immediately but bent down to confirm her guess by scent. "Clover," she said proudly.

"Right again! Here, take some." She shoved a bunch of leaves into Ryan's hands. "Great for sexual health and fertility. You are a single lady, no?" She raised her eyebrows.

"Oh, um," Ryan stuttered, blushing furiously. Agalia let out a great bubble of laughter, delighting in her uncomfortable response.

The botanist smiled weakly at Agalia and passed her, looking at the next set of plants behind her. "Hmm . . . I'm unfamiliar with these."

"Shhh . . ." Agalia whispered loudly. "They're sleepi—"

"Arghhhhh! It's got me!" Ryan screamed.

As she had gently thumbed the innocent-looking leafy plant, a red flower head, about the size of a pumpkin, had whipped around and proceeded to chomp her entire hand so that only her wrist stuck out of its petal mouth. Three other blossom heads looked up at her curiously.

"Constantine, no!" Agalia said sharply, wagging her finger.

The pink lips spat out her hand with a loud *thwock*, and Ryan noticed the tiny, beady black eyes managed to look sheepish. Now that her fingers were released (and completely covered with yellow, pollen-y slime), she took a step back to take in the full plant. It reminded her of a piranha plant that plagued the pipes in *Super Mario Bros.*, except it didn't have teeth; a thick, lime-green stem gave way to a giant, closed-blossom head with enormous human lips. Constantine smacked those lips in distaste, as though it did not care for the taste of Ryan's phalanges.

Agalia patted its head. "These are doe-dee-does. They're like puppy dogs! Aren't they adorable?"

"Uh, yeah, cute. A warning would have been nice," Ryan muttered, her heart still hammering in her chest.

"Why the warning? They're just little things. When they're bigger, look out!" exclaimed Agalia.

Ryan quickly scanned left, then right. "Are any of their, um, parents around?"

"No, no, no, *koukla*, they live in a patch out past the forest. I'm just babysitting for the morning." Agalia put her arm around Ryan's shoulders and guided her back to the greenhouse entrance, where Nicholas and Melina stood.

"So Ryan, Agalia got her hands on some seeds that are unique to this environment—" began Nicholas.

"Very finicky, yes," said Agalia, nodding brusquely.

"—and we'd like to see if you'd be able to grow them into full-grown plants," he finished.

Ryan studied the empty pots in front of her, no inkling of what they could be. "But that's not how it works. It takes weeks for my plants to bloom. It's a science, not magic. And I presumably have no experience with this type of plant," she said, her voice coming out whiny, her fears of being made to perform like a monkey coming to fruition. She bent down to take a whiff of the soil.

"Ryan," argued Melina, "for decades, scientists have been attempting to produce a machine or a solution to the air-quality crisis. And, without even trying to, you create a flower that is the remedy, the miracle that the world needs to clean the atmosphere. It's magic in every sense of the word."

Ryan looked at the empty pots of soil. Pressure and anxiety loomed over her, the task in front of her impossible.

"So what?" she asked. "You expect me to look at the plant and make it grow in a matter of seconds? What am I supposed to do?"

Like a petulant teenager, Ryan crossed her arms in front of her chest and scowled.

"Moro mou, calm down," Agalia tutted, briskly walking toward Ryan and hugging her. "We're not trying to pressure you. You enjoy botany, yes?" She spoke to the botanist as though she were a little girl, though Ryan had to admit she didn't mind the babying.

After a few moments of quiet, she replied, "Immensely. I love the smell of earth. I love the colors; man has tried to replicate them in vain, but they're only possible in nature. I love the patience and nurturing that go into watching something grow. I love how quiet and peaceful it is in a greenhouse. When it's really quiet, you can almost hear the plants growing around you, the beads of humidity slowly forging a path down the windows, the air thick with earthy purity and tangy sediments. I love how horticulture is rooted in science, but it's also such a miracle when you think about how a bountiful plant comes from just a tiny seed."

Ryan looked up. The three Descendants had gone quiet and were staring at her. A beam of sunlight had parted the heavy clouds and shone through the windows of the greenhouse. She saw Nicholas glance at the still-empty pots, hoping that her little speech had miraculously sprouted new life out of them.

"Ryan, we want you to hold onto that peace you just displayed and try to direct that toward your plants," said Nicholas encouragingly.

Agalia chimed in. "Just do what feels natural. We're going to leave you alone to concentrate. We'll be back to check on you in a bit."

Melina walked over to Ryan and wrapped her in a hug. Power emanated from Melina, but the hug was less the raw force of Zeus and more pure love and comfort. It reminded her of sitting in her living room under a sunbeam, completely content; Lester purring by her side, banana bread baking in the oven, a good book in hand, chores done, and nothing on the agenda for the rest of the day except perhaps a snooze. Perfect serenity.

"Ryan, let yourself believe. Give yourself fully to this." Melina released her.

Ryan sighed and nodded. A thought occurred to her. "Oh, Agalia, before you leave, should I be aware of any other, um . . . lifelike, animated, monster plants while I'm alone in here?"

Agalia scrunched up her face in confusion.

"Like, say, the doe-dee-does?"

"Oh, moro mou, I see what you are saying! You don't want another plant coming out to bite you!" Making Godzilla-like roars, she used her hands to make a monster mouth, pretending to chomp Ryan's head. "No, honey, the doe-dee-does are the only mythical specimen of plant in here. Enjoy!"

They filed out, Agalia blowing kisses at Ryan after attempting to smooth back a stray hair on her head.

The botanist looked around the greenhouse, already feeling defeated. She breathed a sigh of relief—she was alone for a moment, glad to be protected from the prying eyes outside the greenhouse.

The aftermath of Melina's hug lingered with Ryan, quelling the anxiety that was rearing under the surface. She took a deep breath, letting the familiar scents fill her lungs and exhaling all the impossible expectations. It was an odd feeling to be in a greenhouse without a clue as to what she should do. She would try to believe, as the Descendants had told her, but in her heart, Ryan could not reconcile the idea that all her years of botany training had been a waste, that she simply possessed an inherent power. If she could do what these people thought, why didn't the flowers erupt from their pots? Agalia could make crops and plants healthier just by being in their vicinity, yet it took Ryan a week to sprout a pea.

Just as a sense of hopelessness and frustration began to overwhelm her, she spotted a pair of gardening gloves. She slipped her hands in and made a very conscious decision to suspend her thoughts as she headed toward the Weeping Dianas. It was like greeting dear friends that she hadn't seen in some time—but as with a true friend, it was as if no time had lapsed and she could pick up right where she left off.

"Maybe if I talk to you on this magical island, you'll grow?" She felt silly, but it wasn't as if she had never carried on a conversation with her plants before. They were great listeners, after all.

"Don't get too used to your new digs. You'll be joining me on a long journey home once they realize I'm not the human equivalent of Miracle-Gro." She finished inspecting the buds, pruning leaves here and there.

OK, stop it right now. You must give this a chance. You have a green thumb AND you've got the wisdom of Oprah, the courage of Malala, the prowess of Serena.

She puffed out her chest, planted her balled-up hands on her hips, and gazed confidently at the half-dozen pots of soil. She felt momentarily invincible in her superhero stance; that is, until a big drop of condensation hit her squarely in the forehead.

Unsurprised yet undeterred, she wiped her forehead and said, "Well, might as well introduce myself. I'm Ryan. I'm the mother of some of your cousins back home. I guess you could call me your aunt . . . anyway, nice to meet you. Hey, if you could do me a favor and just sporadically sprout right now, that would be wonderful." She looked at the pots; as expected, nothing happened.

Checking that the windows were still fogged up, she raised her hands and waved them above the pots like they were a witch's cauldron. She squeezed her eyes shut, imagining the plants growing like Jack's beanstalk, although she was sure that if this were truly happening, she would hear it. In silence, she continued to wave her hands around, smiling to herself—she knew how silly she must look, but this was the first time she'd felt like herself since she arrived. She started singing the song "I Put a Spell on You" from *Hocus Pocus*. Greta loved Bette Midler's version.

She peeked open her right eye. To her utter lack of surprise, the empty pots stared back at her.

Tapping her foot in feigned disappointment, she wagged her finger at the pots. "Now I need your utmost cooperation. With the powers vested in me, I, Ryan Louise Bell, demand that you grow!"

Ryan looked over the empty pots; their lack of cooperation mocked her.

"OK, the hand-wagging doesn't work. Let's try something else."

Squeezing her eyes together, she rubbed her temples counterclockwise, picturing the plants in her mind. She concentrated on them, acknowledging each cell, thinking of the process of photosynthesis to make them grow, visualizing them emerging from the soil and reaching toward the sunbeam. She willed it.

She opened her eyes.

Nada.

"Welp, that's not the ticket either. Maybe they weren't planted correctly. Let me peek under the hood."

For the next few hours, Ryan tended to the barren pots and found that Agalia had planted them correctly—unsurprising, with her being the demigod version of Martha Stewart.

Ryan putzed around in the greenhouse, misting the other plants, pruning here and there, and giving a wide berth to the doe-dee-does (whom she swore were whispering behind her back). Despite her lack of visible progress, the chores did their work; before long she succeeded in forgetting where she was and really started to relax.

ALL THE BLUES COME THROUGH

As she was determining whether the plantless pots were getting too much direct sunlight, the door opened to admit Agalia, Nicholas, and Melina. All three eagerly glanced at the pots—within a second, their faces drooped. Melina and Nicholas were quick to change their expressions, but Agalia walked over to the pots and tutted, "Poor little babies are still hiding."

"Sorry," Ryan said quietly. She'd known it would be fruitless, but she couldn't help feeling like she'd let them down.

As if even the sky were disappointed in her, the beam of sunlight extinguished, transforming the once-verdant greenhouse into a dark and gloomy place.

"Don't apologize, Ryan." Nicholas turned to Agalia. "Agalia, are infants expected to annihilate like Ares? Transfigure like Hera? Strategize like Athena?"

Agalia shook her head vigorously. "Of course not. No. It takes time and training."

"We have the same standards toward Ryan," he said. He looked at Ryan with a smile. "I know you gave it your best shot."

MUCH TO NICHOLAS'S FRUSTRATION—AND RYAN'S relief—
further training was cut short by a stubborn rain cloud that
couldn't be moved by the likes of Kosta, Melina, or Elias.

As all the Descendants sprinted the five miles back to
the mountain, Ryan walked dejectedly through the pouring rain.
Nicholas trekked along patiently beside her, not saying a word, his
paternal support oozing from every fiber of his being. Maybe she was
being dramatic; how stereotypical was it to morosely return after a
day of Greek god boot camp?

Miserably, she realized there was a small part of her deep down
that had hoped she'd be able to perform some type of magical feat.
And along with the failure of the greenhouse training exercise, the
magnificence of the other actual Descendants' powers seemed so far
from the realm of who Ryan felt she was. Artemis was the Goddess
of the Hunt—Ryan couldn't help feeling even further removed from
that skillset than perhaps she would have with a different god's.

She knew that Aphrodite was the Goddess of Love—OK, she
hadn't had any semblance of love growing up besides a begrudging
sense of familial duty. But she was making up for lost time with
Greta and Lester. And she wasn't any sort of vixen when it came to
courting the opposite sex, but she had decently highish hopes with
Cyrus when she got back stateside.

What about Athena? she thought. *I think she's the Goddess of War?* Another stretch. Unless she counted the time she'd gone to war against her unruly, bushy eyebrows and come out relatively un-scathed, albeit with a few hot wax burns and a bare patch that Greta loved to point out.

Wait, wasn't Dionysus the God of Wine? Now there was a god she could get behind. White, red, pink; Ryan was an equal-opportu-nity imbiber. She'd never met a grape she didn't like. If anyone's godly blood ran through her veins, it was the oaky, tannin-filled Sangiovese of Dionysus.

But Artemis. No. Ryan wasn't a hunter. She was nothing like her.

As they entered the warm embrace of the cave, Nicholas smiled at Ryan and said, "I think someone could use some cheering up."

Shoulders slumped, she glumly asked, "What makes you say that?"

Nicholas chuckled. "Yes, it's a perfect assignment for the Muses," he added mysteriously. "Why don't you take a little rest in your room—you deserve it. And then we'll finish the day with a grueling, laborious lesson." As Ryan's stomach dropped, he leaned in playfully. "How Greeks have fun."

Ryan collapsed onto her bed once she arrived back in her room. Annoyed with herself for dampening her bedding with her soggy chiton, she slipped it off and changed back into her own clothes. She knew that Nicholas's vague proposal was meant to pique her interest, but it only added to the bottled-up apprehension she was carrying. Her idea of fun might not translate to these godly people—she couldn't quite picture Nicholas digging around the freezer for a DiGiorno.

Relocating to the window seat, whose magical window accurately reflected the storm raging outside the cave, Ryan grabbed her phone and saw a couple missed calls from Greta. Unable to summon the energy to call her back, Ryan composed a text about busy morning "meetings," a tour of the island's unique plants and the afternoon rainstorm. Next on the agenda was an inquiry about Lester; the botanist requested a photo of him with today's newspaper to verify he was alive and well. Lastly, she mentioned how Cyrus's requests to know exactly where she was and what she was doing had become increasingly urgent. She wondered if Greta thought he was being protective or borderline obsessive; for that matter, she herself wasn't sure. She assured her friend she hadn't accepted his invitation to share her location.

Ryan reread the text, making sure she wasn't outright lying to Greta about doing the scientific research she'd set out to do. It was a fine line, though—if her responses were too vague, she might return to a newly expanded greenhouse *and* the onsite Pilates studio Greta had proposed before she left.

Within a few seconds of hitting send, Ryan checked her phone and burst out laughing—she'd received a request to share her location with Greta. A text popped up:

You considered sharing your location with him and not me? In the words of Stephanie Tanner: how rude.

As Ryan accepted Greta's request, she heard a knock on the door. She tapped out a quick reply: *Simmer down, child! I'm being summoned; I'll give you a call tomorrow. Send pic of Lester. Xo.*

Flinging her phone back to her bed, Ryan opened the door to find Melina and two other girls there.

After planting a light kiss on Ryan's cheek in greeting, Melina gestured toward her companions. "This is Sophia, and this is Helena." She then beelined toward Ryan's drawers to inspect their contents.

Ryan didn't even have a chance to look at Helena; she was staring at the beauty of Sophia. She was fuzzy around the edges, and there were flowers flowing down her back, as though she were wearing daffodil hair extensions. Her soft blue eyes were surrounded with what looked like green eyelashes, almost like delicate stems were growing and reaching out from her eyelids. Her arms appeared normal until Ryan caught a glimpse of the underside of her forearm; her veins were traced in light green, giving off the same effect of a vein stretching through a leaf. Ryan even spotted a few butterflies flitting around her head.

Helena rolled her eyes and snapped her fingers in Ryan's face, as though breaking a trance. "Haven't you ever seen a nymph before?" she asked rudely, running her hand through her long, black hair.

"Is that what you are, Sophia?" Ryan breathlessly asked. "You are beautiful."

"Thank you! It's nice to meet you." As Sophia said this, the butterflies danced around the room in what looked like a synchronized waltz. Helena swatted them away from her, annoyed.

"Ryan," Helena started in a businesslike tone, walking over to the door to make sure it was closed tight. With her back against the door, she asked, "Please tell us everything there is to know about life off this godsforsaken island. What are people our ages out there doing?"

"Oh, of course!" Ryan exclaimed, feeling for once that she had the upper hand on something.

Eyes wide, Melina said, "It's totally against the rules, but . . ." After a moment's hesitation, a mischievous smile broke onto her face. "Tell me everything you know about blue teeth and apples and Wi-Fi."

Giggling, they all piled onto the bed. "Where to start," Ryan wondered aloud. "Oh, duh." She dove for her phone and held it up. "This is basically the single most important thing for young adults. Or anyone, for that matter. Does anyone know what it is?"

"It's a phone!" Sophia shouted, clapping wildly. She gingerly accepted it from Ryan, turning it this way and that.

The nymph carefully passed it on to Melina, who muttered, "It's lighter than I thought it'd be." Handing it to Helena, she asked, "So you use this to call other people to talk, right?"

Ryan frowned, shaking her head emphatically. "No. I mean, you can. But it's actually quite annoying to receive a call, even though that's the original purpose. The main way to communicate with someone else who has one of these, or a similar model, is to type out messages to each other, like this." She demonstrated how to type on the keyboard and showed them the long text conversations between herself and Greta.

"This also has a camera, which takes photos or videos." She turned the camera toward the four of them. "Say, 'first selfie'!"

After the phone snapped, they all inspected it; for some reason, there was only a white, hazy orb where Sophia sat. "Let's try that again . . ." Ryan took a second selfie; seeing the same result, she tried taking a photo of Sophia straight on. "Wow, no such luck," she said, squinting her eyes down at the screen and up at her new acquaintance. "I guess the camera can't possibly capture the beauty of nymphs."

"That's OK! I look great on a fresco," Sophia said brightly.

"What else can it do?" urged Melina, looking at the phone as though it held life's mysteries and hidden secrets. *And just like that, she's hooked like the rest of us,* Ryan thought.

"It can play music! Listen!" She scrolled through her list of musicians and landed on a classic. "This is by a group called the Spice Girls. It's a song called 'Wannabe.'"

Three pairs of wide eyes watched the phone in awe as music belted from its minuscule speaker.

"I've never heard anything like this," Melina whispered. "I like it!"

She jumped off the bed and started dancing around the room. Soon, Sophia and Helena joined her.

Ryan stood up on the bed, nearly hitting her head on the canopy. "Next, you need some killer dance moves!" She lifted her palms in the air, pumping them up and down. "Raise the roof, ladies! Raise the roof!" The three women mimicked Ryan, laughing hysterically.

"Now, shopping cart!" Ryan pretended to push an imaginary shopping cart down an aisle, picking things off the shelf and putting them in her cart.

"Wax on, wax off," she shouted next, miming how to rotate their hands back and forth on an imaginary car.

"You must be the coolest girl out there!" Melina bellowed as she pretended to crash her imaginary grocery cart into Helena.

"Don't forget the robot," Ryan yelled, mechanically moving her arms and rotating her hips.

As the song ended, the girls fell into a heap on the bed, their cheeks red and sore from smiling.

"Tell us more," Melina urged.

"Well," Ryan said, lowering her voice to a stage whisper, "you can also date on this thing."

"Date? Where are the men?" Helena cried, flipping the phone over as if to reveal some hidden compartment.

"Yes, people our age typically date men and women online. You meet someone on the internet through things called dating apps, and if you like their picture and what they say about themselves, you can opt to meet them in person."

The women regarded Ryan as though waiting for her to tell them she was kidding. After a long pause, Sophia said, "That sounds insane."

"Oh, it is," Ryan agreed merrily.

After the botanist showed off a few pictures of Greta and Lester, Melina gently reminded them that they should probably get the guest of honor downstairs before Nicholas banished them to the Furies.

Helena clasped her hands and looked Ryan up and down. "Let's get her dressed and to the party. I want as much face-to-face time with Elias as possible, if you know what I mean," she said commandingly.

"How are things going between you two?" Sophia asked in her serene voice.

Helena huffed. "He's hiding something. I think it's a new woman." She checked her reflection in the mirror, haughtily posing and fluffing up her dark, straight hair. "He's been secretive. More than usual," she grumbled.

Melina strode over with a white robe, draping it this way and that over Ryan's shoulders. "I think we need to go a little more risqué this evening." She raised an eyebrow at the other girls. "Thoughts?"

Ryan began to protest, but Helena cut her off. She grabbed the fabric from Melina and swished it until it turned a deep emerald green. Ryan had to admit it did complement her skin tone nicely. Helena twisted it into a halter top and left the back uncovered; the hemline cut high at her thigh and then fell dramatically behind her. Sophia came behind her and ran her fingers through Ryan's hair— the lifeless, dull locks magically turned to effortless waves, the color so rich and deep that it sucked in all the light around her. Sophia tipped her head, looking at Ryan, then turned around to the girls. "I think I like her hair better the way it was before."

"Are you crazy?! Don't touch it!" bellowed Ryan, grabbing at her hair possessively, admiring it in the mirror.

The girls all laughed. Sophia said, "You seriously don't know how striking you are, Ryan. You're different. You're a breath of fresh air."

It was Ryan's turn to roll her eyes. "Says the girl who puts the nature in natural beauty."

Helena laughed appreciatively and then snapped back into business mode. "OK, let's go."

"Wait! Isn't there anything else you can do? Make my legs grow longer or make my eye color more enchanting or at least get rid of this weird flabby arm jiggle?" She flapped her arm vigorously to demonstrate.

Helena scrunched up her nose in disgust while the other two looked amused.

Melina put her hands on Ryan's shoulders and gently guided her out the door. "Maybe we should talk about your self-esteem on our way."

The girls walked past the rotunda, following a line of Descendants snaking down the path they typically took to the arena, everyone decked out in their finest robes. Ryan's eyes widened as she took in the beauty and grace that unfolded with every step. The pathway was lit intermittently with lanterns of delicate pink fire; there was some sort of charm protecting them from the hurricane-like wind howling over the island.

Soon they came to a clearing outlined with torches. The site was barren save for a large tree in the center, a couple people mingling off to one side. Ryan was confused. She had assumed that they were all going to some sort of welcome party; she had expected a greater congregation and more fanfare.

Just then, a big fluffy cloud floated down the trunk of the tree. A group of people piled onto the cloud, and it slowly glided back up, like an elevator to heaven. Ryan's mouth dropped as her head tracked its progress a hundred feet up to the top of the tree canopy. A minute later, the cloud floated back down, and Ryan hesitantly followed the girls onto the big, soft puff. She wordlessly watched as the ground below them grew smaller and the unmistakable noise of a party grew closer.

At last, they reached the top of the canopy and Ryan gasped: before her was a magical celebration in the sky. The canopy formed an open-air room about the size of a football field, with a big dance floor and a band in the middle. The crunchy leaves below their feet were littered with little baubles of colorful lights that twinkled on and off. Knee-high walls of puffy clouds outlined the arborous venue, with seating sporadically set around two bars on either end of the soiree. Little trays of steaming food were bewitched to circulate among the patrons.

Looking more closely, Ryan saw that the three harpies were rocking out on a keyboard, a lute, and a drum set. Two Sirens accompanied them as backup singers while a raucous crowd danced below. Among them, Ryan caught her first glimpse of the arachne spider-women. Their upper bodies looked human, save for black eyes the size of golf balls. They wore billowy pants of pastel taffeta, gliding around as if each were wearing a Cinderella-esque ballgown. The fairy tale was ruined whenever one of the eight high-heeled shoes kicked to the beat.

A Centaur family of six trotted by. Two proud parents led the group, with four little baby Centaurs trailing behind in bow ties and tiaras. Melina pointed out a group of Graces, all wearing delicate dresses made of clouds. They lit up in a rainbow of colors—mint, lavender, coral—synced in perfect timing to the lightning flashing above the invisible protective shield. A group of kobaloi peered nervously from their huddle, engaged in an illicit game of poker.

The Descendants were interspersed amongst all the mythicals, dancing, eating, and laughing boisterously. Agalia was grabbing the hands of nearby Descendants and starting some sort of Greek conga line, performing steps that everyone seemed to know. Massive plates were piled high with all sorts of delicacies from the buffet. Ryan saw two hulking men pick up what had to be fifty-ounce lamb shanks; they boisterously slapped the steaks together in a toast and tore into them with their mouths and bare hands.

Ryan followed the girls mutely, taking in all the sights. Twice, Melina physically redirected her as she strayed, completely immersed in all there was to witness. They joined a larger group of Descendants around their age, many of whom Ryan recognized from around the cave, most notably Kosta and Elias.

She was introduced to several Descendant friends of the ladies and enjoyed answering their questions about the world outside the island. Topics such as Pop-Tarts, Disney World, and vacuums were discussed in-depth, while Netflix was a concept they just couldn't wrap their heads around. After a while, Ryan saw Nicholas at the bar and excused herself to say hello.

"Nicholas, this is fabulous. Thank you for arranging this! It really has picked up my spirits," she said appreciatively.

"I really can't take credit," he replied, though he looked pleased. "The Muses did most of the work. I was hoping the festivities might reset all the stress you've been feeling since landing on this island."

"Well, a drink couldn't hurt either," Ryan said, smiling.

Nicholas turned around and summoned a nymph bartender, whose chestnut tresses sported tiny acorns at the ends. "What'll it be, Ryan?"

She looked around at all the glowing, unrecognizable bottles behind the bar. "I'll have what you have."

"Two ouzos," Nicholas ordered.

"Oh, I've never had ouzo. What's it taste like?" Ryan asked.

Nicholas's eyebrows nearly shot off his head. "Never had ouzo?" he asked in astonishment.

"Never had ouzo?" the nymph bartender repeated, perplexed.

Overhearing the exchange, a male Descendant next to Nicholas hollered, "She's never had ouzo!"

Everyone around her exclaimed in surprise, and the bartender immediately poured two small glasses in response.

"*Opa!*" everyone around the bar shouted, raising their glasses to Ryan.

Cheeks burning from the attention, Ryan threw back her head and took down the shot in one gulp. Black licorice shimmied over her taste buds, burning as it rolled down her throat; overall it was potent but curiously pleasant.

She smacked her lips appreciatively and opened her eyes to see everyone attempting to stifle their laughter. When she looked to Nicholas for an explanation, he confessed, "I guess I should have mentioned that you *sip* ouzo, Ryan."

Ryan burst out laughing, wiped her mouth, and sheepishly shrugged to the crowd.

Everyone laughed with her, clapped her back appreciatively, and started taking ouzo shots too. Ryan took one more to satiate the crowd and then turned to Nicholas, who had reappeared after going on a secret mission.

"Might need something in your belly now," he said, leading them to a small table. He produced what could only be described as Descendant fast food: shish kebab chicken, fresh tomatoes, tzatziki sauce, and, to Ryan's utter delight, french fries, all wrapped in a grilled pita. She hungrily ate what Nicholas called "souvlaki," all the while sneaking glances at Kosta, who was talking animatedly with a group of beautiful Sirens.

Ryan glanced at Nicholas, then down at his hand, a question forming in her mind. She broke the silence between the two of them, hoping her voice came out breezy and nonchalant.

"So do you guys wear wedding rings, or how do you know if someone's married?"

Nicholas's eyes twinkled, clearly seeing where the line of questioning was heading. Ryan flushed. *For an old man, he sure sees right through me.*

"Unlike Americans, Greeks traditionally wear engagement rings on the ring finger of their right hand." He unconsciously rubbed his naked ring finger while looking at the group of adults her age. Equally breezy, he asked, "Is there someone in particular you're wondering about?"

"No," Ryan answered a little too quickly.

Nicholas chuckled to himself, but there was something sad about the sound. "You and my daughter have a lot in common."

"You have a daughter?" exclaimed Ryan. Her eyes swept over the Descendants in front of her, trying to pick out a girl who shared Nicholas's features, minus the beard. She obviously hadn't met everyone in the cave, but considering the amount of time Nicholas had spent with her, it would make sense to run into his kin sooner rather than later.

"Had." His eyes, dancing a moment before, now looked haunted and worn. "My wife, Kalliope, along with my daughter, Spiras, were among the many casualties from our last clash with Gaea."

This information slammed into Ryan. She'd known that Gaea was their enemy, but she hadn't truly grasped what toll it had taken on the people she'd met.

"When I received my powers as an adolescent," Nicholas continued, "I threw myself into fighting and leading the cause to free the gods, eventually becoming the leader of the group. I decided I couldn't open my heart to love someone I would likely lose." He heaved a heavy sigh and cleared his throat. "But many years ago, the inevitable happened, and I fell in love with a Descendant. I didn't have a choice in the matter, really. My heart recognized who it beat for, and that was that. Kalliope was the love of my life, and she gave me a daughter, Spiras. With those two, I couldn't believe how I had forsaken myself by not opening my heart to love over the past couple decades. I had never felt that much happiness."

Ryan watched Nicholas intently as he continued. "But, now that I had a family to protect, my mission to overtake Gaea strengthened exponentially." A shadow crossed his face, and Ryan got her first glimpse of a different Nicholas. Gone was the gentle and wise old man, replaced by a brooding warrior. "I wanted to hunt her. I wanted to capture her. I was hungry for blood. Her very existence threatened my family. So I pushed our people to go on the offensive."

"You guys fought her?"

He nodded grimly. "I led the charge. But it wasn't enough."

"I'm so sorry, Nicholas," Ryan said sincerely.

They sat together, watching the wild celebration play out in front of them. Luckily, the rain was pounding hard enough off the invisible shield to mute the accompanied cacophony. It was as if the skies were crying for Nicholas.

Finally, Ryan asked, "You mentioned we had a lot in common. Do I remind you of Spiras?" She hoped she did. She wanted to bring Nicholas a little joy, and if this was one way, she was OK with it.

"In many ways, yes. She was stubborn like you. Even when she was wrong, she clung to her beliefs and opinions like a badge of honor."

"Wow, we share some very positive attributes," Ryan replied, raising her eyebrows. Nicholas laughed, and her heart warmed. She was so glad to see a smile upon his face once more.

"She was wickedly intelligent as well," Nicholas said with pride. "She had the ability to hide what she was thinking, never showing her hand, always two steps ahead of those around her. People never made the mistake of crossing Spiras or doubting her."

Spiras sounded like one badass chick, Ryan thought.

"She was also engaged to marry Kosta."

That bitch.

At this bombshell, her eyes moved rapidly in search of Kosta and found him laughing at something Melina had said. Now that she looked at him with this new information, she recognized a hint of sadness in his eyes. How had she not seen it before?

Kosta glanced in her direction, and they locked eyes. Ryan immediately looked down to hide the pain in hers. Was he holding back because he was still in mourning? Because he wasn't interested? Or because she wasn't one of them?

"She is also the reason you are here."

Ryan physically jolted in her seat. Her demigod crush's dead demigod fiancée had believed Ryan was also a demigod? What world was she living in?

Two Centaurs held up a limbo stick, encouraging a harpy to participate; the sight snapped the botanist back to her bizarre reality. Nicholas was speaking again. "Spiras had come to me with her belief that Artemis had a secret baby. Kalliope believed her. But I was too far gone to see reason. I believed we must go to war and that this time, it would work. Had I just listened . . ."

"You can't take on that guilt, Nicholas," Ryan said, patting his powerful yet wizened hand.

Nicholas shook his head as though to clear it and reached for a passing bewitched tray carrying luscious-looking baklava. He handed a small triangle to Ryan. "I am so sorry, Ryan. This party was supposed to be fun and uplifting. And here I am, speaking about the saddest, darkest days of my life. I will punish myself for doubting my daughter and wife until my dying day, but I will also spend the rest of my life fulfilling Spiras's belief. And I have finally found you. So that, my child"—he raised his baklava to Ryan—"is reason to celebrate."

"Cheers, Nicholas," Ryan said, toasting him back.

* * *

After licking honey off her fingers (and furiously scrubbing off a couple drops from her chiton), Ryan parted ways with Nicholas and spotted Helena, who was frowning at the bar. Ryan followed Helena's eyeline and saw Elias flirting with the nymph bartender. *Probably not a good time to bother her*, Ryan thought. As she searched for Melina and Sophia, a deep voice spoke quietly in her ear. "You look lovely."

Ryan turned around to see Kosta standing beside her in a midnight-blue chiton robe. With a tight-lipped smile, she said, "Thanks."

She looked away, knowing full well that she was putting cold vibes out there. Ryan didn't mean to punish him. Everyone had a past. (Well, hers was mostly dotted with the awkward first and last dates arranged by her matchmaker-in-chief, Greta.) But she was already feeling inadequate to this impossible challenge they were putting her through, and now she was competing against the memory of Spiras. She built up a beautiful version of the other woman's head: hair flowing in the wind, icy-blue eyes the mirror images of Nicholas's, pouty lips that got to be nibbled on by Kosta's.

Noticing her grimace, Kosta tapped her forehead. "What's going on in there, *loulouthaki?*"

She smiled in spite of herself. She couldn't deny that there was an unknown force—a magnetism—that kept her going back for more.

They both started talking simultaneously, only to be interrupted by the Muses, who'd begun a choreographed dance on stage. They were spinning hypnotically and chanting when nine hippogriffs joined them, and together they started what could only be described as an interspecies dance-off. It was starting to get very loud as the partygoers congregated closer to the stage, so Kosta gestured toward the entrance of the party. Wordlessly, the two of them stepped onto the cloud puff and floated away from the chaos above.

They stayed near the tree, under the protection of the invisible shield and the glow of the torchlight. Away from the noise, the melodic rain created a romantic and soothing atmosphere as it pattered against the shield.

After Kosta magically conjured up a bench for them to sit on, they both spent some time looking around, watching the lightning illuminate the pitch-black forest around them, then awkwardly laughing whenever they caught each other's eye. The bench was small; their legs grazed, and Ryan was conscious of how much upper thigh the slit of her chiton was exposing. She hoped the lightning didn't highlight her cellulite. Her sly attempt to slowly shift her chiton lower must have drawn Kosta's attention because he chuckled and grabbed something to his right. A warm blanket made of soft, green moss appeared over their legs.

"Thought you might be a bit chilly," the Descendant said, his eyes dancing.

Ryan laughed as she tucked the blanket around herself.

"What'd you think?" Kosta asked, pointing to the treetops. "How was your first Descendant party?"

"It was incredible. Saw my first arachne spider-woman and didn't run away shrieking. Slung back my first ouzo shot. Watched Helena plot the demise of Elias. And then had an uber-depressing conversation with Nicholas."

Ryan stopped suddenly and closed her eyes. She hadn't meant to bring up the conversation with Nicholas. But sitting with Kosta, it was like an itch she had to scratch. As expected, the whole atmosphere around them changed as Kosta turned his body away from hers.

Well, no going back now, she thought. Gently, she prodded, "You didn't mention Spiras."

A disgruntled sigh escaped him. "We've just met. Sorry I didn't feel the need to bring her up."

Ryan rested her arm atop his shoulder. Softly, she said, "You don't have to be defensive. She was a big part of your life, Kosta."

"You don't know my life, Ryan," he snapped.

Ryan slid her hand back to her lap as though she'd been slapped. She could feel her insecurity about Spiras turn to anger, a beast writhing inside her, looking for a target. Restlessly, she stood up and paced a few steps. "You're right, I don't. And guess what, you guys don't know *my* life." She pointed an accusatory finger at Kosta. "You stripped me away from mine so that I could save yours. Even if I do have powers, what makes you think that I would want to use them for you?"

Eyes wide, Kosta let out a derisive laugh. "Wow. That was quite the escalation."

Ryan turned her back to him. "Forget it. Doesn't matter anyway. I'm not one of you, so it's pointless."

Kosta waved his hands in surrender. "OK, then. Want me to take you back?"

"To my house? Or my prison cell?"

"You know you're welcome to leave at any time," Kosta angrily retorted.

"Sure I am! I'm the only hope for an entire people. And now, I have the added pressure of fulfilling the dying wishes of Nicholas's daughter and your lover. Yeah, I can really just waltz away. You'd like that, wouldn't you? Well, I have principles, Kosta. I said I would stay, and I will fulfill that promise."

"Principles. Ha." Kosta laughed callously. "As if you're even trying to explore the powers within you. The reason you're staying is totally self-serving. You just want more flowers."

Ryan stared at Kosta, stung by the words flung at her. Out of her peripheral vision, she saw the cloud lazily float down, filled to the brim with Descendants and mythicals ready to take the party back to the cave. Spotting Elias, she marched toward the descending cloud elevator and grabbed his arm as he stepped off the platform. "Please take me back to my room."

Elias looked questioningly between the moody Kosta and the pale Ryan but nodded, saying nothing.

* * *

Ryan had planned to have a good cry when the door closed behind her, but she saw that Greta was FaceTiming her. Heaving a big sigh and promising her heart she would let the tears flow in a few minutes, Ryan put on a brave face and answered the phone.

"Hi, Greta!"

"Hello! How are—" Greta peered closer into the phone. "What's wrong?"

"Oh, nothing. Long day," Ryan replied, giving Greta a tired smile. "It's, like, past midnight here."

Greta scowled. "You've got your I-just-finished-reading-a-book-and-I'm-depressed-it's-over sad face on."

Ryan laughed, rubbing her face with her palms. "I swear, it's exhaustion from the jet lag and time change. I just returned from a welcome party, so I'm a bit overstimulated too."

"Ooh, fancy! Was there a chocolate fountain? Please tell me they had a chocolate fountain," Greta exclaimed, her eyes bright.

"You are so obsessed with those!"

"Who wouldn't be? You can dip anything in them! Sweet, salty, savory . . ." Greta laughed. "How are the experiments coming along?"

Ryan's brow knitted, confusion spreading on her face.

"Your flowers . . . ?" Greta prompted.

"Oh! Yes, still investigating."

The older woman squinted. "I guess it takes a week or so for the seeds to sprout. Good thing you're there for another week."

Sighing, Ryan said, "Yes."

Greta frowned. "Honey, I can't help but think something is wrong. What's going on?"

"I'm just homesick, Greta. How's Lester? Can he come to the phone?"

"He's taking another call," her friend replied haughtily.

"Ha ha. Very funny." Greta aimed the phone by her feet, where Lester was lying. "Look at you two, getting along!"

Greta bristled. "He's been following me everywhere." She put the phone up to her face. "*Every*where, Ryan. I make toast, he's there. I do the laundry, he's there." She paused, looking down in disgust. "I try to sneak to the bathroom for a solo trip, he's there. I'm backed up, Ryan."

Ryan burst out laughing, so grateful for this moment of release. "I'm sorry, Greta. I love you."

Despite herself, the other woman smiled. "Love you too, Ryan."

THE NEXT MORNING, AFTER SHOOTING off her standard quick *Hello, I didn't die in my sleep* text to Greta, Ryan crawled out of bed, washed her face, and pulled out a fresh white piece of fabric. She managed to fumble together a mildly cute yet durable ensemble. Once on, the cloth magically turned crimson red, a perfect complement to the blood boiling within her whenever she thought of Kosta. Pulling up her hair, she committed to giving it her all in training today.

"Ryan, I'd like you to meet Leonides, Descendant of Poseidon, and Alexandros, Descendant of Athena," Nicholas said after they entered the training arena later that morning. The sun was hidden by ominous, rain-filled clouds, threatening to burst at any moment. Ryan watched idly as Melina tried using her powers to coax them away in the distance. *Must be their rainy season.*

"We've met," Alexandros exclaimed. "I was the owl!"

"Oh, hello again. Nice human body," Ryan noted.

"Thank you," Alexandros said, striking a pose that showed off his muscles, causing Ryan to blush profusely.

"Oh, I didn't mean it that way. Not that your body is bad . . ." she stammered.

At that exact moment, Kosta walked by within earshot. She didn't know if he'd heard pieces of the conversation, but his shoulders were so tense they nearly reached his earlobes.

Leonides pounced in front of Alexandros, striking a different bodybuilder pose. "What about my human body?" he asked, laughing. Alexandros jumped on Leonides's back, and a kerfuffle ensued. Ryan couldn't help but laugh at the men as they tumbled along the ground, pulling hair and tickling one another. They were clearly brothers; both had dark, curly hair and prominent noses. Leonides was a bit taller than Alexandros, but Alexandros looked a few years older.

"That's quite enough, boys. Leo and Al have some exercises for you to try," Nicholas said pointedly. Ryan got the feeling this wasn't the first time the goofy brothers had gotten off track.

After the pair had dusted themselves off, Leo guided them toward an expansive object about the size of the makeshift greenhouse from the previous day, its contents hidden by a giant tarp. Clearing his throat, he tried to smooth his tousled, bouffant hair. "Yes, today I'll display how some of my unique powers align with the Descendant of Poseidon. He is the God of the Sea, so I have honed my ability to control sea creatures with my mind."

He and his brother pulled off the sheet. Underneath was a fantastic aquarium with lovely, colorful fish, huge dolphins, and even a great white shark hiding behind the coral.

"How on earth did you get this gigantic aquarium in the middle of this field?" Ryan was astounded that this entire zoo exhibit was here of all places.

"With these puppies," Leo replied, flexing his keg-sized biceps and then bursting out in laughter. Then, in all seriousness, he added, "The journey was a rocky ride, and the seahorses were pissed."

He affectionately tapped the glass, and four little baby seahorses performed what could only be described as a jig. Ryan stifled a giggle; it was like watching a father gaze at his baby. She stopped short when it dawned on her: it was exactly how Ryan looked at Lester. And her plants, for that matter.

"Ryan, we're not certain how creating life, as you do with your flowers, could fall under a typical 'hunting' power. For the greenhouse training exercise, we investigated whether you could produce a different species of flower but on a godlier timeframe," Nicholas said.

"You expected: *poof*," Ryan said listlessly, blossoming her fingers out.

"Right. *Poof*," Nicholas replied, smiling. "I checked the greenhouse this morning, and the pots were still empty of sprouts." He paused, then said gently, "Don't give me that look, Ryan." She had tried to keep her face neutral, but apparently some doubt mingled with embarrassment had crept in. She gave him what she hoped was a confident smile to mirror his.

Nicholas continued, "For the next two exercises, we're going to follow the more standard definitions of hunting and the powers that could develop from it. For instance, there's weaponry, like the expert use of a bow and arrow, and stalking, trapping, baiting, calling, and flushing, to name a few."

"Does looking like a deer in headlights count? Because this island has really helped me fine-tune that power." She said it in jest, but there was a touch of bitterness beneath it—she knew how these exercises were going to play out.

Ryan knew nothing of hunting. Zero, zilch, nada. In fact, she really didn't like the idea of it at all. She'd never touched a gun and couldn't imagine going out and shooting another living thing, even if it was something gross like a spider or zombie. If they'd asked her to balance a budget in Excel or fix a router or even jazz up a frozen pizza with accoutrements from the kitchen, she'd halfway believe she was a Descendant. But these activities Nicholas mentioned were so out of her realm, she couldn't fathom grasping even an elementary understanding of the skills with consistent practice.

Keep an open mind, Ryan chided herself. *Try for Nicholas. Show Kosta he's wrong.*

Leo spoke. "To hunt is to understand the habits of animals. Animal wrangling is typically done with the assistance of another animal, like horses, dogs, hawks, or falcons. Because we have the power of the gods running through our veins, we don't need the assistance of others. We're a one-stop shop! As I mentioned before, being a Descendant of Poseidon, I can control sea creatures with my mind. My animals have agreed to be compliant as you try."

Ryan waited for more, but Leo just looked at her. "Try what?" she finally asked.

"To wrangle the creatures," he said enthusiastically.

She stared at him. "With my bare hands?" There weren't any tools or nets or apparatus for her to catch them. She thought back to Elias's method of fishing. *Am I supposed to have a Moses moment and part water?*

"With your mind, of course," he said with a little laugh, as though it were the most obvious thing in the world. "Let me give you a demonstration."

Leo stood in front of the tank—immediately, every single fish and living creature within stopped what they were doing and looked at him. Ryan didn't think it was possible, but the fish looked as though they had expressions of expectancy. Even the seaweed, waving in the natural surf of the tank, seemed to lean toward Leo.

Hands behind his back, the Descendant stood very still. Then, the fish began swimming fast, and Ryan soon realized that they were grouping themselves together by color. Soon there was a rainbow of fish—red, orange, yellow, green, blue, indigo, and violet. Just as soon as they got into the groups, they burst apart and swam around frantically, then lined up in order of size, from the tiniest guppy on the left to the giant shark on the right. As if introducing themselves in roll call, each fish moved forward, did a little flip, and got back in line. Ryan broke out into applause after the shark completed a graceful backflip, water splashing over the edge of the aquarium.

"Wow, that was fantastic!" she exclaimed, wiping her forehead off. "Guess I'm standing in the splash section."

"Thank you, Ryan!" Leo responded jovially. "Now it's your turn. First, I'd like you to come up to the glass next to me. We're going to see if you're able to wrangle Balthasar. He's the tiny green guppy—he is very willing to please and easy to control. We start all the young Descendants with an affinity toward Poseidon on Balty.

"I need you to concentrate on his being. Surround it with your mind. Explore his gills, his fins, his scales, his tail, his black eyes. Connect with him and ask him if you can unite with him. He will oblige, and I'd like you to make him rotate like the blades of a fan."

Ryan took in Leo's instructions and wordlessly looked at Balty. He stared back at her. While his head couldn't have been bigger than the face of a dime, his features were expressive. He showed curiosity and focus as he stared back at Ryan, his fins slowly treading water as he remained at her eye level.

A look of concentration on her face, Ryan spoke to Balty in her head. *Hello, Balty. Can you hear me? I'm Ryan.*

The fish continued to tread water before her.

I'd, uh, like to ask your permission to access your tiny little fish brain. Not tiny in power. No, just tiny in size. I'm sure you're a very intellectual finny friend, so I hope you didn't take offense to that. I'm babbling now. Ha, babbling to Balty! Babbling with Balty. You could have your own little aquarium talk show! OK, concentrate, Ryan. Balty, Balthasar, please let me access you.

He stared back at her.

OK, Balty. I'll take your unresponsiveness as a good sign. Could you please turn around slowly?

He stared at her.

Please, if you could use your little fins to rotate, I'd be ever so grateful.

He stared back at her.

Just a quick little turn. You could just go ninety degrees if you'd like. Just a tip.

He stared at her, and then he looked at Leo.

Leo looked at her. "Did you ask politely, Ryan?"

"Yes, I used my best manners. He's not doing anything."

"Try again," he said lightly.

Ryan screwed up her face in deeper concentration. It was hard blocking out the fact that the others were watching her like a hawk. Or like a guppy.

She took a deep breath and continued her internal conversation. *Balty, I would be eternally grateful if you could let me access your brain and your body and your being.*

He stared at her.

Please, turn around. Spin for me. Do something to let me know that I've accessed your brain. She was pleading now.

Suddenly, Balty wiggled his tail fin vigorously, looking from Ryan to Leo.

"OH MY GOD, I DID IT," Ryan exclaimed, her arms pumping in the air. "I did it!" she cried as she hugged Leo beside her.

Leo politely hugged her back, which wasn't the type of reaction she'd expected for such an enormous feat. Sure, it was just Balty, but he'd done something on her command. This was huge!

Leo stepped back and bracingly said, "Sorry, Ryan. That's actually his sign that he has to go to the bathroom."

Sensing the dismissal, Balty darted behind a piece of coral.

Ryan's jaw dropped as she processed what had just happened. Miserably, she scanned the nearby area to see who could have witnessed her blunder. Of course—Kosta and Elias had witnessed the entire thing. Elias made an extremely poor attempt at hiding his smirk, but Kosta watched on with an expressionless face. Ryan hung her head. She didn't know what was more embarrassing: being defeated by a strong-willed, gill-bearing fillet of fish or actually having believed she could do this.

A distant rumble of thunder sounded behind her as she turned to Leo and said, "Sorry, doesn't look like I can do it."

"Do not apologize, Ryan." He jostled her shoulder a bit, nearly knocking her off the ground. "This doesn't mean that you aren't powerful. It may mean that this particular power isn't possessed by Artemis's Descendant."

"Well, I guess that's OK. I don't really see how this skill could be used against Gaea. Do you round up enemies, sit them down, and entertain them to death?" asked Ryan, snickering.

As she was about to turn around to ask Nicholas where they were to go next, the shark within the aquarium violently torpedoed about—to Ryan's horror, she saw that it was going on a bloody rampage, eating everything in sight. It took an enormous bite of the dolphin, and she could hear the wounded animal cry in pain. The water turned red with blood; the other fish swam about in terror, trying to hide from the maniacal shark. It darted wildly, blind with rage. Leo just stood there, calm, with his hands still clasped behind his back.

Ryan realized that the shark hadn't gone insane; Leo was controlling it.

"Stop it! *Stop it!*" she bellowed, shaking the Descendant's calm, at-ease shoulders.

"That's enough, Leo," Nicholas said gently.

Finally, the shark's rage subsided. As it turned its back to them, Leo turned to Ryan, all signs of cheeriness gone.

"Looks can be deceiving. Remember that while we may look and act harmless, we are deadly when it comes to warfare."

A flash of lightning doused the carnage in bright light. Ryan shivered as the thunder rolled ominously. The field of Descendants looked up at the sky.

"Stubborn," Nicholas noted with interest, watching a group of Descendants that had joined Melina in trying to push the clouds apart. A small opening of blue sky would materialize above them, only for the cumulonimbus thunderheads to resolutely surge back together.

Jogging toward the group of cloud wranglers, Leo turned and yelled, "I'm going to join them."

"My turn." Alexandros strolled up, rubbing his hands together. "We're going to be trying our hand at camouflaging."

"As long as it doesn't have to do with slaughtering," Ryan said wearily. "May Balty rest in peace," she added, throwing Leo a dirty look.

Nicholas smiled. "The Centaurs will heal all the marine animals in the aquarium. Balty will reign over his little guppy empire again. And chin up; your powers could come flooding to the surface with this training."

Ryan cringed; Nicholas's pep talk may have come from the heart, but his imagery hit her apprehension about camouflage right in the jugular. Unlike most women her age, she consistently failed miserably at following contouring tutorials on YouTube, somehow drawing *more* attention to her occasional adult acne. She highly doubted disguising herself was a power in her supposed godly wheelhouse.

In the end, Ryan didn't have to worry about a thing. Alexandros's lesson was so laughable, she thought it more productive to try making plants erupt in the greenhouse or give the now-revived, post-potty Balty another go around the aquarium. Alexandros was a human chameleon, able to change the color of his skin to anything behind him. After meticulously explaining his process, he left Ryan to sit in a grassy meadow, saying that when he was younger, he'd needed peace and quiet in order to hone his colorful talent.

With her arms wrapped around her knees, Ryan sat motionless, not even trying at this point. She felt exposed; a pathetic red lump in a green field, a conspicuous reminder to all the Descendants that she was a failure. She was also exposed to the incoming storm that rumbled threateningly.

As the skies opened and a torrential downpour began, the Descendants around her started to pick up their equipment and sprint back toward the direction of the cave. Ryan just sat there, lightning horrifically flashing and thunder rattling her eardrums, and looked at Nicholas. The defeat in her face was not reflected in his. He gave her a kind smile, pulled her up, and said, "Great effort today, Ryan."

With that, Alexandros stood up not three feet away from her, gave her an emerald- and lime-colored bow, and headed back toward the caves with the rest of the Descendants.

* * *

Back inside the mountain, Nicholas departed on an errand. Looking around, Ryan realized there was no one there to guide her back to her room. She caught Kosta's eye but pushed her shoulders back and walked in the general direction of her room. She might not have possessed powers, but she certainly had a good sense of direction.

She peeked inside a tunnel, confirmed there were no harpies or arachnae, and continued toward her room. A pep in her step, the botanist stretched out her arms, wondering about the Weeping Dianas and hoping that the greenhouse could withstand another torrential storm. She took a left and thought, *Look at you, just walking through these halls like you own the place. Hot damn!* She imagined herself in a Beyoncé-esque stage leotard and began singing quietly as she strutted through the tunnel.

She turned around and did an awkward little moonwalk, rounded a corner, and realized that she was not in the corridor she had expected. Despite being alone, her cheeks flushed: Ryan had embarrassed herself, to herself.

She was about to backtrack when she saw a cracked doorway. *Maybe I can flag someone inside to help me find my way back.*

Crossing her fingers that she wasn't entering some sort of dragon lair, or the entrance to another dimension for that matter, Ryan approached the door—and gasped. Melina had described this place: it was the room of the Fates.

Unseen, she backed out of the doorway, but curiosity got the better of her. She peered in stealthily, taking in the enormity of the room. Shelves upon shelves stretched into darkness, but instead of books, there were long, vertical wooden dowels stacked with spindles of shimmery thread in every color, texture, and size. There seemed to be no rhyme nor reason to the organization of the shelves; they looked like giant abacuses, the spools ranging from the size of footballs to refrigerators. The hues varied from mauve to mustard to cyan, each shimmering as if alive, although Ryan noted that some were duller than others. It was a library of lives, she thought, awestruck.

Recalling her conversation with Melina, Ryan located Clotho sitting in front of a rapidly spinning wheel, mesmerized by the silver spool of unborn lives slowly increasing in width. Eyes closed, her foot rhythmically tapped the ground as her hands guided the string. Despite holding the most dazzling thread Ryan had ever seen, Clotho wore a dowdy robe of faded gray. Her hair was straggly and unbrushed, her skin wrinkled and discolored. There was no denying that she was ancient. The slack around her jaw hinted at the absence of teeth; her back was awfully hunched, the consequence of spinning for centuries.

Another sister came into view, nearly identical to Clotho, save for a smaller stoop. She hobbled over to a chair with a fresh spool of ivory thread. *Lachesis*, Ryan thought. Her gnarled hands placed spectacles upon her face as she sat down and tore a two-foot length of thread from the spool. She studied it, reading it left to right, took out a pencil from behind her ear, and made a tiny mark about halfway across the string. Then she set the delicate thread down at her side and started the process all over again, the only difference where she marked the piece. Sometimes she'd study the thread for long periods of time, while others barely received a passing glance. Ryan's heart dropped when she saw the sister make a mark at the very beginning of one string, knowing that some young life would be cut devastatingly short. Chewing the inside of her cheek, Ryan tore her eyes away, searching for the third sister.

Atropos finally appeared from the inner depths of the room, carrying a bundle of strings in disarray. She sat down next to Lachesis and, piece by piece, picked up a string, found the nearly invisible mark made by her sister, and cut it carefully with a sharp little dagger.

The thread then turned black, disintegrating into fuzzy, almost feather-like tufts that collected at her feet. She did this quickly, scanning each colorful string before she cut the life in front of her.

Suddenly, she stopped cutting, squinting at the string. She passed it to her sister, who studied the piece with her crippled hands. Lachesis nodded her head once to her sister, got up, and hobbled to Clotho at the wheel. She held it in front of her third sister, who glanced at it and nodded her head as well. Lachesis returned to her chair, made a second mark on this string, and put it in the pile to her left.

Ryan recognized the black pile of used thread at Atropos's feet as the same stuff that Clotho was weaving into the beautiful silver string. She realized with a jolt that they were using the discarded lives to weave new lives.

Without looking up or giving any hint that she knew Ryan was there, Clotho said, "Ask your question, child." Her calm and pleasant voice was a complete juxtaposition to her wild, disheveled exterior.

Ryan jumped in fright, dangerously close to emptying her bladder as she retreated out of the doorway behind the wall. Her heart racing, she knew that she had been spotted, but the women and their "professions" scared the piss out of her.

She gulped, smoothed her robe, and walked fully into the doorway. "Oh, I . . . didn't mean to disturb you. I'm lost." Ryan feigned her best look of innocence.

Lachesis put down the string in her hand and looked Ryan over.

"Many have come before you to ask the question. Many will come after," she replied in a similarly youthful voice.

At this point, both Clotho and Atropos had also stopped what they were doing. All three surveyed Ryan with their dark, knowing eyes.

Ryan remained calm despite herself. "What's my destiny? Am I the one they're searching for?" She paused, twisting her clammy hands. "Does Artemis even have a missing bloodline? Was Spiras right?"

Ryan hadn't even known she was going to ask these questions until they were already out. She watched as the sisters looked at one another. A silent consensus passed between them; they all abruptly stood up and headed down the aisle that divided the shelves of spool. Clotho stopped, turned around, and motioned for Ryan to follow her.

The botanist looked left, then right down the hall, unsure if she should follow. Melina's introduction of the Fates had mentioned they'd gone crazy, unable to fully execute their job. Ryan didn't know if it was wise to follow them deep into the room.

Curiosity won out as Clotho guided her into the maze of thread. They passed endless shelves of spools, Clotho's candle illuminating only three shelves in front and behind. Ryan stopped counting after seventeen and soon realized that a candle was no longer needed, as a silvery white light was coming from ahead.

As they happened upon the last few shelves, Ryan stopped in her tracks, jaw dropping at the spectacle in front of her: there stood a huge hundred-foot tree with countless gnarled branches that stretched out across the room. Instead of leaves, the two-foot-long threads hung from every branch, like colorful tinsel on a Christmas tree. Inexplicably, the tree glowed; there was no obvious source of illumination that caused the billions of pieces of thread to shine and reflect light all over the room. The threads danced, shimmering and swaying as though the tree were alive and breathing. A steady stream of strands gracefully drifted down to the floor; seeing a bare spot in front of her, Ryan concluded that Atropos must have picked up a heap and brought it back to the front of the room to cut.

"This is the tree of life," said Atropos, her voice pleasantly melodic. She raised one of her arms and made a gesture with her hand, like plucking something with her thumb and pointer finger. As she did this, one of the silvery strings untangled itself from a branch fifteen feet above and lazily floated down to her outstretched hand.

Clotho and Lachesis huddled around Atropos, studying the shimmery thread that Ryan unquestionably knew to be her own. It was a deep plum color, the width of an uncooked spaghetti noodle with a satin finish.

"Not too close to the flame," Ryan cautioned with a nervous laugh. They either didn't hear her or ignored her ill-timed, poor excuse of a joke.

The women started murmuring to one another, hunched over the thread. Ryan leaned in, trying to make out their conversation while squinting to see if she could discern Lachesis's dreaded mark, but her efforts were in vain.

The women stopped talking and peered up at her with great interest. Atropos raised her arm once more, lifting the little lifeline above her head. As she let go, it snaked its way back to its original resting place.

"Spiras spent a lot of time studying this tree. Being the Descendant of Apollo, she had an aptitude for prophecy and divination," Atropos said. "We Fates read what each individual lifeline tells us. We do not judge or interpret them as a whole. But Spiras's powers lay in reading the lifelines like they were lines in one big book."

Clotho chimed in. "Spiras was desperate to find something. She read and read the lifelines, climbing the branches as high as she could reach. She spent days and sleepless nights camped out here, searching. Until one day, she found it. The lifeline she was looking for."

"Was it mine?" Ryan whispered.

"As soon as she read it, Spiras tossed it back on the tree and ran out of here," Lachesis responded.

Disappointment washed over Ryan. If only they'd seen what had enthralled Spiras so obsessively.

"So am I on track to fulfill my destiny?"

Lachesis looked at her hard before responding, "A lot of work remains, my child."

Brow furrowed, Ryan's eyes ping-ponged between the three sisters, searching their faces for meaning. "My fate . . . did you assign me the right destiny?" As an afterthought, in a small voice, she asked, "Who am I?"

"Fate and identity are two quite different things, Ryan. Your fate is sealed, but your identity remains fluid," Clotho responded, hands clasped behind her back.

Ryan screwed up her face, trying to understand what they were telling her.

"And so does her allegiance," Atropos noted to her two sisters, who both nodded.

Frustration bubbled within Ryan. These women literally had her life in their hands and weren't giving her any sort of help. She watched Atropos stoop down to gather another pile of fallen threads. All three sisters turned around and shuffled back to the front of the room.

As she followed the sisters out of the room, Ryan studied the tree of life once more. Shivering, she morosely hoped that Greta's long and prosperous thread hung near hers.

All three returned to their original places and began their duties once more.

Ryan stood in the doorway, watching them for another minute.

Before turning to leave, she decided to give it one last effort. "Can you at least tell me if I'm the Descendant of Artemis?"

Without looking up, Lachesis responded simply, "Why tell you what you already know?"

T HE NEXT MORNING, THERE WAS a note on parchment from Melina, asking Ryan to meet in the rotunda. After a lengthy period of wandering, the botanist wondered to herself if even following simple directions was too much for her.

"Where have you been?" Melina called to Ryan as she hesitantly peeped out of a tunnelway. Relieved, Ryan saw she was back in the rotunda.

The botanist threw her shoulders back and strode over to Melina. She shrugged. "I took a little walk."

Melina squinted her eyes. "You got lost."

Ryan dropped her shoulders. "I got lost. You guys really need Google Maps in here. Turn left at the sea nymph. Take a right at the Siren. If you have arrived at the old woman who cuts the length of your life with a dagger, you have gone too far. Rerouting," said Ryan in a mock-robotic voice.

They both giggled.

"Let's go to the *fournáki*, or bakery," Melina suggested, physically guiding Ryan in the right direction.

A few moments later, they arrived at a little storefront with a steamed-up window. Even with a snaking line out front, the smell of honey and fried dough was reason enough to wait. Ryan was quite content chatting with Melina and Descendant-watching.

As they moved up in line, an older woman with radiant skin the exact match to Melina's umber strode up. Just like Melina, intricate black ink ran up and down her arms and neck. When the women were a couple feet away from one another, their ink momentarily glowed, as though recognizing kin.

"Ryan, this is my mother, Phaidra."

"Hello, Ryan. I am pleased to meet you. My daughter tells me that you are pleasant and likely very funny by American standards."

Smiling, Ryan made a mental note to relay this "compliment" back to Greta; she'd get a hoot out of it. "Melina has been a wonderful friend and teacher to me while I've been here."

"You are very welcome here," Phaidra said to Ryan. Looking at Melina, she said, "I ran into Nicholas. He said you are to pack in as much training as possible this morning and then head to the council meeting around noon."

"But Mom, we haven't eaten yet," Melina whined, pointing to the bakery.

Phaidra let out an exasperated sigh. "Don't kill the messenger, Melina." She quickly scanned the Descendants around her, adding before she turned to leave: "And you didn't hear it from me, but Nicholas is holed up in a meeting with the Seers, so if you guys have a quick bite to eat, you won't be busted." She shot them a mischievous smile and strode away.

A few minutes later, Melina gave an "*efharisto*" and Ryan a "thank you" to the woman who handed them a flaky phyllo-dough pastry, dripping with honey and dusted with powdered sugar, along with a steaming demitasse of espresso.

Melina led them to a little table where weak sunlight shone down on them. Looking up, both Ryan and the sun seemed unconvinced it was going to stick around much longer. The two women both sipped on their espressos in companionable silence, watching the mountain come alive with Descendants going about their normal morning routines. After gobbling her pastry, Ryan hastily dusted off the front of her chiton as Kosta appeared and joined the line for some baked goods.

"What exactly happens at these council meetings?"

Melina shrugged, examining her empty cup. "Overall management of the island. Mythical-Descendant relations. War prep and training updates."

"Hm," Ryan responded. "And a representative of each god is present?"

"Yes, there are eleven of us that are elected."

"So why can't I come? Since I'm supposedly the only Descendant of Artemis?"

Melina looked uncomfortable. "It was decided before you came that the meetings would be off limits for you. Just like the rest of the Descendants."

"Why? It sounds very mysterious."

"Oh yes. Trying to mediate arguments amongst the harpies is riveting stuff. Particularly when property lines of their bunk beds come up," Melina responded sarcastically. She gestured toward Ryan's cup. "Are you finished?"

"All done," Ryan said after slurping her last bit of bold espresso. "Are we headed to the training field?"

"I met with Nicholas last night. We are going to change strategies; perhaps you don't work well in a traditional training setting. So we're going to immerse you in our culture, working side by side with Descendants as they use their powers to carry out our everyday activities. We think if you feel closer to our way of life, you'll feel closer to the gods. If you feel closer to the gods, your powers will blossom like your magical flowers," she said, slowly opening her hand like a bloom.

"Is Nicholas freaking out that I haven't shown powers yet?"

Melina pulled out a piece of parchment from a pocket on her chiton robe that hadn't been there a moment ago. Studying it, she said, "He just wants to make good use of the time while you're here."

"So that's a yes," Ryan said bitterly.

Melina ignored her. "First you'll meet with Maria in her restaurant as she prepares for the lunchtime crowd. She has a unique way of cooking; as the Descendant of Hera, she's all about family. So every morning, Maria goes on a walkabout around the cave to get a sense of the overall emotional atmosphere. How are people feeling? What ails them? And how can her food assist in remedying the needs of her people? Afterward, you'll plan a menu with her."

"I have an *appetite*," Ryan said with a cheeky grin, "to *hunt* out hunger. Get it?"

"Ignoring you," Melina sang, looking back down at her list. "Next, you'll meet with the Furies. When the gods were free, Tisiphone, Megaera, and Alecto patrolled and imparted justice to those mortals who committed a crime against the gods."

"Gulp," Ryan responded, eyes wide.

"These days, there isn't much crime on the island, but the harpies reported that someone or some*thing* had bewitched the gods to sneeze every hour on the hour."

As if on cue, a deafening roar erupted from above. Jumping out of her seat, Ryan's eyes shot up to the ceiling, where the twelve statues had just recovered from their epic sneezes. Getting her wits about her and climbing back onto her seat, Ryan felt little droplets rain down on her skin; she prayed it was water and not godly snot.

"So you'll go on the *hunt* for clues to uncover the perpetrator. See, I can do it too," Melina said smugly.

"Whose god handles the antihistamines?" Ryan grumbled, still shook up.

"Lastly you'll meet with the Muses. There are nine of them, each of whom represents special art associated with Lyric, Music, Comedy, Tragedy, Dance, Astronomy, History, Hymns, and Epics. They are to give you a lesson on genealogy and where we come from. Their lesson is less about physically honing your powers and more about giving you a foundation."

"They're the ones who threw the party, right?" Ryan asked, moving her neck and her shoulders around to an imaginary beat.

"Espresso makes you . . . jokey, doesn't it?" Melina asked with eyebrows raised. "Yes, they're in charge of parties and holidays, as well as theater. You'll see . . . they can get pretty dramatic."

Turns out, dramatics played a big part in their lesson, as Ryan was shuffled into an empty amphitheater by nine identical sisters with nine pairs of lips all simultaneously trying to carry on a conversation with her.

After a lackluster performance of menu planning with Maria (Ryan's suggestion for unlimited salad and breadsticks to soothe the rainy-day blues landed on deaf ears) and a mea culpa with the Furies (Ryan's investigation had embarrassingly pointed back to the Furies themselves; they were not amused), the Muses explained that, being the record keepers of the past, they were going to put on a performance for Ryan.

They wore their hair the same, wrapped up in tight buns on top of their heads, and shared the same pale-green eyes. They were scurrying around in yellow robes, but in different shades—dark mustard to lemonade mist. They were a living, breathing yellow paint swatch.

The Muse in the canary yellow robe stepped forward, flourished a deep bow, and, in a dramatic voice, bellowed, "*Kalispera.* Good evening. Tonight's performance is called The Truce." Bright white fire exploded from the torches, and then everything went to black.

Blue mist rose a couple feet from each torch, and a beam of light from an unknown source above illuminated the stage. The woman who'd announced the title of the show was no longer seen, but her voice boomed, narrating the story that was playing out in front of Ryan.

"*Once upon a time, the gods were banished to Mount Olympus by Gaea, Mother Nature herself.*"

A Muse walked out onto the stage, no longer clad in a yellow dress but wearing an elaborate costume with twelve huge dolls draped around her like a sunburst. They were so real, each god's face expressing a range of emotions and animatedly talking to one another.

A giant, dark-brown boulder rose from beneath the stage, raising the Muse up toward the cave ceiling. One of the goddess heads wailed, "Let us out! It's up to you, Descendants!" Her tearful cry echoed eerily throughout the amphitheater.

"*The Descendants tried in vain to save their godly counterparts.*"

As the Muse on top of the mountain grimly watched on, a group of Muses entered the stage, miming different types of magical spells. As real sparks emitted from their fingertips, the Muses became more desperate and despondent at their futile attempts to save the gods from exile. Ryan's heart broke for the actors, their pure anguish palpable. She supposed they weren't even necessarily acting; even after centuries, their emotions were still raw as they reenacted their family being mercilessly torn apart.

"*It was no use. Their magic was not strong enough to break them free.*"

A scarlet curtain dropped down in front of the scene, but unlike a curtain hanging at a theater, it completely fell, disappearing into the floor. The mountain and all the Muses vanished with it, leaving the stage empty.

"It was time to utilize other measures."

From both sides of the stage, Muses stormed out, a battle scene unfolding. On stage right, Muses dressed in chitons brandished golden weapons of tridents, arrows, and swords. Muses in magnificent Centaur and arachne costumes followed them, screeching battle cries. On the other end of the stage, a Muse was dressed all in black, her dominance and unbridled power emanating from her place on the stage. Her long, green hair fell in thick, mossy tendrils over her shoulders. She looked at the Descendants with fierce hatred in her eyes, as other Muses dressed as abominable, hulking creatures hurled themselves threateningly toward the Descendants. As the battle progressed, the side representing Gaea overtook the Descendants, and realistic rivers of fake blood spilled over the edge of the stage. Ryan's stomach lurched, barely breathing from the stunning and violent reenactment.

"Time and time again, they were unsuccessful. Many have come. Many have gone during this valiant fight.

"Meanwhile, as we healed from our fight against Gaea, the world outside the island was waging its own war against her. Her earthly children had become powerful, and Gaea recognized that she was not strong enough to counter what the humans were making of her world."

Another scarlet curtain fell from the sky, the battle and blood all disappearing into the floor as the top of the curtain reached the ground.

A man walked to the center of the stage, his robe a swirl of layers; sheer black organza, chiffon, and satin stretched and floated, the robe moving in slow motion on its own accord. Even from her vantage point a couple rows up, the man's magnificent eyes captivated Ryan. Thick, dark braids wove around the crown of his head.

"Who is that?" Ryan whispered to herself.

The Muse narrating must have had superhuman ears; she boomed back a response. *"Samir is a Seer. Their eyes are a medium we use to see what's happening outside the island."*

With a flourish that competed with the drama of the Muses, Samir turned his back to the Ryan. A white tarp fell from the ceiling, like a screen. Suddenly, light cast from his eyes, revealing moving pictures, like a movie projector.

News reports, video clips, and aerial footage portrayed a highlight reel of doom. "The Industrial Revolution . . ." Ryan whispered in comprehension.

Clip after clip of the effects of the Industrial Revolution were shown, occasionally accompanied by a news reporter or an unseen narrator projected audibly through Samir's mouth. A time lapse of burgeoning population growth followed an aerial pan of bald acreages from deforestation. Another clip showed dizzying factory lines of mass production; smokestacks billowing ash into the air; sewers spewing waste into a river; a toddler wearing a child-sized face mask jumping in puddles amid a barren yard. Another clip showed bulldozers driving amongst overflowing landfills; contaminated crops being fed to cattle; disintegrating ice caps falling into the ocean; farmers looking on at a dusty, dead cornfield; coastlines under water from rising sea levels; parks littered with dead monarchs; African elephants looking at dried-up watering holes. The reel faded to black.

Choking back tears, Ryan thought, *This highlight reel would give Sarah McLachlan a run for her money . . .*

The Muse continued her narration. *"Gaea, unable to heal the*

world from the human-caused climate change, has shown reckless aban-
don as punishment on a world she feels has let her down."

Samir's eyes came back to life, showing scenes of a different cause. News reports of the last few years showcased all the unexplained mysteries that scientists assumed were related to climate change: devastating earthquakes in countries where there were no fault lines; long-dormant volcanoes that erupted without warning; wildfires that burned for months in frigid weather. It ended with the sinkholes Greta had described a few nights ago.

The reel again faded to black, and Samir sashayed off the stage.

"Wait, they're saying Gaea is responsible? For all the random mass atrocities?" Ryan whispered incredulously.

"Yes, Ryan," the narrator boomed, breaking the fourth wall. *"Specifically, the Titans. They are Gaea's army of monster children and have been using earth as a playground to wreak havoc and mayhem."* She cleared her throat, going back to her script. *"But the humans, pitifully powerless, will no longer suffer alone!"*

From the wings, an unseen choir of Muses cried in harmony, "THE TRUCE!" while the torches exploded with fireworks, eerily illuminating the twelve marble faces watching the show from above.

Two Muses entered the stage, and Ryan snickered; one of them was unmistakably playing Elias. Dressed in his standard slate-colored chiton robe that complemented his espresso hair, the Muse emphatically frowned at the audience and then showed off her muscles in various positions. She then swaggered toward the other Muse who played Gaea.

"Wait, Elias left the island to talk to Gaea?" Ryan asked in wonder. The narrator didn't respond this time.

The Muse playing Elias said, "Gaea, let us use our powers in the open, without threat of your persecution, and we'll help you heal the world against this human-made illness, global warming."

The Muse playing Gaea said, "Only if you forever end your fight to free the gods. You will have to seal the gods with your own power before I will let you roam freely."

The Muse narrator said, *"The decision to agree to the alliance has been excruciating."*

Gaea left the stage, and more Muses came out, dressed like members of the council; they debated back and forth, gesturing wildly, arguing wordlessly.

The Muse narrator continued, *"Some argued that the time was now, as the world was in dire peril. Some argued that we cannot give up on the fight to free the gods. But alas, the fate of the Descendants on this island is what reigned supreme."*

A Muse, undoubtedly playing Nicholas with his trademark long silvery beard, mimicked his gravelly voice: "We are turning our backs on the gods. We must find the missing link."

Muse Elias responded: "We are slowly dying on this island. They are slowly dying out there. Nobody will survive if we don't do something."

Everyone departed the stage, except Muse Elias, who was joined by a sauntering Muse Gaea.

The narrator gravely said, *"A timeline for the final decision was made."*

The two Muses shook hands, and the red ribbon of curtain fell, revealing an empty stage.

The Muse narrator: *"With the clock ticking, a Seer picks up something interesting."*

Samir glided back onto stage and projected a scene of Kosta, Elias, and Nicholas watching news coverage of Ryan and her discovery.

Passionately, Nicholas said, "She's the missing piece to why we can't overthrow Gaea and free the gods."

"She's showing signs of being all powerful," Kosta agreed.

Elias retorted, "You can't prove Artemis had a secret child and an unknown bloodline out there. We already gave our word. The truce is done."

Nicholas looked at both of them and said with an air of finality, "Bring her here."

Glad for the shield of darkness, Ryan felt her cheeks burn red hot. Kosta had fought for her even before he knew her. And she hadn't known Elias felt so strongly against her.

Samir gracefully exited, and the Muse narrator, for the first time since the beginning of the show, presented herself by walking across the stage. *"Our future is uncertain. Will she be the one? Or will we fulfill the truce? Only time will tell."*

The theater was quiet as the torches turned from cool blue to their normal, fiery glow. Ryan felt like the Muses were paused in their last poses, waiting for her to applaud or cheer, but the gravity of the revelation made her bolt from the auditorium.

Kosta had just rounded the corner. "Hey, I brought you some lun—"

"THIS IS ALL ON MY SHOULDERS? YOUR ENTIRE LIVELIHOOD?"

"What? What are you talking about?" Kosta blustered.

"The truce," Ryan hissed.

Still confused, Kosta studied Ryan and then looked back toward the amphitheater. Comprehension dawned in his eyes. "Did the Muses tell you? Ryan, calm down," he said, resting his hands on her shoulders.

She whipped back around, running her hands frustratedly through her hair, her mind moving a mile a minute.

"Is it true? That you made a pact with Gaea? But you're all crazy with hope that I'll somehow help you free the gods?"

"Yes, it's true," Kosta said softly.

"You didn't think to tell me this?" she beseeched.

"We didn't want to overwhelm you."

"Quit underestimating me!" Ryan bellowed.

She whipped around and smacked straight into the chest of a lion with an eagle head. It flapped its wings to get back its balance, looking perturbed at Ryan.

"Are you kidding me right now?! You have griffins here?"

"Hi, Shervin," Kosta said. "You OK?" The eagle head nodded, and she heard it mutter, "Typical American," under its breath.

Throwing up her hands in disbelief, Ryan paced farther away from Kosta, slower this time, avoiding another run-in with a mythical beast.

"Ryan, a few of us have always thought there was a missing piece. Every time we've gone to war with Gaea, it's like our powers are incomplete. When we saw you, it just felt like you had to be using powers to do what you do."

She kept striding toward the direction of her flat.

"We have to search every avenue before officially sealing away our gods forever. Do you know what that means for us? For our fight? It means we've been living on this godsforsaken island in vain for twenty-seven hundred years. We're dying out here."

She stopped and turned around. Sneering, she spat, "I'm not one of you, Kosta. I never will be."

Kosta's patience waned, his voice growing louder. "I don't understand why you're so angry."

"You guys withheld this information from me. You're not being straight with me."

"Be reasonable, Ryan. If we'd laid it all out on the line the moment you stepped foot on this dock, would you have believed us?"

She sighed. "No."

Kosta took a deep breath, his voice calm again. "Look, I'm sorry. We were going to tell you about the truce. The council decided to give you a couple more days of training under your belt. Allow you to 'accidentally' run into a griffin"—his lips turned up into a smile—"and then get into the gritty-nitty."

"Nitty-gritty," Ryan corrected, unable to suppress a smile momentarily.

"That's what I said."

She rolled her eyes at him and let out a deep breath. "OK. I've calmed down. Nothing like seeing yourself on a gigantic screen by the eyes of a human projector. And then learning you're the last chance of hope for a civilization of people."

"Five more days. Please. Just try your hardest these next five days. You now see what's on the line for us."

"Yes, and I now see what's on the line for *us*," Ryan said to herself. Kosta's eyebrows shot up questioningly. Louder, she said, "Us as in humans. My plants can counter greenhouse gases, but they don't exactly know any hand-to-hand combat against Titans." Cracking her knuckles out of habit, she said, "Five more days. And then you guys are going to move forward with the truce."

"Yes. The day after you depart."

"Wow," breathed Ryan.

Kosta let out an enormous sigh. "I know."

"I need to process all this."

"Where were you going?" he asked.

"To my room . . ."

He chuckled.

Once again, her face flushed. "This isn't the way, is it?" He shook his head. "See! I am hopeless!" she said, only half joking.

Kosta gestured toward a doorway a quarter of the way around the rotunda. They walked together in silence. Ryan noted their arms grazing gently with every step. There was plenty of room down the hallway, but they remained close. She peeked up at him at the exact moment that he peeked down at her—they both immediately whipped their heads back forward and then awkwardly laughed, their cheeks matching the curtain from the show.

"Here we are. I need to run and mend the pterippi fence—" He stopped at the questioning look on Ryan's face. "You'd probably associate them with Pegasus—they're winged horses."

"I knew you had unicorns here," Ryan muttered.

Kosta chuckled and continued, "Then bring in some fresh water for the Sirens and attend another council meeting."

"A super-secret council meeting?" Ryan probed, again only half joking.

He shrugged. "Look, I'll ask Nicholas if you can come to the next council meeting, OK? Would that make you happy?"

"It'd be a start," she said, smiling.

He gave her his hallmark lopsided grin and extended a clenched fist at her, palm up. He then opened his hand and yelled, "BOOM."

She frowned at the open hand and then up at Kosta, mystified.

Sensing her confusion, Kosta quickly added, "Did I not do it right? Sometimes, when Samir gets drunk on ouzo, he'll teach us some greeting or gesture that's current in the outside world. He said that young adults use this as a form of hello."

Ryan realized that he was attempting to do a fist bump and

"explode" it at the end. A laugh bubbled up. She corrected his form, turning over his fist so that the knuckles were up; a shiver ran down her spine as she manipulated his beautiful bronze hand. She then used her fist to bump his, knuckle to knuckle, and made an exploding sound with her mouth as she opened her hand, fingers stretched out wide.

A grin erupted from Kosta's face, triggering an explosion in Ryan's heart. He gleefully repeated the gesture, and although still a bit mechanical, he seemed to have gotten the hang of the action. "See ya later!" he called as he turned to go.

"Not if I see you first!" Ryan hollered back, cringing at her dorky goodbye.

ALREADY MIDWAY THROUGH THE FIRST of Ryan's two-week superhero sabbatical, days settled into a predictable rhythm: meet with a different Descendant and try some vague iteration of hunting that related to their own power. Nicholas prowled from the sidelines, either impatiently imploring her to try harder or cheering her on with empty words of encouragement, his eyes all the while growing as bleak as the weather that hounded them. His stress was palpable, and it kept Ryan in a constant state of agitation. She wanted to snap at him: *Do you think I'm purposefully holding these powers back?*

Although she couldn't truthfully relay what was going on to her friend, Ryan was in desperate need of Greta. And Lester. She was so homesick, and through poor internet connection (or was it technically a Seer connection?), the time change, and pure happenstance, the two of them kept missing each other's calls. Greta sent perfunctory updates about the greenhouse construction and the latest global catastrophes while still harassing Ryan to send photos of Nicholas. Ryan harassed Greta right back, insisting she send photos of Lester with fur intact. But there was only so much one could convey through texts and emojis, and Ryan was eager to return to Greta's maternal presence.

Melina watched with a commiserating smile as the botanist

spilled all these feelings over breakfast. "The feeling of missing home is so foreign to me," she said.

Ryan tilted her head, studying Melina. "Isn't it going to be quite a shock to the system if you all move forward with the truce and live out there? Not only living in a whole new world with technology you haven't had access to but also the social implications."

Melina nodded. "It's something we've been discussing during our council meetings ever since the truce has become a viable option. We think most people will still live here, but they'll be free to come and go. It'll be a gradual transition, so that people can dip their toes in versus diving headfirst."

Ryan squinted her eyes at her friend. "That's what *you* would want to do?"

Melina looked down at her empty cup of coffee. "No," she whispered fervently. "I want to stay in a really fancy hotel, where they bring food to your door and have little bottles of hair soap by an enormous white bathtub. And then I want to discover a coffee shop where they'll make me a mocha-chocha-flappacino and I can sit in obscurity, not knowing one single person but blending in with people my own age. And then I want to walk to my job, where I'm an assistant for a major magazine editor in one of those breathtakingly tall buildings with the security guards. And after work, I'll slip on an outrageously fabulous outfit to meet my friends for pink cocktails in those fancy clear glasses where we dish on all the adventures we've had in love and life."

"Sounds like an episode of *Sex and the City*," Ryan whispered to herself.

Melina blushed and nodded. "It's where I learned about cosmopolitans."

"How—?"

Melina slyly looked around and whispered, "There is a black market of sorts for more 'modern' information. Befriend—or bribe—a Seer, and they can show you recent television shows and movies. That's how some of us stay up to date on popular culture. Officially, as someone on the council, it's strictly forbidden. It does not reflect our ideals and lifestyle, and we're afraid it will create longing for what inhabitants on the island cannot have."

It dawned on Ryan that the first time she'd entered the cave with Nicholas, he'd busted a group of teenagers watching *Friends*. Sandrine must have been a Seer.

"Well, I don't know how realistic *Sex and the City* was, but we can make that a reality," Ryan said, patting Melina's hand. "But it's also important to know a few things before you fall head over heels into the plot of *Devil Wears Prada*."

"I teach you now, Ryan. And then you'll teach me," she said warmly. "Speaking of, you're going to shadow me while I work through my responsibilities for the day. I need to redirect a stream for the Centaurs so their field of wolfsbane doesn't flood from all this rain, visit the Seers to hang some new projector screens, and help the Muses with laundry. Each time, we'll have you try to work up your magic."

"I'm great at spot removal," Ryan joked.

When Melina raised her eyebrows, Ryan continued, "Lesson one: laundromat humor."

"Is everyone out there as strange as you?" Melina asked, nudging Ryan's ribs in jest.

"You betcha," Ryan replied with a laugh, shooting her with little finger guns. "Pew! Pew!"

Walking arm in arm with Melina, the botanist looked around, smiling. The sun had parted the clouds and was shining beautifully into the atrium. As they made their way outside, Ryan waved a little hello to the Muses, gingerly walked around the harpies so as not to step on their tails, and stopped to show a group of teenagers how to do Madonna's "Vogue" pose.

Taking a big breath of fresh island air as they stepped outside, Ryan realized she was falling in love with this island, with its inhabitants and their magic.

Melina guided her toward the vegetation near the beach, where Elias was waiting. "Ooh," Ryan squealed. "Birds of paradise!" She squatted down to look at the flowers up close. "I've never seen one in person," she explained as Elias and Melina looked on.

"How did you get interested in botany?" Melina asked.

"Well—" Ryan began.

"Actually—" Melina cut her off, looking off in the distance. "Hey, Samir! Come over here!" she called.

The Seer from yesterday's Muse performance glided over from his walk along the beach. Tipping her head to the side, Ryan carefully studied the man in front of her in wonder. Up close, she was able to fully see the eyes that had so captivated her the night of the Muse performance. Their deep, black pupils dominated, with only a hint of an iris surrounding them. As though the pupils seeped out of his eyes, black fine lines, not unlike tattoos, swirled around his forehead and cheeks, creating the effect of lace draped around the upper part of his head. Paired with the floating dress, he looked like a dream personified.

"Unbeknownst to us, the Muses gave you an introduction to Seers, the vessels of godly transmissions," Melina told her.

"Hello, Samir. It's nice to meet you," Ryan said.

Samir nodded, his voice a deep baritone of energy. "When the gods ruled, we served as the middlemen between them and mortals, working as a mouthpiece for both parties. Mortals traveled far and wide to us oracles, hoping for insight into their fates and misfortunes, ways in which to appease the gods and to seek out prophecies."

"Wow," Ryan breathed.

Melina said, "When the gods were banished to Mount Olympus, the communication channel broke between them and the Seers. Shortly into their refuge on the island, all the Seers went blind. Without any purpose or sight, they wandered around the island, muttering to themselves while we helplessly looked on."

Samir shook his head sadly, glancing up at the indiscernible peak of Mount Olympus. "When it became evident that there wasn't a quick fix to free the gods from Mount Olympus, we recognized a need to monitor the world outside our island. Isolation made us vulnerable to what Gaea was doing. It wasn't an option to use traditional communication methods with anyone beyond our forcefield, as we'd risk Gaea pinpointing the island's location. We needed eyes on the ground, without being on the ground.

"Sensing a purpose, the Seers slowly came back to life. Their foggy, cataract-plagued eyes cleared up, and with every blink, their vision came into focus. Soon, we noticed a mysterious brightness shining from their eyes. The Seers' eyes were projecting scenes from outside the island, as though they were watching from above. We determined their magical eyes could channel different wavelengths throughout the atmosphere, like X-ray and radio waves, and that they could broadcast what was happening all over the world."

Samir regally lifted his chin up with pride. "As technology burgeoned with mortals, so did it improve with us. With the invention of television and internet, we've managed to tap into it all, keeping the council abreast of what is going on outside the island. That's how we found you."

Ryan cringed at the thought of the council and Kosta seeing her

Weepy Willow ugly-cry interview. *Is a girl not safe from internet infamy on a remote, hidden island?* she wondered.

"Touch Samir's arm and show us," Melina said.

"Huh?" Ryan said.

Samir touched a finger to his temple, gazing at Ryan. "Seers can see what's playing inside your head."

"We'll see what you see," Melina told her, pointing to her own temples.

Questioningly, Ryan looked at Samir, who gave a nod of encouragement. Warily, she touched his arm, and his eyes projected to life, two blinding white beams. In a trance, Elias and Melina angled Samir so that he was projecting toward the dark bark of a wide tree. Immediately, the botanist watched as the pictures projected in her mind's eye were reflected upon the tree.

Watching intently, Melina asked, "Do you want to tell us what we're watching?"

"Uh, yeah, sure," she began awkwardly. "I don't think I'd be where I am today if someone had paid more attention to me. Isn't that the silver lining of being woefully neglected?" she added to herself with a laugh. "My path toward botany all started when I was around ten years old. My aunt insisted I go play outside whenever I got her in way. So I was left to my own devices for hours at a time."

Samir projected a scene of a rundown house, where a preteen Ryan was handed a sandwich and unceremoniously shoved out a screen door. They watched as she morosely looked out at the broken-down swing set and plopped down on the crumbling cement step to inspect her lunch. Ryan's youthful face scrunched with abhorrent disgust as she slowly slid out a tomato from in between the two slices of bread.

"Gagging down the snot-like, fleshy booger of a tomato wasn't an option, but neither was risking a lecture from my aunt on how I was wasting food that could be allocated to her 'real' children," Ryan said, using her fingers as quotes.

They watched as Ryan eyed the screen door behind her back, carefully tucked the tomato back into the sandwich, and marched to the side of the house, strategically out of the way of any windows. The resourceful youth grabbed a stick and started digging a hole.

"I had the sudden inspiration to secretly bury it. It was a win-win scenario in my head: I wouldn't be punished for being ungrateful, and the worms would certainly enjoy a treat."

The projection fast-forwarded to Ryan in a different outfit, albeit just as shabby, joyfully inspecting a little seedling peeking out of the soil.

"Much to my delight, a week later, a brave sprout came up to greet me. I became obsessed with the discovery that I could grow something that was completely my own. I'd never really had anything that was my own my whole life. Soon, the little hidden area next to the fence became my first laboratory, as I experimented with any seed I could get my hands on."

A montage of Ryan digging holes, dropping in seeds, patting down the soil, hauling water, pruning, and weeding followed. She couldn't stop the rather embarrassing moments that popped in as well, such as a scene of her reading *The Secret Garden* to her plants, and another showing her covering them up in the middle of the night with her own bedcovers.

"And then one day, my aunt found out . . ."

A woman with frizzy blonde hair stalked around the corner of the house, where Ryan shot up, dusting her hands of dirt and trying to use her body to shield her plants from her aunt. The aunt's face twisted in rage as she pushed Ryan aside, yelling obscenities and threatening to traipse over the nicely manicured rows of plants.

"As the summer days grew longer, my aunt discovered that a side of her nasty, pathetic lawn had been relegated to a patch of random veggies and beautiful flowers. After a Grade-A temper tantrum and confirmation that I—a third grader, might I add—wasn't growing 'Mary Jane,' my aunt realized she could cash in on my green thumb."

Ryan glanced at Samir, who still stood motionless in his fugue-like state of projection.

In the next memory, she and her aunt were sitting side by side in the kitchen, Ryan eating a chocolate chip cookie while her aunt pointed to some photos from *Good Housekeeping* magazine.

"My aunt found bouquets she liked and asked me if I could grow them for her. After an exhilarating trip to the local nursery, I doted over a lush flowerbed full of beautiful blooms for many years."

As an afterthought, Ryan added softly, "My aunt never put a tomato in my sandwich again."

Melina and Elias watched as the lawn became beauteous and green, with an abundant flower garden that overtook one whole half of the yard. It was a bevy of reds and oranges and yellows, butterflies and bees.

"My aunt became a local floral celebrity, the book club and church ladies swooning with garden envy. She opened her own floral business for weddings and events, cashing in on my talent yet never crediting her secret weapon," Ryan said bitterly.

"A Descendant with beautiful powers," Melina breathed.

"A niece with a powerful green thumb," the botanist corrected her. "But when I was fifteen years old, there was news."

They watched as Ryan's aunt snagged a cookie out of her niece's hands and shoved a positive pregnancy test under her nose. Her aunt pointed to the front door. In the next scene, they watched as Ryan pulled the pitifully barren suitcase with a wonky wheel to the backyard, where she gave one last look over her floral empire, tears running down her face.

"My aunt was pregnant with twins. It was unplanned. Despite a surge in income from me, they wouldn't have room for me with the new babies, so I got the kick-boot and was unceremoniously passed along to the next family member."

They watched as Ryan looked up at a tall building in a densely populated metropolitan area. She walked into a drab apartment with a guy who barely acknowledged her; he just pointed to another empty, sad room.

"My bachelor uncle lived in a depressing high-rise apartment with zero green space. Fed up with the family roulette, I graduated high school early and applied for emancipation. From there, I attended college for botany and started my real life, without faux family members pretending to care."

Gently, she lifted her hand off Samir's arm. Blinking rapidly, he rubbed his eyes, looked sadly down at Ryan, and patted her arm. He murmured, "Thank you for sharing that with me," nodded at Melina and Elias, and walked back toward the beach.

"Humans are so cruel," Elias said. She expected to see a consoling look on his face after witnessing the uncaring nature of her family, but she saw contempt instead. He turned and walked away from the sandy beach, inland toward the tropical greenery.

"Some are . . ." Ryan agreed.

"You are one brave woman, Ryan," Melina said, with sympathetic eyes and a kind smile. She flicked her head toward the direction of Elias and followed him into the jungle.

The humidity had risen; Ryan looked behind her shoulders and saw clouds building up in the horizon over the ocean. She tried to pat down the frizzy hair around her face, but the sweat from her forehead just made it look like wet fur.

She turned to follow Melina, leaving her emotional baggage on the beach.

Catching up to her, Ryan carefully guided her clumsy feet around the foliage. "Last night, I was thinking about what life would be like if the gods were off the mountain. Like, what would change? How would life be different? I took a mythology class in high school, so my knowledge is limited, but I have a general foundation of the Olympians and their powers." She scrunched her face in concentration. "I can't imagine how it'd work. And I don't want any of this to sound offensive, but haven't humans done OK without them?"

When she glanced at Melina's face to gauge her reaction, she was met with a warm smile. "You mean besides killing the planet?" her friend teased.

"Yeah, that minor setback."

"It all goes back to Gaea. She is the creator of all things on this earth, but when it comes to ideals or behaviors or complicated mortal constructs, she has no expertise, nor does she care to help solve or influence those who may ask for help. She leaves the mortals to fend for themselves; humans are left to do their own bidding. This is where the gods come in. They rule over destiny, justice, and luck. Every god has a purpose, a power. When a mortal calls upon a god for help, they can use their power to alter that person's fate."

"So with the gods present, humans can, what—make a wish to a god and it'll come true?"

"Not exactly. I don't want you to think that freeing the gods will have this monumental positive effect on humanity. They're flawed like mortals. But with Gaea solely in power, the balance has been off. They'll be able to shift things back, so humans have an easier go at it."

"If the humans accept the gods at all," Ryan noted.

A few paces ahead, she saw Elias stop abruptly. "What do you mean?"

Ryan let out a low chuckle. "Say you save the gods off their mountain vacation home. And they just appear to everyone out there," she said, pointing to the horizon, where ominous clouds were assembling. "It will cause an uproar, to say the least. Mayhem. Pandemonium. Likely World War III. A holy war. Two thousand years of beliefs, crumbled in an instant."

Elias gave a dismissive grunt, but Melina was looking at her, eyes wide.

"There are fervently religious people out there who believe in one god. They will be absolutely shook if their values, the very foundation of their beings, are suddenly turned on their heads. Even the people who are agnostic or atheist—to suddenly have proof that there is something out there that wants to rule them, beyond their wildest imaginations?" Ryan shook her head. "It's going to cause major problems."

"They wouldn't have a choice," Elias said gruffly.

"Exactly my point, Elias," Ryan shot back.

They had arrived at a rippling creek, narrow enough for Melina and Elias to effortlessly hop over. Ryan stared at the width nervously, knowing her uncoordinated leap could leave her sopping wet. Melina and Elias were surveying both ends of the stream, pointing and planning.

Melina pointed to the right. "That is the direction of the patch of wolfsbane that the Centaurs want to protect from flooding."

Elias continued her thought, "So we'll have to redirect it . . ." He looked behind his shoulder. "Around this way."

Melina nodded in agreement.

"You want to wrangle it and toss to me?" Elias asked.

"Sure." As Melina was about to bend down, she stopped. "We should let Ryan try to help, though."

"Of course," Elias said, crossing his arms. "Be my guest."

For some reason, despite having no realistic chance of performing any sort of magical skill, she wanted Elias to believe she could.

"I'm ready," she said, bending her knees and shaking out her hands, as though that would somehow show her physical prowess. "What do you need me to do?"

"I'm going to scoop up the stream, and we're going to throw it to one another, moving it thirty paces in this direction."

Ryan's confidence faltered a bit at the sentence, but she pushed her shoulders back again and said, "OK, great. I'll watch you; just let me know what I need to do." She clapped once and rested her hands on her knees, as though she were going to catch a softball.

Melina smiled encouragingly and then bent down. She used one of her muscular midnight-black arms to scoop one side of the stream; the water was bound together as though in a clear plastic pipe. Melina gathered the other side and hefted the heavy stream onto her shoulder. She yanked one end like a stubborn garden hose, and Ryan saw that she was straightening out the stream ahead of them; it physically writhed in the ground, changing its path.

"OK, walk about ten paces over there and I'll toss it to you. Concentrate on using your powers to hold the water, like almighty Poseidon himself." As an afterthought, Melina added, "Elias, why don't you get behind her and catch it if she's unsuccessful?"

Walking toward Elias, Ryan tripped over a root; Elias's boa

constrictor arms swiftly caught her across the midsection before she fell. Mumbling her thanks, the botanist got into position, Elias taking his place a couple feet behind her.

Squeezing the watery tube in her arms, Melina said, "OK, I've managed to narrow it out, so you should be able to get your arms around it when you catch it. One. Two. Three!"

Lifting her arms open wide, Ryan watched as the tube of water gracefully flew into the air, as though in slow motion. Internally, she commanded herself: *Come on, powers, come out NOW.* Knees bent and slightly shaking with anticipation, she waited as the water came barreling toward her. *Ryan Bell, you've got this!*

A huge whoosh of water smacked Ryan hard in the face, her arms grasping nothing but wetness, the force of the watery python knocking her flat on her back.

Every inch of her soaked, she wiped off her face and tilted her head up; Elias had tucked the stream under one arm and was offering her the other, all while trying to hold in his laughter. After she accepted his hand, Elias effortlessly righted her for a second time.

At least it's not frizzy anymore, she thought miserably, wringing out her sopping hair.

Melina marched over and asked if she were OK. Ryan nodded, studying her pair of teachers. "Jeez, you guys would have been handy during Hurricane Katrina."

They really would be able to help in dire situations if they could use their powers off the island, she thought. But say they accepted the truce and were able to live in the real world with their magic: how could the 126 of them be useful on a planet so big? With so many problems and issues that could use their attention, how would they choose which deserved their demigodly intervention? And what about Melina's aspirations to lead a "regular" life? How would this work out for them?

Melina interrupted her thoughts. "We'll try again. Follow me. OK, Elias?"

He grunted, tugging one end of the stream to follow his path while Ryan and Melina walked on another ten paces.

"OK, I want you to really envision Artemis. Her power. Her strength. Her love of nature. Just like your love of nature."

"Her love of her offspring . . . her love of abandonment," Ryan muttered, peeling a soggy leaf off her inner arm.

Melina frowned. "I don't think that attitude is going to help your case."

The botanist shrugged, attempting to wring out some water from her sodden chiton.

"Please try. You promised you'd try," Melina said quietly.

Ryan stopped fidgeting and looked at her friend. "Of course, yes, I'm sorry." Taking a deep breath, she prepped her stance for the very probable outcome of a watery whack in the face again. Turning toward Elias, she watched as he juggled the water around in the air for fun.

"Show-off," Melina muttered to herself.

"OK, I am the bloodline of Artemis. Artemis, use me as your tool. Let's save some wolfsbane," Ryan said.

Knees bent, Elias wound up and tossed the stream into the air, lightly, like a father tossing a Wiffle ball to his toddler. As it came careening down upon her, she prepared herself for the inevitable explosion of cold water over her face.

WHOOSH! Knocked flat onto her back, Ryan wiped off her face again and looked at Melina, who cradled the stream in both arms like a baby. "Refreshing," Ryan sputtered, picking herself up and wiping the debris from her muddy back.

"It is a big stream," Melina said consolingly.

Elias walked up and gingerly picked something out of Ryan's hair. "There's a minnow." He flicked it back into the stream. "I think one more should do it?"

"Agreed," Melina said.

Elias walked on. Neither he nor Melina urged her to try a third time; instead, Melina smoothly tossed the stream over to Elias, who gently set it back down into its new home. Walking back toward the ladies, Elias kicked the stream a little here and there, making sure it was in the precise route he'd imagined.

"Back to our conversation, Ryan, you believe the gods are real and you aren't having a hard time," Melina pointed out.

Ryan shrugged. "I believe that you guys possess powers." She looked out in the distance. "And I am starting to see evidence that there is something fishy going on out there in addition to the climate change." Her head whipped up as she heard a rumble of thunder, unsure if Zeus himself was disagreeing with her admittance. "But I don't know who is up there . . . or if it's best they come down," she admitted.

"Well, you wouldn't have a choice either, now would you?" asked Elias, lightness in his tone but fire in his eyes.

"Elias," Melina said in a warning tone.

Ryan jutted out her hip and crossed her arms. "Well, if I'm who you say I am, I think I do have a choice," she retorted. She turned her back to Elias and spoke directly to Melina.

"It's hard because, when I think back to my own life, there were so many things out of my hands, out of my control. So many things I was fighting for and against, just to survive. Had the gods been present, would my life look any different? Would it have turned out better?"

Melina gave an understanding smile. "Mortals currently have no way of taking a more hands-on approach to their futures or their fates. They're left with the cards dealt to them by Gaea."

"But humans can overcome the life they're born into. They can work hard, study, resist their reality, and dream for a brighter future," Ryan said with conviction.

She couldn't help thinking that Melina and perhaps the other Descendants were looking at all this through rose-colored glasses. They were so close to the situation, yet so far from knowing the plight of living like a normal human being, a mortal. Adding the gods into the mix sounded like another complication in an already complicated world.

But what is the solution? she asked herself. To release the gods, or to release these demigods on the world? To let humans figure out how to combat climate change themselves? But what about Gaea and her campaign to give up on humans? Ryan's stomach churned with uncertainty; humanity was being pushed into a corner, and currently, she didn't see a way out.

"I'm going to jog over and tell the Centaurs that the stream has been redirected," Melina said, as if sensing her friend's indecision. "Want to come, Ryan?"

"I think I'll go get changed," the botanist replied. "I smell like a swamp."

Elias leaned over for a sniff. "She's right. I need to head back to the cave, so I'll come with you."

"Great, see you guys later," Melina said, walking in the opposite direction of the mountain.

Ryan followed Elias in silence. Once they got back to the beach, they both stopped to admire the purple lightning and unsettled waves. As the salty brine of the ocean breeze whipped her hair around her face, the botanist peered up at her companion.

"So . . . have any secret rendezvous with a special lady lately?"

Elias shot her a piercing look.

"What? I can't ask about Helena?"

As the muscle in his jaw unclenched, Ryan laughed. "Who did you think I was referring to?" She shook her head. "I'm guessing there are lots of ladies out there that you . . . *entertain*."

He grunted, neither a denial nor a confirmation.

"Elias, do you like being a demigod?"

Eyes bulging in surprise, he let out a bark of laughter. "What kind of question is that?"

She shrugged. "You don't seem happy."

"Who has time to be happy when you have to do all this?" he cried, pointing toward the stream behind him.

"Will you be happy if the truce goes through?"

"Well, there will be a change in management, for one thing. That's a start," he said under his breath.

Ryan frowned. "You don't see eye to eye with Nicholas?" She'd never seen any outright tension between Elias and Nicholas. *Well, that's not true,* she thought—Elias had underlying tension with everyone.

"I didn't exactly apply for this job. I was granted these powers, which is an honor, don't get me wrong," he said to her with a scowl. "But I've had no say into what my destiny is. My fate has been chosen for me. For us."

Ryan nodded. "I understand. It's like if I wanted to be a botanist but was forced to become an influencer." She performed a few halfhearted dance motions, trying to recall the moves from Greta's latest dance challenge.

"Something like that," Elias grumbled.

"So what do you want to do?"

He let out a snort of derision. "This has nothing to do with what I *want* to do. It's what I *must* do."

Taken aback by his response, Ryan gently said, "I meant, as in a job . . ."

"I know what you meant, Ryan. But get your head out of the sand. You know what we're up against. Humans need to be ruled. They don't know what's best for them."

"That's a wildly inaccurate blanket statement."

"Look what you've made of the world. Look at how Gaea has turned her back on you—now we are your only hope of salvation!"

"I thought I was *your* only hope," she said with an attempt at a smile, trying to defuse the tension.

He looked at her and pointed. "Are you?"

". . . no."

"Well then, this whole conversation is pointless. If you ask me, we need to carry on with this truce. As soon as possible. It's urgent out there," Elias said, gesturing to the horizon.

"You want to get rid of me," Ryan said softly.

Thunder boomed, quickening her heart. She started to head toward the cave, unsure whether she was more afraid of the impending storm, or of the man who stood in front of her.

"I want to get off this island. I want to fulfill my destiny, a destiny of my choosing, and I want to use my powers," Elias said to her back.

Ryan turned around. "For good?"

He laughed. "Who's to say?"

WHAT HAVE YOU GUYS BEEN up to?" Kosta snapped as Ryan and Elias entered the cave, windblown and disheveled.

Taken aback by his tone, Ryan frowned at him. Elias raised his eyebrows and smirked. "More 'training,'" he replied, wiggling his eyebrows up and down.

"As if, Elias," Ryan mumbled as he sauntered away. "Will you point me in the right direction to my room?" she asked the other Descendant. "I need to change."

Kosta nodded brusquely. "Right this way," he muttered, keeping two strides ahead of her.

"What's gotten your toga in a knot?" Ryan asked.

He shrugged his shoulders, muttered something under his breath, and continued walking without turning to look back.

The botanist rolled her eyes, exasperated by the second brooding demigod in the past five minutes. "Pardon me?" she asked testily, attempting to inconspicuously dislodge her damp chiton robe from her butt cheeks. She was not in the mood, and she didn't need ancient Greek god magic to verbally spar with anyone.

"I was looking for you," he said loudly, his words echoing off the wall. He turned his head back at her and paused so she could catch up with him, then lowered his voice. "I thought Melina was going to train with you this morning, so I was surprised to see you with Elias."

Ryan flushed at his admission, but there wasn't much warmth in his voice. "Elias and I were just having a lovely chat, watching a hurricane lazily blow in. Now, if you don't mind, I'll escort myself to my room now."

"Wrong direction," he called. "You're so stubborn."

Ryan crossed her arms and stopped in her tracks. "Wait, what? *I'm* stubborn? I have been nothing but tolerant while you people put me through these absurd experiments."

Kosta whirled to face her, his eyes blazing. "Do you even recognize how incredibly stubborn you are, Ryan? It's no wonder your talents remain dormant rather than face such obstinance."

He took a deep breath, staring into what seemed like the depths of Ryan's soul. "I see right through you. You're purposefully sabotaging yourself! You let your emotions get the better of you."

"I get that you guys think I'm your salvation, but you do not get to judge how I'm dealing with all this. You have never been where I am."

Kosta huffed in frustration, both hands on his head, clearly struggling to retain his composure.

"And you think *my* emotions get in the way?" Ryan continued. "Look at that scowl on your face! I bet you couldn't even transfigure a pile of . . . donkey poo into a . . . squirrel, what with you constantly being up and down and up and down," she sputtered, making exaggerated waves with her arms.

They were inches apart, frowns deeply imprinted on each of their faces. Kosta was the first to break, bursting into laughter. "You get awfully creative when you're angry."

Ryan tried to hide her smile by turning her head and letting out a big sigh. "Well, I call 'em like I see 'em." She looked up at him, relieved the tension had dissipated. "Are you jealous of Elias?"

Looking uncomfortable., Kosta simply ran his hand through his silky locks.

I would choose you a million times over Elias, every single day, forever, Ryan thought, overcome with lust. "Kosta, I think Elias is the type of guy who is only in love with himself," she responded with a small smile. She couldn't believe that this man was feeling in any way, shape, or form threatened by Elias. "I'm not interested."

"Oh . . . well, I wasn't sure," he said awkwardly. "It's OK if you were. I could put a good word in . . ."

"Let's just say a date with a squirrel made of donkey poo sounds more appealing at this point," she said emphatically.

He shifted to lean on the wall of the tunnel. "I really did just want to make sure you were OK and check in with how you're doing."

His words melted Ryan. She simultaneously felt her cheeks blush, her heart swell, and her nose sting as he spoke. Quelling her teenage rush of hormones, she responded, "I think the whole island knows how I'm doing. Even the weather is reflecting how much of a tragedy this is."

Kosta, quiet now, simply gave her a small smile, then invited her to follow him down another tunnel. They commenced walking in silence and eventually came to a fork in the pathway. She looked up tiredly to see which way he would lead her.

"Do you want to have a little fun?"

Ryan stared at him dubiously; she hadn't expected this question. She noticed he looked tired too, but he had a hint of mischief in his eyes. She thought longingly of her little cave sanctuary, with its magical fireplace, its fake window looking over the fake ocean, and its all-too-real bed. A refusal was on the tip of her tongue when she thought, *What exactly do they do for fun around here?* She didn't see a neighborhood Applebee's with endless appetizers . . .

Letting out a big sigh, she said defeatedly, "Sure." She couldn't in her right mind pass up what could be a date with an almost–Greek god.

"Don't sound so excited," Kosta replied in response, his face clouding up again.

She smiled. "This is me not being stubborn."

Turning to the left, Kosta called, "Follow me," over his shoulder.

They walked wordlessly down a path, Ryan following closely behind her companion. As they walked, her mind began to wander; she couldn't help comparing this mountain to a giant anthill, with its rooms and tunnels spreading for what seemed like miles in all directions.

"We haven't been down this way before," she noted. Then, "Whoa," she said, stopping in her tracks.

On one wall of the tunnel, adorned with torches on either side, was a beautiful, intricately painted fresco. Peeking past Kosta, she saw that the whole tunnel ahead was lined with them, walls adorned with murals.

"The real estate listing on this mountain cave home didn't mention an art gallery. Is this what you wanted to show me?" Ryan asked, bending closely to inspect the vibrant pigment. The rocky wall had been planed down, creating a smooth canvas.

"Nope, just a perk," he said with a grin. "These frescoes have been here forever. Well, since before I was born. The seven of them portray the progression of how the gods became stuck on Mount Olympus." He clasped his hands behind his back and, with the air of a scholar, said, "Please, allow me to be your docent on this tour through our history."

Ryan laughed and replied, "Oui, oui."

The first fresco portrayed a beautiful woman hovering over the planet earth while an indomitable man stoically sat on a throne amongst the galaxies and stars. The intensity of the woman's gaze resonated with Ryan; she recognized how the woman longed for the man with every fiber in her being. Although the man returned the look with interest, her passion was not reciprocated with the same magnitude.

"Gaea fell in love with Uranus, who was Lord of the Universe. While Uranus was feared as the mighty father, Mother Nature was loved because everything sprang from her—she was the beginning of life. She nurtured every being that she created, delicately choosing a special place and purpose for them."

"This is more of the Mother Nature I know," Ryan said, studying the woman closely in the painting. The Gaea in the fresco was such a contrast to the Gaea in the play the Muses had put on; this one was ethereal, while the one in the play—the one who had been described to her—was rotten and evil.

They slowly shuffled to the next fresco. Ryan drew in her breath—her immediate reaction was grotesque curiosity. Gaea was in the throes of labor, her head thrown back, her hair a flow of raging rivers, her eyes bewitched with violent ecstasy. But that wasn't the disturbing part. There were several arms sticking out from between her legs. On the other side of the fresco was a line of horrifying abominations that appeared as though they had just come out of her.

Kosta continued, his face screwed up in disgust. "Much to her delight, Gaea bore children with Uranus, but because she was so smitten with them, she failed to realize that they were truly monsters, each more gruesome and ruthless than the one before. First came six Titans and six Titanesses, followed by three Cyclopes," Kosta said, pointing to each of them. "After them came three more sons, each with fifty heads and a hundred arms, named the Hecatoncheires. As each child came, Uranus became more and more disgusted by his offspring with Gaea."

Kosta was getting into it now, bounding to the next fresco. Ryan didn't mind leaving this fresco behind; she hoped the next one was less disturbing.

It showed Uranus, who looked tremendously fierce, hatred burning from his eyes, aiming a golden trident at his monster children, forcing them all into a dark hole in the center of the earth. Gaea was hysterically weeping, trying in vain to grab the trident out of Uranus's hands.

"Eventually, their own father threw the Cyclopes and the Hecatoncheires into Tartarus, the deepest, darkest pit of the earth. Gaea was devastated and asked her Titan sons to break their brothers free."

"Wow," Ryan breathed. "Did anyone stand up to their super-intimidating, universe-ruling dad?"

"Five denied Gaea's desperate requests, but the sixth one, Cronus, agreed to appease his mother. Cronus was the youngest but strongest Titan, and when he successfully overpowered his father, Uranus fled and relinquished his powers to his son in his defeat." Kosta pointed to the next fresco over; they walked toward it.

A Titan, looking just as ferocious, if not a teeny bit less intimidating than his father, surveyed the mortals below from his throne in the clouds. Gaea, surrounded by woodland forest creatures, looked up at him from a tree. Ryan tried to gauge her expression; she looked proud, yet the botanist thought she saw a little tension as well. Was it malice?

"Cronus became the Lord of the Universe and sat on the highest mountain, ruling both heaven and earth with a firm hand. His rule was the golden age in which gods and mortals got along together—he was obeyed and respected by the gods and worshipped by man.

"And while he respected his mother, Cronus did not quite deliver on his promise to her, as he realized Uranus may have had a point in keeping his monstrous brethren locked up. Deeply upset by this betrayal, Gaea sought revenge on Cronus. Unfortunately, there weren't any gods strong enough to take him down, so Gaea was patient, biding her time. She knew that eventually Cronus would have a son stronger than him. Cronus learned of this prophecy as well and feared its implications; so, every time his wife, Rhea, bore them a child, Cronus swallowed the newborn god to ensure that all his offspring were safely concealed inside him."

"Talk about heartburn . . ." Ryan muttered as they walked to the next fresco. Gaea, cradling a baby, was on a ship. Her appearance had changed; the lightness in her eyes was gone, replaced with a cold concentration as she fixated hungrily on the island in the distance.

"Cronus's wife, Rhea, was heartbroken and jealous of her sisters, who were surrounded by their own Titan children. When Rhea became pregnant with her sixth son, she asked Gaea for help. Gaea jumped at the opportunity and hatched a plan. When Rhea bore Zeus, she wrapped a stone in baby clothes and gave it to her husband, Cronus, to swallow. Meanwhile, Zeus was secretly swept away to the island of Crete, where he trained to become as powerful as his father.

"Years later, Zeus married a Titan daughter named Metis, who convinced Zeus that he must have allies in order to overtake his father. So the crafty Metis fed Cronus an herb that made him vomit up all his children: Hades, Poseidon, Hestia, Demeter, and Hera. They all joined forces with their brother, and once Cronus saw them as a united force, he fled, surrendering his powers to Zeus."

Ryan snorted despite herself. "That's one monster puke."

The next fresco showed eleven gods and goddesses, sitting upon thrones in the clouds. They watched with interest as Zeus used his lightning bolt to open an enormous crater in the earth. The hideous monsters with the many heads and arms cheered as the Titans replaced them inside the big hole.

"Zeus was now the most powerful god, but he did not wish to rule alone; instead, he shared his supremacy with his brothers and sisters. The Titans refused to live under the reign of the Olympians and revolted against the gods.

"True to his word, Zeus freed the Cyclopes and the Hecatoncheires from Tartarus. They were allies to Zeus and in gratitude forged the most powerful weapons for the gods, including Poseidon's trident and Zeus's lightning bolts. The Titans were no match for the power and the weapons of the gods. Zeus locked them up in Tartarus, where the hundred-armed monsters stood guard at the gates to make sure they never saw the light of day.

"Although half her children were now free, Gaea was livid that Zeus had locked up her first-born Titans—but she accepted her defeat, and there was a time of peace. Gaea, however, was once again lulling the gods into a false sense of security."

With an air of finality, Kosta walked to the last fresco, which showed a lavish party in the clouds while Gaea and all her monsters, reunited, watched with delight from below.

Gaea had changed over the progression of murals; in this last one, greed and hunger for power shone through her eyes, her sharp features portrayed as though rotting.

"Nearly twenty-seven hundred years ago, when all was right and balanced in the world, Gaea decided to show her gratitude for the peace that the gods were abiding by, so she invited them for a celebration. She asked that all the gods meet her at Mount Olympus, where she would have a great feast awaiting. Never ones to turn down a celebration, the gods happily obliged. As the party was in full swing, some very unexpected party guests arrived with Gaea: the Titans and Titanesses. Zeus was shocked and enraged when he saw they were free and angrily called on the Cyclopes and the Hecatoncheires to capture them. However, the Olympians quickly realized that their one-time friends had turned to foes; the weapons their allies had once forged for them were now used against them, sealing them to Mount Olympus. Gaea, reunited with all her monster children, finally executed her revenge."

Ryan shivered at the thought of the monsters in the frescoes. If Centaurs were real, did these merciless creatures really exist outside the island, causing all sorts of chaos and havoc to innocent humans? *A mother's love can truly be blinding*, she thought to herself. "But how could Gaea be so apathetic to her mortal children? I don't understand it," she asked softly.

Kosta shrugged. "She created this one world for all those born to her. And then watched humanity destroy it," he answered simply. He took one last look at the hall of frescoes and then turned, gesturing Ryan to follow.

The botanist noted a sharp increase in the humidity as they continued on their path. She couldn't tell if they were far underground or not, but things were beginning to feel damp. The path slowly turned from smooth, well-worn slabs of mountain rock to larger, uneven stones, so that Ryan had to take each step with care. Head down, she concentrated on her footing, thinking to herself that this hike was not her idea of fun. Swallowing a bitter remark about her chaffing chiton, she lifted her head to politely ask Kosta how much farther until their destination. Instead, Ryan came to a sudden halt and uttered her second, "Whoa."

Unbeknownst to her, the ceiling had risen higher and higher, exposing a large cavern with a cenote in the middle. Ryan's eyes traveled up in awe as she observed a large hole in the ceiling, made where the earth above seemed to collapse, exposing a natural pool of groundwater below. Tree roots, brush, and green vegetation hung down, surrounding the hole. A stream of pale light from the sky above illuminated the cenote, and rain poured into the pool below, creating a small waterfall. The water dazzled like a turquoise gemstone and seemed to glow in different areas. An occasional flash of lightning illuminated the cave and rumbles of thunder echoed within, but the stalactite ceiling and walls protected the underground lake from the stormy elements above.

It was nice and humid inside the private paradise, perfect for swimming. *Ohhhh, that's what he had in mind.* She thought self-consciously about her unshaven legs and then wondered what exactly the Descendants wore underneath their chitons. She had on the polka-dotted bra she'd arrived in, worn with the straps tucked in to not ruin the effect of the one-shouldered robe that was now covered in mud and still damp from her escapades with Melina and Elias. She also wore a pair of underwear with little cartoon sloths all over them, bearing the message, "I Love You a Sloth."

She didn't have to wait long to find out what was under Kosta's robe. He pulled it off in one smooth movement, his tan line–less buns staring her straight in the face.

"Oh my god!" she shrieked, shielding her eyes.

"What?!" He looked at her in alarm and then turned to survey the water, trying to figure out what had caused her to panic.

"You're naked!" she bellowed. She was beginning to feel as though she were overreacting. *Pull it together, Ryan, it's just a little skinny-dipping.* She pasted an awkward smile upon her face, trying to mask her surprise at his brazen disrobing.

"Oh," he said, looking puzzled. He grabbed the fabric and covered his crotch. "Do you not want to go for a swim?"

"No, I do. It looks refreshing," she responded, peeking between her fingers and seeing that he was covered now.

"Great!" And with that, he dropped the fabric again and began climbing a ledge to the left. There were a few large vines that were tied back, originating from the vegetation above. He untied one and catapulted himself out, swinging madly to the middle of the pool, letting go in time to do a triple flip at the peak of his arch, and gracefully finished with a swan dive. He was underwater for quite a while as Ryan nervously searched the recesses of her brain back to her middle school water safety class, but to her relief, he finally popped up a few feet away from her in chest-deep water.

"Come on in! I just let the cetea know we were here."

Ryan looked nervously at the once-enchanting-but-now-foreboding water, trying to see whatever monster the cetea were. Long forgotten was her fear of Kosta's nakedness. "Um, what's a cetea?"

He splashed around, lazily treading water, and replied, "They're sea monsters."

"Oh, sea monsters, he says so nonchalantly," Ryan said, nodding her head. "I think I'll stay out here." She backed up, distancing herself from the edge of the water.

Kosta shot up, treading water. "Why?"

"Why? Oh, I don't know. It's been less than an hour since I ate last, and I don't want to get a cramp," she replied sarcastically. "Oh, and I prefer my bodies of water free of sea monsters."

"Oh, the cetea are harmless! They live in an underwater burrow below. The babies like to come out and play when we're swimming. Here come a few now."

Out of the water came six monster heads. They swam excitedly around Kosta, coming within a foot of him and then bolting away as though shy. One jumped a few feet into the air, and Ryan was able to get a glimpse of what a cetus looked like: it had the head of a frog, the front paws of a dog, and a fish tail. They were all about three feet long and bulky; she guessed about fifty pounds each. As she watched them get braver and greet Kosta, she got the sense that the cetea were unmistakably happy. Their frog mouths were turned upward, their eyes squinted with pleasure, and they were wagging their fish tails in delight. Ryan laughed out loud; they were genuinely like little puppies of the sea.

"Is there anything else in there that I should be aware of?" she asked pensively.

"Nope, just the cetea. Their parents are about ten times larger than their babies, but they typically stay below, happy to have a break from their young. As you can see, they have a lot of energy."

About ten more sea puppies had arrived and were jumping and splashing with their brothers and sisters.

"Are you coming in, or are you rooster?" Kosta asked, looking at her.

Ryan looked at him, puzzled. "What?"

"Are you rooster? Isn't that what your people say when you're afraid to do something?"

"Oh, do you mean am I chicken?" She doubled over laughing, hands on knees, tickled at his misspeaking.

A huge tidal wave of cool water erupted over her—it was Kosta's turn to laugh gleefully, proud of the epic splash he had summoned.

Ryan stood in shock, drenched. With her jaw set, she was hell-bent on getting even.

"Turn around," she said.

"Why?" he asked.

"I'm changing. Turn around."

He rolled his eyes, apparently unused to such modesty, but reluctantly turned around, splashing the cetea.

Ryan stripped down to her bra and undies, wishing she'd at least put on her matching set so it would sort of resemble a swimming suit. Next time she was catfished to a mythical island, she'd be better prepared, she thought.

"I saw it, by the way," he said.

Ryan froze. "Saw what?"

"That dimple on your cheek that you try to hide," he replied.

Ryan immediately covered her butt cheeks with her hands before realizing that Kosta was referring to the secret dimple above her mouth. She let out a weak laugh to acknowledge his observation, both sets of cheeks now blushing fiercely.

She looked up at the ledge and started climbing, wanting to get her Tarzan on and swing into the water on a vine. She hadn't realized how high it was—she had to be at least twenty feet above the water. Kosta turned around, spotted her and shouted, "Go, loulouthaki!"

Before she could talk herself out of it, she grasped the vine and leapt off the edge, swinging wildly. Instantly, she regretted her bravado, panicking as she reached the peak of the arc. Willing herself to release the vine and avoid pancaking back into the wall, Ryan flailed gracelessly into the water, executing an acoustically resonant belly flop.

Flesh burning, she broke to the surface to hear Kosta roaring with laughter and clapping. Ryan swallowed her pride and did a little water curtsy. Her embarrassment quickly dissipated as she watched the cetea swim around her, trying to get in a good sniff but then shyly retreating back to Kosta for safety. Slowly, they warmed up to her, and she was delighted by how gentle and sweet they were.

Together, they all swam to the cenote opening, where the rain fell in perfect rhythm. The cetea dragged Ryan around the water, each arm wrapped around their frog necks as she giggled uncontrollably. They all wanted a turn playing with her. She found herself treating them like children, making sure they all got their fair share. Four or five cetea would dive deep underwater and then furiously swim up to Kosta's feet, propelling him thirty feet out of the water. A few times Ryan thought he was going to shoot out of the opening. What a sight it would be to see a beautiful naked man shoot out from an underground geyser, she thought. She had gotten less shy about the fact that he was in the nude, although she avoided looking at his nether regions as much as possible, besides a quick glance here and there (for Greta's sake).

She decided she had to redeem herself, so she rounded the cetea up and half gestured, half spoke her wishes for them to push her into the sky. Being significantly lighter than Kosta, Ryan rose higher and faster than him, her fingertips grazing the ceiling above. On her way down, she managed to corkscrew her body and dive beautifully into the water. When she came up, Kosta was clapping again, this time with a look of admiration on his face.

Suddenly, an enormous, fully mature frog head peeked out of the water. Measuring ten feet across, it glanced at Kosta and Ryan, then let out a deep gurgle to its pups.

"Hi, Doreen," Kosta called. He looked at the cetea, who had all stopped and were staring at their mother. "I guess Mama says it's time to go."

They all wailed in unison to their mother, as though in protest. She let out a stern gurgle and then sank back from where she had come. The cetea knew that the battle was lost; they each came over to gently brush up against Kosta and Ryan before following their mother below.

The cenote was quiet and still after the departure of the cetea, and Ryan reveled in the peace that followed. She floated on her back and slowly swam the perimeter of the calm pool, the gentle rain echoing off the rocky walls. Kosta followed her.

"Thanks for this. This is exactly what I needed after the day I had," she said to him, still looking up.

He didn't respond, just floated a couple feet next to her.

"And I'm sure you're wondering if I actually tried and if I believed I could do it. I did."

He was still silent.

"I mean, as best as I could. I want to please everyone." She pushed out into the water, trying to catch Kosta's eye.

"Look, if it were up to me, I'd be one of you. I've never fit in anywhere all my life. I've always been a loner. I've never had a family. The prospect of finding out that the reason I've had a tumultuous life and upbringing is that I was supposed to be here . . . it's extremely enticing. It would explain why I'm able to invent this miracle flower when no one else around me can, or maybe mean that there's a greater purpose for me. I wish I could be like you. It'd make so much more sense. This would put all the puzzle pieces of my life together. I wanted this."

As she was saying the words, she realized she was speaking the truth.

Kosta looked at her, his head tilted thoughtfully. "You had a tough go of it, growing up, didn't you?"

"Hmph—you could say that." Smiling ruefully, she pushed off the rock wall, catapulting her body away from the shore.

"What happened?" Kosta asked quietly, following in her wake, closing in until she was only a foot away.

Ryan's face twisted in a grimace as the memories materialized. She hated recounting her grim beginning, but the tenderness in Kosta's face encouraged her to share the painful secrets she carried within.

"I guess I was a colicky baby. I cried day and night those first few days after my adoptive parents brought me home from the hospital. According to my grandparents"—Ryan listed them off on her fingers—"and my other set of grandparents, and aunt, and uncle, I was unable to be soothed. I just cried and cried and cried." Ryan scoffed. "I can't imagine, waiting years to become approved to adopt, finally being selected for a closed adoption, and then you're handed this baby that will not stop crying." She emphasized the last few words with irritated exasperation.

Ryan turned her back on Kosta and swam on, swishing to where the rain fell from the nature-made skylight.

"My aunt once mentioned that while it agitated others, my adoptive mother was never bothered by my wails. Her only concern was to soothe me, to get to the root of why I was in such discomfort. This little tidbit of information that my aunt arbitrarily mentioned one day was my lifeline. It filled my spirit. It sounded as though my mother really did want me. That she really did love me. Maybe I was her miracle baby." The melodic plink of rain hitting the water filled the silence between Ryan and Kosta.

"But I was also her demise," Ryan said, her voice low and husky. "Apparently, she was convinced, after reading every parenting book she could get her hands on, that a soy-based formula would bring some relief to her darling daughter. Disregarding my father's warning that it was dangerous outside, she headed out to the twenty-four-hour pharmacy."

Ryan swam back to the water's edge, her limbs and demeanor suddenly exhausted. "The remnants of the snowfall had mostly been blown off the road, but the black ice . . . the paramedics said she died instantly."

Kosta sidled up next to her and grabbed her hand in both of his.

"Ryan, I'm so sorry," he said quietly. They sat like that for a minute, both looking at their hands clasped just below the surface of the water. He then asked, "What about your father?"

Ryan looked up, giving Kosta a watery smile. "My new father, delighted at my arrival a mere couple weeks before, couldn't bear to look at me. His parents—my grandparents—decided to take charge and moved in shortly after. They never said it, but I knew they blamed me for what happened to my mother and subsequently the shell of a human my father became."

"How could they blame a baby?" Kosta asked, bewildered and angry in equal measure. "That's cruel!"

She forged on. "They were only able to take it for a few months. I had apparently outgrown the fussiness by this point, but there was no room for me, what with the profound grief as an unwanted houseguest. I was moved to my maternal grandparents' house for a few years. I don't know if they had agreed with their daughter's decision to adopt in the first place, so love was expressed in the form of a favor to the memory of their dead daughter. After another few years and the early signs of Parkinson's in my grandmother, I landed at my aunt's house. And then my uncle's. And then I finally gained my own independence when I was old enough to take care of myself."

Kosta squeezed her hand. "You have overcome so much."

Ryan let go of his hand and floated on her back, gazing at the ceiling. Although empathy was fleeting in her life, she always shied away from those who offered it. "It's a twisted cycle of abandonment. My biological parents didn't want me. Then there was a brief respite of love, and then, with a horrible twist of fate, it was all taken away from me again."

Kosta gave her a half smile and said, "Grief can change people, Ryan . . . a lot."

She sighed, recognizing he spoke from experience. "I know. I've come to terms with it all, I really have, despite this pathetic story." She gave him a sad smile. "I've fought my entire life to change the ending—or should I say the middle—of my story, so that it's not a tragedy. I fully recognized at a young age that my destiny was in my own hands, and that I had the power. . ." Ryan paused and chuckled softly. "Well, not *your* type of power, but the ability to mold my future into whatever I wanted it to be. Some might look at my life as small and insignificant, but . . ." She grinned to herself, imagining her little haven back home. "But it's mine."

Ryan turned to Kosta, surprised at how comfortable she felt spilling a lifetime of trauma to this handsome fella. "So now do you believe me when I say I wished I fit in here? How I wish I was always meant to be here?"

The Descendant was staring at her. "You are so powerful, Ryan, in your own way."

A shy smile crept across the botanist's face.

He continued, "Do you feel this when you're in training? This desire to belong?"

She let out a little laugh. "Between trying to get a fish to follow my commands, catching a babbling brook with my bare hands, and avoiding humiliation in front of the whole camp, my mind was kind of at capacity."

Kosta laughed. "What, like it's hard?"

Ryan froze mid-paddle. "Was that a *Legally Blonde* reference?"

Kosta grinned proudly. "I've been waiting to insert that Elle Woods quote into an appropriate conversation since your arrival."

Ryan laughed and gave him a round of applause, and he bowed his head appreciatively.

"But in all seriousness, I get it. Not only are you expected to believe something unfathomable, but you also didn't grow up in this community, and you've never had the chance to feel the gods. You've seen some of our powers. You've gotten a glimpse of what life used to be like with the population of mythicals. But you've never felt what's ingrained within each of us since birth."

Ryan nodded her head. "Yeah, I guess that's true. I feel like I understand the current predicament and why you guys are so invested in freeing the gods, but I don't have a sense of who they are and why they should matter to me." She squinted at Kosta. "But you were never around when they roamed the earth at will. How do you feel it? Why do you feel close to the gods?"

Considering this question, Kosta simply said, "It's my legacy."

She thought for a moment, scared to say the words that had been in her head for a time. "But how do you know it'll be better? I mean, no offense to the council, but I can't help but question your judgment. How do they know that releasing the gods will make the world a better place? Everyone has been hidden away on this island, untouched by the real world. I understand that Gaea has taken away the gods' ability to rule, and that's a grave injustice on your end, but I haven't experienced a sense of unbalance. The rest of humanity doesn't see that. There is strife and pain and war and terror and evil out there"—Ryan pointed toward the ocean—"but there is also joy and kindness and love and happiness. It's not perfect by any means.

But it's life. Life gets messy out there . . . that I can say for sure." She sighed. "I just don't know how life is going to be once the gods are back. I'm so conflicted on whether"—she dropped her voice barely above a whisper—"releasing the gods would be a good thing for mankind."

She snuck a peek up at Kosta to see how he was taking her little speech. He was frowning deeply—not out of disappointment or anger, but in concentration, plunged into thought, as though she had perhaps brought up some good points.

"I don't have the answers to your questions," he said slowly. "But I can tell you that a world where Gaea has stripped the gods of their powers and mercilessly hunted my people for the past couple millennia is something worth fighting against."

"But what makes your people's race more important than all the people out there?" she asked quietly.

"I guess I've been indoctrinated to believe that saving the gods from exile will be for the greater good," he said with a small, nervous laugh.

Ryan smiled at Kosta, signaling that she appreciated his diplomatic response. "So are you all in for moving forward with the truce?"

A muscle in his jaw clenched. "This is all I've ever known," the Descendant said, looking around the cenote as they treaded water idly. "So there's a huge element of uncertainty. But what keeps me up at night is: What happens when Nicholas dies and the power isn't replenished to another Descendant? And the number of demigods continues to dwindle? What does that life look like for my future children and theirs?" He shook his head. "I'd rather make some very tough decisions now as a united team, to secure a future for us and generations to come, than risk extinction on this island."

When Kosta mentioned having children, Ryan's ovaries nearly

burst. She momentarily imagined Kosta Jr., Greta Jr., and Hermione Jr. splashing along with them in the cenote.

"What are you thinking about, loulouthaki?" he asked, noticing her dreamy expression.

"Nothing," she replied quickly. "What does that name mean?"

"Donkey poo," Kosta replied with a smirk.

Ryan burst out laughing, and he joined in. She swam around and ducked underneath the water, keeping her eyes squeezed shut so as not to accidentally see Kosta's sea monster. She finally burst up to the surface as her lungs protested angrily. Kosta had been following her progress in the water, an amused expression on his face.

"As a united team, you're all certainly on a spectrum of how strongly you feel about the truce," Ryan observed. "Elias definitely wants off the island, like, yesterday. Melina is dutifully bound to what's best for the island, but she's such a free spirit; she would thrive out there, and I see the longing in her eyes for a life bigger than this island. Then there's Nicholas, on the other end. I can feel his hunger, his almost obsessive desire, to free the gods."

"Nicholas's passion to release the gods from exile has become even greater since Spiras and Kalliope died." He turned away from her, swimming on his back.

"I know I said it before, but I'm so sorry, Kosta. I can't imagine the pain you've gone through."

Kosta let out a deep sigh. "Nicholas blames himself for their deaths. I think in his mind, their deaths won't be in vain if he's able to free the gods."

Frustratedly swishing the water in front of her, Ryan asked, "And he's still convinced, even after all this time, that there's a chance to finally defeat Gaea and free the gods? Didn't Einstein say something like the definition of insanity is doing the same thing over and over again and expecting different results?"

Kosta shrugged. "Every generation born on this island has gone to war with her. For centuries, it's been a cyclical cataclysm of building our army of mortals and demigods, generating this campaign of narcissistic invincibility and goading Gaea to battle. Then, after we're mercilessly beaten into near extinction, we return to our hidden island, bury our dead, mourn, and then start rebuilding."

"I thought you guys never leave the island."

"Well, once a lifetime, we get to leave to fulfill our destinies and hope we don't come back in a body bag," he said bitterly. "We're only safe from Gaea on this island, so when we go to war, we choose a battleground far away from our home and from humans." He let out a little laugh. "Some of our past battles have left . . . unexplained oddities around the world. Ever heard of Stonehenge in England? Or the Bermuda Triangle? Or Blood Falls in Antarctica? Scars from battles past."

Eyes wide in wonder, Ryan thought back to the many harebrained conspiracy theories she and Greta had discussed over past Friday night cocktails; godly battle wounds were not one of them.

"But what happens if you kill her?"

"We can't kill Gaea . . . we don't know what that'd mean for earth itself. The plan is to capture her and let the gods deal with her as they see fit," Kosta replied.

"Wow," Ryan breathed. "So you prepare and are always ready to fight . . . just in case."

"Just in case . . ." Kosta trailed off.

Ryan shook her head. "Seems senseless."

"But this time, it's different: we have you," he stated resolutely.

"I'm with Nicholas. I wholeheartedly believe that you could be the reason why we have always gotten so close but never succeeded."

It was Ryan's turn to twist her mouth with bitterness. "Artemis's dirty little secret."

She swam ahead of Kosta, considering the most direct route to her robe, then reached the shore and darted for cover. Behind her, she heard him get out, stretch, and then pick up his own robe. She was hurriedly trying to figure out exactly how to convert the long piece of fabric into the beautifully draped outfit she had been wearing when she felt Kosta pick up an end of the fabric.

Hesitantly, she turned toward him, allowing him to essentially dress her like a small child. He had the cutest expression on his face, eyes slightly furrowed in concentration, his mouth pursed. A few strands of dark hair hung over his forehead, sending little droplets of water traveling down his face like tears.

Before she knew what she was doing, she tucked the deviant hairs behind his ears and gently wiped away the water from his face with the palms of her hands. Their heads were inches apart from each other, Ryan's hands on Kosta's face, and his hands on her waist—as if they were ready to embrace. He gazed into her eyes and then down at her lips but took a step back, using the excuse of tying the robe around her hips to create a healthy distance between them.

Her whole body was hot, from both the humidity and the moment. When Kosta turned toward the exit, she fanned herself feverishly, trying to calm down.

"Kosta," she called. He turned around.

As she lifted her eyes to meet his, Ryan paused. Kosta's face was muddied with heartache—she couldn't justify causing any more pain or confusion or uncertainty. She couldn't make him relive it again. Instead, she whispered, "I just want to thank you. For everything."

She awkwardly put her hand out, realizing too late that she didn't know what its purpose was. She squeezed his bicep and grabbed the other one with her other hand for good measure. "Thanks for introducing me to this little Olympian oasis—it was so fun. And thanks for listening to me. And hearing me. And believing in me."

She had unconsciously stepped forward so their bodies touched, her hands still on his arms, her eyes raking his face, which looked passionately down at her. His hands slowly reached down and wrapped themselves around her back. His pupils dilated infinitesimally, but Ryan was close enough to notice. As she leaned in closer, her lips a mere couple inches from his, their breath sharing the same air space, she felt his hands travel upward and gently pull hers off his arms.

He pulled away, his face impassive but his eyes almost angry. She couldn't help the look of hurt that escaped her face, but she quickly forced it to reflect his.

He cleared his throat. "Let's get you back."

She followed in silence, the rejection stinging every pore in her body as it sunk in. *How stupid am I to think I actually had a chance with a demigod?* She thought she had read all the signs right, but clearly she could never live up to the memory of Spiras.

Feeling dejected, she trudged along—her heart longing for the reward of a magical kiss. Despite all these emotions, Ryan realized what she wanted most of all was to remedy the source of Kosta's deep and utter despair so that she never had to see his face contort that way again. It really broke her heart.

The botanist finally started recognizing her surroundings, and soon they were at her door. She could not wait to get inside and hibernate. *Oh, what I would do for a glass of deep red wine*, she thought.

Avoiding his eyes as she opened the door, she said in a deadpan voice, "Thanks again."

"Ryan." Kosta turned her around so they were face to face.

"It's OK, Kosta," she said, still not meeting his eyes.

"It's—"

"No need for any explanation," she replied quickly.

Frustrated, he ran his fingers through his hair—adorable, she thought bitterly. "I just need to . . ."

Looking up into his eyes, Ryan made a decision. She put on a big smile, put both her hands on his shoulders, and said in as convincing a voice as possible, "Kosta, it's OK. Besides, I've got someone waiting for me back home."

She squeezed his shoulders and then entered the room. She gave him another smile as she closed the door, and then burst into silent sobs as soon as the door clicked shut.

THE FOLLOWING FEW DAYS WERE a washout in more ways than one. Ryan failed miserably at all the training sessions, the demigods trying with increasing desperation to wriggle the powers out of her; and the weather had taken a turn, stubbornly raining buckets day and night, making the entire island a soggy mess.

Becoming exceedingly inventive (or scraping the bottom of the barrel, as Ryan thought), the Descendants even scheduled some training with the healer Centaur, Sylir. A visit to the infirmary proved not only that she had no special talents but also that she was prone to vomiting when healing a harpy with an infected ingrown toenail.

The only superpower she recognized as hers was the ability to blush furiously or forget how to properly operate her limbs whenever Kosta was in the vicinity. He could be clear across the atrium, doing some chore to keep the island running, and Ryan's sweat glands would go into overdrive. Both went out of their way to avoid one another, which made being around Kosta quite dangerous for others; he accidentally knocked over a marble column of the Parthenon while skirting her path. Between her premenopausal hot flashes and his calamitous clumsiness, they were a match made in heaven.

To make matters worse, her one outlet, her lifeline, had become noticeably absent in the past couple days. Ryan guessed Greta was punishing her for the vague calls and texts; responses grew fewer and further between, texts reduced to one word. What if Greta were hiding something from Ryan, like Ryan was hiding something from her? What if something had happened to Lester? What if her cancer had come back? What if there were more atrocities happening near their home?

Despite Greta's absence, Cyrus was still blowing up Ryan's phone. She wasn't exactly ghosting him; navigating between deity drills and a demigod's heart was quite taxing on Ryan's schedule, and it didn't leave much time to respond to his volley of texts and calls. Plus, Cyrus was becoming increasingly unreasonable in his requests. She argued that he was being protective, but after an onslaught of tsunamis had bombarded Spain, Morocco, and Portugal, he'd gone as far as saying she was unsafe and he was going to come get her, demanding to know the exact coordinates of her location. Ryan recognized the latest natural disaster had been in her proximity, but for someone she'd only met once to declare that he was going to fly internationally to save her . . . it was a bit too Nicholas Sparks for her.

Melina spent most of her time bringing Ryan this way and that, all the while producing the promised Weeping Dianas as fast as she could. Hands down, Melina was her closest friend on the island, but Ryan refrained from discussing Kosta or Cyrus with her. She'd also remained mum about seeing the way Melina looked at Sophia.

"What is this place?" the botanist asked, rubbing her arms from the chilled air and overall creptastic environment.

Melina looked around a little guiltily. "Um, the crypt."

"Why here?"

She shrugged. "It's the only place the other Descendants won't get into my things."

The room was the size of an airplane hangar, with a high, rocky ceiling and rows and rows of beautiful marble resting places. Cheery fireballs floated lazily above them, casting a warm glow over the dank final resting place of the deceased. Ryan turned her head left, then right, taking in the enormity of the space, amused by the juxtaposition of the life Melina was creating amongst her audience of dead folks.

"Also, my dad is buried over there," the demigod said quietly, tilting her head toward a deep gray headstone a few feet away. "I like to spend time with him when I can."

"Oh, Melina. I'm so sorry for your loss," Ryan said, kneeling down to wrap an arm around her friend.

Melina smiled her thanks and pulled over an empty pot of soil. "He lost his life fighting to free the gods. He's been gone seven years, and I can still remember the scratch of his beard when he'd peck my cheek goodnight and hear his roar of thunderous laughter echoing across the atrium. He was so godsdamn loud." She smiled down at the pot, flicked her pointer finger upward, and—*POOF!* —a fully grown Weeping Diana burst from the soil, making Ryan flinch.

Ryan bent down to tenderly stroke the velvety leaf of the newly born flower. Awestruck, she said, "I bet he was so proud of his powerful demigod daughter."

"I try to carry on his legacy and be strong for my mom." *POOF* went another flower.

Picking up the pots and adding them to the end of a row of flowers, Ryan said, "I guess they don't need sunlight when they're made from magic." The spooky atmosphere rendered the blue petals lackluster and subdued, as though the plants dialed down their magnificence out of respect for the dead.

"Well, there's not much sunlight out there anyway," Melina muttered.

"True. I'm worried about the boat ride out of here." Ryan took the newly created flower and added it to the row.

"It'll clear up soon."

"Melina," Ryan said, turning toward her. Her serious tone made Melina stop mid-*POOF*, resulting in a light blue mini bloom. "I know I committed to staying the two full weeks, but let's be real here: nothing is going to happen in the next three days. It's time for me to go home."

Just as Melina opened her mouth to argue, they heard quick footsteps echoing against the rock tunnel growing louder. A few seconds later, Kosta popped into the doorway.

Seeing Ryan there with Melina, Kosta's face went from neutral to frosty. "He's getting ready to leave."

Melina got up from her plant assembly line. "OK. Guess I should say goodbye."

Furiously searching their faces, her stomach dropping, Ryan asked, "Who's going where?"

Not meeting her eyes, Kosta responded, "Elias is going to accept the truce."

"What?" Ryan bellowed. "When was this decided?"

"The last council meeting," Melina said quietly.

"Those damn council meetings." She rounded on Kosta. "You said I could go to the next one."

Kosta shrugged.

"What does it entail?" the botanist demanded.

"Accepting it. Then we'll set a date and time for Gaea to come here and witness us perform the ritual to seal the gods to Mount Olympus for good," Melina said grimly. "In exchange, we're free to go."

Ryan shook her head emphatically. "You guys can't do this. You're not ready."

Kosta turned to leave. Melina looked between Ryan and the retreating demigod.

"You're giving up," Ryan shouted.

Kosta whipped around. "Giving up? Giving up? It's been two millennia, Ryan," he bellowed back to her.

"Then why am I still here?" Ryan yelled, her voice reverberating off the walls. She looked around the crypt guiltily; she didn't care to wake the dead.

"Good question," Kosta said disdainfully. A moment later, his face softened, recognizing the harshness of his own words.

Pleading, Ryan said, "Look, I know you aren't making this decision lightly, but I don't think you guys coming out to save humanity is the answer."

"What is the answer, then, Ryan?"

"People are going to freak out. We need to—"

"Your own people are dying out there, Ryan. Do you want us to decline the truce and watch as you mortals suffocate yourselves while Gaea's monsters destroy everything you've built? For us to stay here on this island as our powers slowly die, helping only ourselves, trying in vain to save the gods who will never be released?"

Quietly, Ryan asked, "But can you trust Gaea?"

"No. But that's a risk we're willing to take," Kosta said bitterly. "And once everything out there is smoothed over, who knows who will ultimately rule in the future?"

"As in, you're going to try to overthrow Gaea?" Ryan asked, surprised.

Kosta responded by icily staring at the other Descendant. "Come on, *Melina.* They're waiting for *us.*"

He turned around to her one more time. "Once Elias gets back, he'll pick you up to deliver you home."

Not one to be dismissed, Ryan followed the two up to the main level, where members from the council were making their way out to the dock with Elias.

"Nicholas, you can't do this," Ryan pleaded.

"Ryan," he sighed. For the first time since she'd arrived, Nicholas looked like the old man he was supposed to be. He had lost the hallmark joy that usually twinkled in his eyes whenever Ryan was near.

Taken aback by his reaction, she timidly asked, "Are you mad at me?"

"Mad? No," he said, shaking his head. He started walking toward the beach, Ryan following.

"You seem mad."

"Disappointed."

"In me?" she asked, stung.

"Yes."

"Why?"

Nicholas stopped and turned, the mouth of the cave opening up to the raging ocean in front of them. "You didn't try hard enough."

"Are you kidding me? Nicholas, all signs point to no. Look at the testing. I've been here for almost two weeks."

"Are you kidding *me*, Ryan? You've been leaving a trail of magic the moment you came."

Ryan shook her head, confused. "Nicholas, what are you talking about?"

Nicholas sighed heavily. "You didn't try, Ryan, and I'm trying to figure out where we went wrong."

"A trail of magic," she said, dumbfounded.

"Yes. Look at the weather. Every time you get grumpy, it rains," he replied, pointing up to the black, churning clouds.

She balked. "That's ridiculous."

"The weather turns at the tip of the hat," he said, grouchily observing the clouds above.

"Nicholas." Ryan uttered his name in disbelief. *Please let his disappointment in me be a horrible joke.*

"And I'm a little frustrated by how lightly you've taken this."

"I've been anything but—"

"Have you? Because all I see is a self-conscious girl going through the motions, just trying to get through it," Nicholas said, now facing her and looking hard into her face.

Through clenched teeth, Ryan snarled, "I've tried." In response, there was a crackle of thunder. Annoyed, she said, "That was a coincidence."

Nicholas shook his head, a sad smile on his face. "Are you sure, Ryan?" He walked into the pouring rain to send Elias off into the stormy sea, to seal their fate. And hers.

STUNG BY THE DOUBLE WHAMMY of Kosta and Nicholas's dismissal, Ryan wandered around the island, silently saying her goodbyes. Her heart broke with every step, already missing its people and beauty. The Sirens were rehearsing a haunting melody that echoed mournfully off the rocky cave walls. Ensconced within her misery and the gut-wrenching tune, Ryan started slowly inching her way toward an overlooking precipice. At once, a harpy walked over and took her hand in his scratchy paw, patting it until she was out of her stupor. Giving him a nod of thanks, he cartwheeled over to his two waiting brothers. Although Ryan smiled at everyone, she was in mourning—life was tough here, but they didn't stand a chance of acceptance in the real world.

That evening, the botanist squirreled away to her solo suite, avoiding the judging eyes of her supposed friends. They'd flipped on her, she thought—certain she was one of them one moment, giving up on her the next. Angry, she threw things pell-mell into her suitcase. She even snuck one of the clean, white chiton robes in there, certain that its magic would falter but at least provide a souvenir from the incredible, emotional adventure.

Although her heart was breaking, she did feel it flutter in excitement knowing she'd get to see Greta and Lester soon. She'd even text Cyrus that she was coming home after neglecting him for the past day. Yes, his texting was intense, but only because he was convinced she was in danger. And he was right; in danger of Kosta breaking her heart over and over again.

* * *

Early the next morning, she heard a knock on her door and smelled the welcome scent of coffee. "Come in," she croaked.

Nicholas entered. She hated to admit that her whole being had hoped it was Kosta, every atom in her wanting him to stalk through the door and apologize profusely for the love roller coaster they both couldn't get off. She eyed Nicholas warily as he set down a tray with a steaming coffee press and little cookies twisted like a braid.

Sitting up, she shot him a small smile to see how it was received. He took the bait and returned a gentle one, the twinkle in his eye back after its brutal absence.

Belatedly, the botanist wiped at her face, sure she looked like crap—her hair was matted to her forehead from the sticky tears that came in her sleep, and her eyes were puffy and aching. But she didn't care. She felt like she could be raw with Nicholas.

"You're awake," he noted. "You've slept the clock around. I think you must have needed the rest."

Extricating herself from the tangle of blankets, she joined Nicholas by the fireplace. "Disappointing a colony of people *and* failing to be the only hope for the survival of mankind is exhausting."

Nicholas chuckled.

Tap-tap-tap.

The demigod was swinging the little beads at the end of his beard, his hand working of its own volition to make the soothing tapping sound while his eyes were squinted deep in thought. Ryan asked, "Are those prayer beads?"

He looked down at the two rows of beads tied in his long beard, the amber color radiating against the sea of contrasting grays. "They're called kombolói; you could call them Greek worry beads. You'll find that most people carry them on their persons, but seeing as this is my constant companion . . ." He gently tugged the thick, scraggly tendrils reaching to his knees.

"Do you use them to pray?" Ryan asked.

"No," Nicholas said with a hint of a chuckle. "In fact, the sound irritates Elias. Many times, he's tried to cut them off while I wasn't looking."

Chortling herself, Ryan asked, "So they're used more to relax? Like a soothing habit?"

"Exactly." He demonstrated for another minute as they both silently watched, swinging his hand up so that one row of beads hit the other row. With his index finger and his middle finger, he tipped the beads down and then flipped them again, the collision emitting the calming *tap-tap-tap*. "I see you've packed up."

She nodded. "Melina and I are going to collect the plants from the crypt and determine how many freight trucks I'll need to coordinate once I get back to port."

Nicholas sighed and dropped his beard and beads. "Shall we go to my favorite spot on the island and have a goodbye coffee?"

"Let's," Ryan agreed with a smile.

After quite a hike, they arrived at a room on the edge of the mountain with a panoramic view of the ocean. It was a spectacular view, and despite the massive storm taking place, a rocky overhang protected them from the elements. About three feet from the edge of the opening were two chairs set up to take in the vista.

"Wow," Ryan breathed. "This must be the penthouse view."

Nicholas smiled. "Yes, it's a wonderful resting place for watching the sunsets, although we haven't seen many of those lately. Please, sit down."

The storm raged with enthusiasm for its audience of two. Ryan noted that on this island, there was a quite the different between the "vanilla" weather she was used to and this highly orchestrated spectacle of the elements. Lightning flashed with varying degrees of gigajoules, a bright shock even in the late morning light. Thunder rolled continuously, a low growl threatening to crescendo to a deafening roar at any moment. The angry sea pummeled waves against one another, like cymbals during a never-ending finale.

"Why are there two chairs up here? Do other people know about your secret hideout?"

"Others know but do not visit. It's a bit of a sacred room for me," replied Nicholas, gazing outside.

Ryan plopped herself unceremoniously into one of the chairs, her feet lazily hanging over the arm rest. "Oh, why's that?"

"This is where Kalliope agreed to marry me. We spent many evenings up here, watching the waves roll in as the sun set in the sky. And the shooting stars up here? Simply breathtaking. I cherish those memories more than anything."

Ryan closed her eyes, mortified. Of course—how self-involved could she be?

"I'm sorry," she said heavily. Moving her feet off the ground, she rubbed her face tiredly with both hands. "I can't seem to do anything right these days."

They sat there in silence, the wind's indecisiveness shooting fat raindrops and ocean spray in all directions.

"Since the loss of Spiras and Kalliope, many have lost their confidence in me. For the first time ever, there has been dissension. Dissension at a time when we need unity the most."

Ryan looked down and said quietly, "Well, we know the reason for that."

"No, Ryan," Nicholas replied forcefully. "You are our one unifying piece. Some may not see it, but you are our redemption."

Lightning struck with such force nearby that Ryan tasted tangy metal in her mouth.

"How could you say that?" she asked loudly. "I can see why they've lost confidence in you when you put all your confidence in a mere mortal like me. Nicholas, I hate to break it to you, but could your hope be blind? How long until you realize that I'm not the one?"

The wind screeched as though agreeing with her sentiments, but its spookiness lent little reassurance. Ryan shivered, grateful for the protection of this little mountain hidey-hole.

"I feel it, Ryan."

Her insides clenched with rage; all her angst and anger at Kosta and Nicholas, at being pegged for someone she wasn't, rose like a volcano inside her. She took a deep breath, steadying herself to not lose her temper, before saying, "I don't believe that for a second, Nicholas. How could these all-powerful, mighty gods get stuck on a mountain? How am I supposed to believe that they can't come down and save you? How can you have so much faith in these gods that have failed you? They are the reason you lost Kalliope, and Spiras, and all the other countless souls that have been stripped away from you. They are the reason you've been stuck on this island for two-eff-ing-thousand years! Who cares if you can't save them? What have they ever done for you?"

Sneaking a glance at her companion, Nicholas simply peered

back at her with interest. "You certainly are angry for someone who is apparently so far removed from this whole situation."

"What do you mean?" she asked, exasperatedly throwing her hands in the air.

"Where is this fury coming from?"

"Um, I dunno, maybe being lured here under false pretenses only to be put through ridiculously embarrassing tests . . . just a guess," she said, though she regretted her tone immediately. She sank back in her chair and examined her cuticles, ignoring the squall outside and the guilt she felt within.

Nicholas was quiet for a while, staring off into the distance. "Looks like Elias is back."

Ryan jumped up and headed toward the door; the temptation to try her hand at goading a giant wave to swallow up Elias and his little dinghy of lies was overwhelming. "I'll go get my things," she said, without a last look back.

On the way to her room, she suddenly remembered that there were some stray Weeping Dianas left over in the greenhouse, back from her very first failed attempt at magic with Agalia. Ryan cursed herself for forgetting to remind Melina to grab them and cursed the weather she knew would reduce her to a soggy tissue on her rescue mission. But she couldn't leave any soldiers behind.

Out of breath and drenched, she launched herself into the muggy structure after a terror- and adrenaline-fueled jog through the storm. She leaned against the door, massaging the stabbing stitch out of her side while surveying the greenhouse. Although the pounding rain rattled the glass panes like gelatin, she knew she'd made the right decision: there were rows and rows of Weeping Dianas in different growth stages, including the couple pots she'd planted the first evening she arrived. *And their little sprouts have finally emerged*, she noted happily.

Ryan sagged down the doorframe, landing on her soggy bottom. She recalled the hope she'd felt when she received the postcard from the Descendants, the hope she'd felt when Kosta and Melina were waiting to greet her on the dock, the hope she'd felt once she spied her Weeping Dianas grown by someone other than herself. The hope that she could, at last, provide humanity with a fighting chance against the toxic atmosphere caused by their own recklessness.

But now, Ryan was faced with a monster greater than herself, one she had absolutely no chance of stopping.

She had never felt so alone. Alone in a greenhouse, in a field, on an island, in the middle of the ocean. Even as a child, in and out of loveless families, Ryan had never experienced this raw ache of loneliness because she'd never known the feeling of being loved. But now that she had Greta and Lester, the absence of their affection was overpowering. And while the Descendants had welcomed her with open arms, her lack of progress had replaced the embrace with frustration and gloom.

Thunder clapped, causing her to jump and bonk her elbow on the doorframe. Frustrated, she pounded it back with her fist. She scooted forward toward a fully mature Weeping Diana, hoping it could somehow photosynthesize some cheer into her spirit, but an awful realization washed over her: in her haste, she hadn't fully thought through how she was going to carry the couple dozens of pots back with her to the cave. A tear fell down her cheek. She was such a failure.

She heard the door open a crack and immediately yelled, "CAN I JUST GET A MINUTE?!"

"Heavens to Betsy, what a welcome!" a familiar voice bellowed right back.

"GRETA!"

17

RYAN FLUNG HERSELF INTO HER best friend's arms, open-mouth sobbing into Greta's floofy white hair, pausing only to take a gasping breath and grab the older woman's face between her palms. She was real. Greta's familiar scent enveloped her—honeysuckle shampoo, fabric softener dryer sheets, a tinge of Baileys—its effect instantaneous. Her aroma, paired with the power of her embrace, worked as a miraculous medicinal antidote to the stress and anxiety of the past weeks. Everything was going to be OK.

Once Ryan could string a few words together after a very guttural greeting, she uttered, "What are you doing here?"

Pragmatically, Greta responded, "Coming to save you, of course."

"From what?"

Greta paused, glancing behind her as the Descendants slowly filed into the greenhouse behind her. "I don't know, exactly." She threw suspicious glances toward Kosta, Melina, and Nicholas, but her face relaxed as she appreciatively eyed Elias up and down. "I had a feeling you needed me."

Ryan laughed, a snot bubble erupting from her nostril. Hastily wiping it, she cried, "I did. I really did."

Greta pushed Ryan behind her small frame, reached for the closest weapon within reach—a small trowel—and menacingly brandished it toward the others. Ryan giggled. "But I'm not in trouble!

It's all so . . ." She looked at Nicholas. "I can now appreciate how hard this was to explain." She turned back to Greta. "They think I'm a Descendant. Of the Olympians."

Greta's garden-tool-wielding arm dropped to her side. "A what to who now?"

"A lost bloodline of a god. Or goddess, technically. Artemis," Ryan said, her mouth unconsciously puckering over uttering the deity's name.

"Sounds like I'm going to need a stiff drink," Greta responded, leaning back against a table lined with clover plants.

Nicholas chuckled. "Let me try to catch you up." As he ramped up the prelude to his long-winded explanation, Ryan mouthed *Nicholas* to Greta and wiggled her eyebrows. Greta distractedly mouthed back, *Be cool.*

With some help from Melina and Kosta (and some terse interjections from Elias), they unraveled the myth for Greta, who stood uncharacteristically still. When they'd finished, her penciled-in eyebrows were arched and her rouged lips pursed.

Holding her breath, Ryan waited in silence for Greta's response.

"Well, of course you are," her friend said matter-of-factly.

Ryan's knees wobbled, threatening to give out on her. "What?!"

"What?!" Melina, Elias, Nicholas, and Kosta echoed in unison.

"The evidence is right in front of you. The flowers."

"Greta—"

"That's exactly what I've been telling her," Kosta interjected.

"So what's the problem?" Greta asked.

"Am I hearing this right? Is this real life?" Ryan sputtered.

"She won't allow herself to do the magic," Nicholas replied with fervor. All of them were talking about Ryan as though she weren't there.

"It's not magic, it's science!" Ryan bellowed.

"Well, that won't do," Greta said, surveying the botanist with disappointed eyes.

"Greta, I think you're jet lagged. Maybe we should give you a rest," Ryan said, walking toward her friend to guide her out of the greenhouse.

Greta slapped away her hand. "I've always known you were special, child."

"I'M NOT SPECIAL," Ryan shouted, her fists resolutely clenched by her sides.

Greta slid on her magenta readers to study the botanist. "Ryan Louise Bell, don't spaz out."

"Hmm. I guess it's not so curious that a Descendant of Artemis would feel a sense of betrayal," Nicholas said, comprehension dawning on his face.

Scowling, Ryan said, "What? She has nothing to do with this."

"She has everything to do with this."

Ryan harrumphed. "Well, I have to admit, it is so laughably perfect. It's *so fitting*. After feeling restless and abandoned and unimportant my whole life, it's because I'm actually part god! An heir to a goddess! And I'm part of this wonderful, magical, loving community of superheroes! And you've been searching for me my whole life!

"But of all twelve Olympians, I get the real *winner*. I love how everyone glosses over the fact that my great-great-grandma Artemis decides that her child, her only Descendant, is not good enough to reveal to the other gods. It's just so fitting that I live a crappy life and I get the crappy god. The one who deserted the bloodline, and because of that has spurred a cycle of abandonment for the past 2,700 years. Washed her hands of any commitment, responsibility . . . love," Ryan said, trailing off.

Her voice rose again. "Well, guess what? Maybe Great-Great-Grammy Artie is getting a taste of her own medicine up there, banished on Mount Olympus, stripped of all the things she loved and held dear. As you guys are literally dying to free them, sacrificing your lives, she hid the fact that her bloodline is the key to both your and their redemption."

Ryan's shouts echoed off the walls of the greenhouse, everyone watching wide eyed as her wrath played out. She turned her back to them all, stomping back and forth like a petulant child.

"And now, you guys have a pact with Gaea and are going to create even more mayhem out there once people are faced with the fact that magic exists, and it all goes back to one person: Artemis. So yeah, maybe I am a little ticked off at the idea of being related to her."

Quietly, Greta said, "Uff da, honey. You're going to scare Lester."

Whipping around, Ryan saw a cat's groggy head peeking out of Greta's carry-on bag near the greenhouse door.

"LESTER!"

Ryan pounced on her fur baby, scooping him up into her arms as another bout of sobs and snot released themselves. Over Lester's purrs, she vaguely heard the group titter, but she dismissed her curiosity in favor of motorboating Lester's fuzzy tummy. The reunion was like a dream, bathed in a golden glow with a parade of floral aromas that overpowered his fusty feline fragrance. "I can't believe you're here! My little trans-Atlantic kitty! Oh gosh, I guess you're trans-Atlantic and trans-Mediterranean. Ooh-la-la. I can't wait to see your passport stamps. I'm surprised border patrol didn't stop you for all your naughty kitty warrants." Picking cat hair off her tongue, Ryan looked back to see everyone beaming at her. "Sorry, I'm a little obsessed with my cat." She squeezed Greta's shoulder. "And my Greta."

Nicholas's ice-blue eyes were crinkled with joy. "Brilliant. Absolutely brilliant."

She nuzzled Lester. "He is, isn't he?"

"Not him, you crazy cat lady. Look behind you, Ryan," Greta exclaimed.

Ryan turned around and followed their gazes to the pots of Weeping Dianas—only they weren't weeping. Their trademark droopy heads were instead reaching high and proud, their bells open toward a bright sun that was busy drying the rain-dotted greenhouse roof.

Slowly kneeling down, Ryan delicately thumbed the velvety petals of her Weeping Diana. "Look at you," she whispered. "Cornflower, sky, tiffany, navy. All the blues come through."

Feeling others hovering behind her, she turned, pointing numbly. "How?"

"Ryan," Nicholas said, "like it or not, you are the Descendant of Artemis. You are fiercely independent. You are stubborn. You are intellectual. You are a fighter. You have a thirst to succeed."

Ryan shook her head.

"You're just like her. And seeing as you're able to control the weather, and do it more powerfully than any Descendant I've ever witnessed . . ."

She crossed her arms. "You think I . . ." She trailed off, eyes unfocused toward the back of the greenhouse, where an entire bay laurel tree shimmied its branches as though to wave at her. "But there's no way . . . you've got it wrong."

"No, Ryan, we haven't. We never did, in fact," Nicholas said, beaming. "We've always been right about you. You are a Descendant. A powerful one, at that. I had found it irksome that the moment you arrived on our beautiful island, the weather took a turn for the worst.

I was afraid you'd reject our home for a sad, dreary, pathetic place. My worry became a reality when I saw the weather worsen along with the progress of your training and decreasing faith. It wasn't helping anyone's spirit, least of all yours.

"But as the weather progressively worsened, and the other Descendants were unable to contain its wrath, I started to think outside the box, as I am prone to do. While others were worried that Gaea was letting her monsters wreak havoc on the weather surrounding our island, it didn't feel like a storm whose purpose was to destroy or cause harm. And we certainly know that a weather pattern doesn't cause storms like this, so I concluded that it had to be an inside job.

"Before I had a chance to consider who amongst us was responsible, chance had it that you walked by after training. You didn't see me, but as I observed you, you looked like a rain cloud personified. You were a walking, breathing, living thunderstorm. Your morale was so low, it seemed to decrease the barometric pressure around you. After that, I felt like it was no longer a coincidence that your arrival turned the island into its own little El Niño.

"To test my theory, I studied your emotions. I knew you were saddened by leaving the island, but I hadn't counted on you being mad as a hornet. I think all this deep-seated animosity toward Artemis hindered you from consciously controlling and exploring your powers."

Ryan shifted her weight, crossing her arms across her midsection. "I mean, yeah, I was miffed when I learned I wasn't supposedly the Descendant of Athena or Zeus or something. But I think my ill will toward Artemis was more surface level."

"I think it's bigger than just you. I think it's hidden in your genes;

this rage and anger, spanning generations, all aimed toward an unnamable source—Artemis, the ancestor of your bloodline."

Stunned, Ryan stared at Nicholas. Then she turned her gaze up through the glass roof to the cerulean sky, dotted with picturesque, puffy clouds, the angry storm clouds a distant memory.

"But I didn't feel like I've been doing that—I mean, I didn't do it," she said, tripping over her words.

"You did," Nicholas said simply. Melina nodded emphatically, pride written all over her face.

Ryan looked down at Lester, who was gazing back at her as if to say, *I've always known you had it in ya, Ma.*

"But why now? Are you saying that I've been controlling the weather at my home? In Minnesota?" asked a nonplussed Ryan.

"My understanding is that Minnesota's weather is pretty unpredictable, so I don't think people would have identified a noticeable difference when you started unconsciously revealing your powers. But from what I hear, your little town has been largely unscathed from the natural disasters that have been occurring on a regular basis around the world, so I'm thinking that your presence had something to do with that."

"We've been lucky," Ryan said, glancing at Greta, who arched an eyebrow at her. "Well, if this is true—and I'm still not quite convinced—why can't I feel like I'm doing something? Why is it unconscious?"

"The blood that flows in your veins is hers, but unless you accept her as well as accept who you are, you will not be able to control or grow," Nicholas replied sagely. "And while I did see how you came to your opinion on the abandonment of Artemis, I don't think you considered her situation. Of course, this is all my theory, but around the time she must have had a baby, times were tough. Things were unstable. Everyone could see relations with Gaea were becoming frayed. Her own twin brother, Apollo, killed Orion when he found out they were fond of each other. Who knows? Maybe he found out more than that. Gods were unpredictable, and while she made Zeus promise that she didn't have to marry, she didn't know if she could extend that protection to her baby.

"And I, for one, understand that. Because I wasn't able to protect mine. And if I could, I would have made the same decision that Artemis did. To give her child a life and a future," Nicholas ended heavily.

Ryan frowned, absentmindedly booping Lester's nose while he batted her fingers away. "I guess I never thought of it that way."

She searched for Kosta, who had been watching the events unfold from the back of the group. Their eyes met, and he gave her a lopsided smile that was equal parts smug and exasperation, perfectly conveying an *I told you so.*

Ryan grinned back sheepishly, rubbed her face, and stood up. "I have to admit, Artemis sounds like a pretty kickass lady."

"So you don't think you'll continue calling her Artie?" Melina asked.

Ryan laughed. "If I ever meet her face to face, I owe her hell for what she put me and my bloodline through. I have a feeling calling her Artie would get on her nerves, which I love."

They all laughed.

"I still don't understand how I'm related to the Goddess of the Hunt when I've never shown any sort of ability to 'hunt.'"

"Ahh." Nicholas nodded knowingly. "Although we tried seeking out your powers through different definitions of 'hunting,' we were a little too literal in our endeavors. To hunt is to search. Correct me if I'm wrong, but you've spent much of your life searching for belonging, searching for acceptance, searching for a life and for love. Artemis did these things too! Even with your flowers, you've been exploring and investigating and examining and seeking, all things involved in hunting."

Ryan thought back to her upbringing and to the life she had made in Grayville. Nicholas was right—she was on the hunt to belong, to be happy, to be nurtured. As an effect, she'd breathed life into the Weeping Diana, she'd domesticated the seemingly feral cat in front of her, and . . .

Suddenly, her heart stopped as it hit her. "Greta," Ryan whispered. "Your cancer."

Tears in her eyes, Greta smiled and nodded. "It was you, baby girl."

Ryan nodded, at first shyly and then confidently. *Yes*, she thought, *it was me.*

It IS me.

She could hear voices beyond the greenhouse walls. Walking outside, Ryan saw Descendants filing into the training arena, dodging giant puddles and taking advantage of the rare sunny weather to hone their magical talents.

She gazed up at the puffy clouds, closed her eyes, and lifted her palms up to slowly coax them away. When she opened her eyes, the sun had an unobscured path to make its proud descent into the horizon. Surveying the damp training arena, Ryan let a slow breath escape through her lips. The trees around the perimeter of the field shook and waved their leafy branches wildly, as though heralding her. The wind blew hard for a few seconds and then receded to a gentle breeze, the grass dry and the puddles gone.

With a bashful grin, an aloof cat in her arms, and Greta by her side, Ryan faced the crowd of astonished Descendants. A voice thundered across the arena: "To Artemis!"

The entire field shook as everyone responded, "TO ARTEMIS!"

Kosta yelled, "To Ryan!"

"TO RYAN!"

R OBERT REDFORD? REALLY, RYAN?" GRETA muttered in a disappointed tone.

"*That's* what you want to talk about?" Ryan asked incredulously. "My description of Nicholas?"

"Quite frankly, it's the most unbelievable thing I've seen since I've arrived," she said, tapping the glass of the charmed window back in Ryan's room. "And that's saying something."

Ryan put her hand on her hip. "So you're completely unfazed that there's this whole group of magical people, that the gods exist, AND that I've got powers."

Greta shrugged. "Gandalf would have painted a more complete picture. Or at least John Hammond from *Jurassic Park*." She paused, then turned toward Ryan. "There aren't any dinosaurs on the island, right?"

Ryan shook her head.

"Had to ask," Greta said as she sat down on the loveseat, watching Ryan dote on the snoozing Lester, who'd tuckered himself out stalking the ever-swishing Centaur tails the remainder of the afternoon.

"How are you totally unaffected by what's going on around you?" Ryan asked.

Greta looked into the distance, a faraway look in her eyes.

"Kiddo . . . you're something special. You've been surrounded by all sorts of mysteries since I've met you. So for me, this is a perfectly legitimate explanation to a perfectly legitimate, albeit unexpected, mystery."

"Have we met? I'm like the least mysterious person around," Ryan responded petulantly.

"I didn't say *you* are mysterious. Look at Lester. He was a feral cat, Ryan. You domesticated him."

"Pssh. He saw the opportunity for a warm house and food at his beck and call. I'm just the first idiot to open the dang door for him."

"Well, I'm sure glad a black bear didn't walk in," Greta replied tartly.

Ryan rolled her eyes.

"And then there was my cancer."

"It's entirely possible that you responded positively to the treatment."

"That killed everyone else?" Waving dismissively, the older woman got up and sat down next to Ryan. "You are my miracle friend, Ryan. I knew it then, and I know it now. So no, for me, I don't need to run screaming with flailing arms, unable to process what I've seen. Because I've been living with a slice of this place for the past couple years. You, my love, are the one that didn't know it." She got up and picked up one of the white chiton robes that was peeking out of Ryan's drawers. Holding it this way and that over her body, Greta continued, "And I'm also a little disappointed that you didn't dish on the heat between you and Kosta. Oof. Call Nelly, because it's getting hot in hurr."

Ryan looked away. "There's nothing between us. It's too complicated."

Greta looked around and up at the rocky ceiling, nodding. "I get that. But lots of good things in life are complicated. You deserve goodness and love, Ryan." She handed Ryan the sheet and stretched her arms out, a queen ready to be clothed by her lady-in-waiting.

Chuckling, the botanist started draping the cloth over Greta. "He doesn't love me, Greta," she murmured. "I've been here for, like, less than two weeks."

"Don't tell me you can't fall in love in the blink of an eye, Ryan. You fell in love with Lester the moment you freed him from the neighbor's underpants." She threw a disgusted look at the cat, who'd sauntered over and sat next to her. Together, the pair surveyed Ryan as though she were sitting in front of a judge and jury. "And don't forget *our* love story; we fell in friend love mere hours after meeting in the grocery store. Time does not bound love. When you know, you know."

The fabric slowly revealed a shocking shade of chartreuse. Greta studied her reflection with her magenta readers; Ryan heard her whisper, "Hells yes," under her breath.

Opening the door for Greta, she said, "Time may not bound love, but love has caused a catastrophic cycle of my familial line. Artemis fell in love, and look what happened. Even Gaea fell in love and was betrayed. Nothing good comes out of love."

"Now, who is Gaea?" Greta asked.

On their way to the rotunda, Ryan filled in her friend on Gaea, her disdain for both the gods and the humans of earth, and the truce—a tall order for their short walk, but knowing Greta's attention span, Ryan condensed it to the key points.

Face grim from the realization that humanity hung in the balance, Greta said, "Well, it sounds like this world could use a little more love. I'm glad it's not with Cyrus, though . . ."

Ryan frowned. "Why do you say that?"

Greta looked tense. "He paid me a visit a few days ago."

"At our house?" Ryan asked incredulously.

Greta nodded. "Yes. He demanded I tell him where you were."

"What?"

"I told him the truth: that I didn't know your exact whereabouts. I was about to tell him I was worried about you too and that I was also trying to search for you, but then I took a good look at him. He looked different. Not only was he coming off a bit deranged, but his skin looked . . . shiny yet sallow . . . almost granite-like. He wasn't well." She shivered. "He scared me, Ryan."

Entering the atrium, they caught up to Kosta. "Who scared you?" the demigod asked, observing the tense expressions on both Ryan and Greta's faces.

Greta bounded toward Kosta and linked her arm in his. "Oh, just catching up on an ex-lover of Ryan's. Nothing to be jealous of." She shot a conspiring grin behind her.

They joined Nicholas, Elias, Melina, and Agalia, who were all chatting on the steps of the Parthenon. "Greta, I want you to meet Agalia!" Ryan told her friend. "She's fantastic with plants and has made me feel right at home."

In response, Agalia patted Ryan's cheeks kindly and then said, "Kalispera, Greta!"

Greta looked her up and down. "Pleasure," she said crisply, her smile not quite reaching her eyes.

Agalia heartily grasped onto Greta's hands. "I've become awfully close with Ryan since she's been here. Dare I say like a mother?" she said with a laugh, gazing fondly at the botanist.

Patting Agalia's hand rather firmly, Greta replied, "Oh, I'm sure more like a grandmother."

Agalia laughed, dropped Greta's hands, and sat down next to

Nicholas. Ryan noticed that Greta took up the other side of Nicholas as she eyed Agalia.

Nicholas turned to his new seatmate. "Greta, please tell us how you arrived here."

Now that the focus was on her, Greta suddenly beamed. "Oh, it was quite the odyssey." She paused, waiting for everyone to comprehend her joke. "So great, you'll think it's a myth. It took Herculean efforts—"

"Greta," Ryan interjected.

She shot Ryan an affronted look. "I expedited my passport, which usually takes eight business days, but Vern at the county office owed me one after I caught him in a rather compromising position with his assistant, Loraine." She wiggled her eyebrows up and down suggestively. "So I bought a one-way ticket to Athens in hopes I'd find my girl."

"Why did you come in the first place?" Kosta asked, skeptically eying Greta.

"I just had the feeling Ryan needed me. She was hiding something from me." Greta gestured around her. "And boy, was I right on the money."

"And you chose to bring the cat?" asked Melina.

"It wasn't so much a choice as him planting himself inside my carry-on bag. No amount of catnip or coaxing would get him out of there." Greta lifted her arms up to reveal fresh scratches. "But he paid dearly for his decision to come along. Let's just say one of us got airsick, and it wasn't me . . ."

"But how did you find us?" Kosta asked.

"I shared my location with her," Ryan replied.

Kosta shook his head. "This island is unplottable."

"Through our phones. The GPS on my phone told her phone my location."

Kosta looked aghast.

Greta nodded. "I landed in Athens and went straight to the seaport. As I was miming to a non-English-speaking fisherman how to commandeer the Greek navy to storm a nonexistent island on the Aegean, I recognized Elias from a photo Ryan sent to me. I persuaded him to take me here."

"You sent a photo of Elias?" Kosta said, perplexed. Elias smugly grinned at him.

Ryan huffed. "It was a photo of the boat that I rode on when I came to the island my first day. Elias happened to be in it."

"Thankfully! I'd recognize that tall drink of water anywhere," Greta said, winking at the drink of water in question.

"Well, we're glad you're here," Nicholas said to Greta, who beamed and peeked at Agalia to see whether she'd heard the compliment. "Yes, you and Lester were instrumental to Ryan's powers coming out."

At this, Greta's smile drooped a little, dismayed to share credit with her feline nemesis.

"The truce . . . are you still going forward with it?" Ryan asked desperately.

"We have to," Elias replied, throwing his hands up in the air.

"We haven't performed the physical treaty yet," Melina reasoned. "There's still time."

"That's dishonorable," Elias growled. "I made a promise."

"We are a complete set now. We must rethink our future," Kosta added.

"Has anything changed? Do you feel anything different? Has anything shifted?" Ryan asked, looking each Descendant in the eye.

"Everything feels the same to me," Elias said with a shrug.

"We haven't tried to overtake Gaea now that we have Ryan," Nicholas pointed out.

"Gaea is coming tomorrow. We can't train Ryan in that time," Elias argued.

"Well, we have much to discuss." Turning to Ryan, Nicholas asked, "Would you like to join us at the council meeting?"

"Oh! Yes," Ryan said, her chest puffed out like a teenager who'd passed their driver's test. "What should I do with her?" she asked, pointing to Greta.

"I'm not a child, Ryan. I'm a grown woman. I can take care of myself while you're gone," Greta said, looking around the rotunda with wonder.

"Very grown," Ryan heard Agalia say under her breath.

"Grown, yet youthful," Greta hissed back.

Ryan could picture Greta rubbing elbows with the Sirens, only to fling herself off a cliff. Melina must have had similar thoughts; she loudly suggested, "How about I grab my mom and she can show Greta around?"

Ryan watched as Melina guided Greta toward Phaidra, all while the older woman shot threatening looks behind her at Agalia. The botanist snorted with amusement; typical Greta to get feisty once she sensed a little competition. Whether it was for Nicholas's affection or Ryan's attention, she wasn't so sure yet. Leave it to Greta to sashay into an island full of gods and vie to be their queen.

* * *

A few hours later, it had been decided: the Descendants were going to ambush Gaea. Per Elias, Gaea was to show up alone to meet with Nicholas, who would be the Descendants' representative. Meanwhile, the rest of the Descendants would hide around the training field, waiting for the signal to capture Gaea once and for all.

Ryan was uneasy about this plan for several reasons. First off, her powers were strange. The Descendants had explained ad nauseam during her training sessions how they wrangled their powers, but with Ryan, it was less about control and more about surrendering herself to the magic within her. She felt more like a conduit. But every time she described her method to the Descendants, they chalked it up to her still being a rookie and not having had a legitimate amount of time to train.

Secondly, she didn't agree with the plan. Gaea sounded conniving, and Ryan didn't think she'd fall for it. Ryan kept arguing to the other council members that if she were Gaea, meeting her long-lost enemies in their home court after 2,700 years, she wouldn't carelessly strut in.

Thirdly, with Greta and Lester underfoot, Ryan felt extremely vulnerable, fearing that her loved ones would be nearby when they attempted to capture Gaea. She'd told Greta repeatedly that she would be under the protection of the Centaurs at the other end of the island, but Ryan knew Greta would make a trade with the devil himself to witness everything go down. She was tempted to use Lester's kitty travel tranquilizers on her friend and store her someplace safe.

Most importantly, she couldn't shake the feeling that Elias was hiding something. She hadn't expected a happy dance from him once her powers had finally reached the surface, but he was more tense than ever. He'd been distracted in the council meeting, and Ryan caught him studying her with intensity on more than one occasion.

Kosta and Ryan were the last out of the meeting room. They watched the others scurry to get the rest of the island prepared for tomorrow's ambush.

"Well, my first council meeting was exciting, but I'm a little disappointed I didn't have to take an oath on Poseidon's trident, or learn a secret handshake," Ryan said to Kosta after the meeting as they walked back toward the rotunda.

When he didn't respond, she looked into his glaring face. "What's wrong?" she asked slowly.

"I cannot believe you shared your location with Greta. I thought you were smart enough to see how much danger we Descendants would be in if we were ever discovered," Kosta said, seething.

"I *am* smart!"

"Who else have you shared it with? The guy you were talking about? Your lover?"

"Oh yes, Cyrus, and let's see . . . the local news station and my UPS driver for all my Amazon shipments." The fury in Kosta's face made Ryan spurt out, "Kidding! I only shared it with Greta, and I can absolutely guarantee that I didn't expect her to actually use it."

"You have been reckless with our trust and with our lives," Kosta grumbled.

Ryan rolled her eyes. "Cool it, Kosta." She remembered that he had uttered those same words to Elias the first time she saw magic. If he had been near a body of water, Ryan would have been tempted to try her hand at using her magic to toss him in the water. But she wasn't quite sure her own powers would let her.

"Gaea is coming *here. Tomorrow*," he said, slowly emphasizing each word. "I can't 'cool it.'"

"Aren't I supposed to be the answer to all of this?"

"Are you?"

They glared at each other, each silently goading the other to say something else, an unspoken dare hanging in the air.

Instead, they lunged toward each other, their faces locked in a passionate kiss, Ryan's fingers hungrily combing through Kosta's hair while his fingers grasped her back and waist possessively, as though he couldn't get close enough despite their bodies being deliciously intertwined. Her skin reacted every way it could—tingles, chills, goosebumps—physically manifesting the inevitability of this moment. This moment the Fates had glimpsed on her lifeline. This moment her heart had throbbed for, egging her on with every beat, quickening when it got closer to its match, its partner, its home.

Just as suddenly as it had begun, they parted, panting with bruised lips while staring at each other.

Ryan took a deep breath and slowly walked toward Kosta. She cupped his chin in her hand, using the other to delicately trace his lips. She searched his eyes.

"Am I finally enough for you?" she whispered.

Loud, frantic footsteps echoed toward them. Melina rounded the corner, wide eyed. "She's here."

THEY RAN AS FAST AS they could, merging into the steady flow of Descendants and mythicals down the long path to the arena. Nicholas's original plan for a solo meetup was abandoned; Gaea's unpredictability called for all hands on deck.

Well, almost everyone. Before exiting the mountain, Ryan pulled a harpy aside and demanded that he lock Greta and Lester in her room—under no circumstances was he to let them out. The harpy saluted Ryan and, along with his two brothers, skipped toward the direction of her room.

When they all arrived at the training arena, everyone watched as several large platforms made of clouds came into focus, each holding a handful of . . . well, Ryan wasn't sure what she was looking at. Their silhouettes were inhuman and grotesque. Her eyes landed upon the largest platform in the middle, where a woman stood menacingly. She knew immediately that this must be Gaea.

The woman who stood before her was anything but motherly. Her skin had an earthy brown tinge, making her look unwashed and rank. Her hair consisted of clumps of green moss that hung down her back. Ryan didn't know if it was the wind or if the ends were alive, but the strands stretched out like creepy tendrils. She wore a tunic of shiny black kelp, her hands and legs sallow and brittle, revealing talon-like nails. This woman was not quite human, and

Ryan couldn't fathom that she had once been beautiful—she now resembled a dirty, strung-out vagabond.

Standing next to Kosta and Melina, she leaned over and hissed, "You guys can't do the truce."

"What truce?" Despite hovering thirty feet away, a boom of laughter exploded so loud that some of the Descendants had to cover their ears. Gaea abruptly stopped laughing and said, dripping with haughtiness, "I've changed my mind."

"What?" Kosta asked Gaea in incredulity.

"Yes, it's just less complicated if I get rid of everything that possesses godliness." She shrugged her arms emphatically, looking wide eyed and innocent, then let out a haunting cackle of disdain.

"I bet you all feel very clever, hiding practically in the backyard of the place where you traitorous, filthy rats originated. And on this beauteous island, an object made of all my earthly goodness."

Nicholas's powerful, stern voice boomed in reply. "I can assure you, Gaea, that none of your earthly poison lives on this island. And I'm surprised that you still consider the fruits of your labor as 'objects.' You once nurtured the product of your powers. Now, your maternal nature is gone, replaced by a vicious appetite for destruction."

"Silence! I am the sole power behind everything on this earth. Every mountain, every animal, every plant. All you see is from me and only me. For thousands of years, you've falsely worshipped many who purportedly create and enhance what I do. Well, they've been gone for a long time, and look how the earth is still able to thrive and prosper."

"We have very different ideas of prosperity, Gaea."

"I'm assuming you've been admiring the fun we've had over the past couple weeks. It's been a ball, stretching my muscles, really unleashing my superiority." The atmosphere crackled with Gaea's vitriol. "Those humans—"

"—who are your children too," Nicholas interjected.

"—have forsaken me, poisoning all that I have created for them. Using and abusing the planet, as if they can simply create a new one once they're finished with it. No, it's time for a new reign of Gaea. The humans will be wiped out so that I can heal the world and my *other* children"—she gestured to the monsters around her—"can live free and out of hiding."

She beckoned, and her monsters slowly came into view.

Ryan's knees threatened to give out on her as she studied the monsters next to Gaea. There were hundreds of hideous beasts in all shapes and sizes, their eyes rolling uncontrollably, teeth bared and venomous drool seeping to the ground. She spotted a serpent the size of a water slide and followed the forty-foot body to its head, which was the size of a VW Bug. She peered at the other end, wondering if a school-bus-sized rattle was there, but to her horror, she saw that what should have been the tail was another hideous snake head.

Behind the initial line of monsters were what could only be described as giants. They towered over the other atrocities, their powerful knuckles dragging on the ground behind them. One had hundreds of eyes all over its head; they all blinked at different times, creating a dizzying effect. She spotted a few other monsters with one eye and realized, with a gulp, that Cyclopes did indeed exist. There were three tall women to the right of Gaea, and Ryan's stomach heaved as she saw that their hair was made up of snakes the size of pythons. She averted her eyes, wondering if one of the Gorgon sisters was Medusa.

But what shook Ryan the hardest was the familiar monster standing next to Gaea. "Cyrus?" Ryan gasped.

He was discernible only by the tuft of jet-black hair and the Windex-blue eyes she'd once salivated over. The rest of him resembled the Hulk, veins bulging out of his bulky muscles, the angles of his jaw and limbs sharp and disconcerting. Instead of green, the Titan's skin was silvery; it looked not like normal, flexible flesh but as though it were rock solid. Actually, Ryan thought, it looked like he'd been chiseled out of granite.

"Who?" asked Kosta, looking between Ryan and the Titan next to Gaea.

Cyrus looked down, as though ashamed of his rocky body. "Ryan . . ."

"You're a Titan," she said, aghast.

Although all the Titans and Titanesses resembled one another— they were about five times the width of a normal adult and reached fifteen feet tall—all were different shades, seemingly carved out of different pieces of boulders and mountains. They looked terrifyingly powerful in strength—and, knowing that they could morph into a normal human as Cyrus had, Ryan was anxious about the powers they possessed.

"We had to make sure," he said with vehemence, although his eyes pleaded an apology.

"Sure of what?" Ryan asked.

"That you weren't . . ." Cyrus glanced at Gaea. ". . . one of them."

Gaea made a clucking noise and feigned sadness. "So sad. Your love story would have been one for the ages!"

Nicholas interrupted. "We cannot allow you to kill off the humans, Gaea. We can help you restore the earth with our powers, and with Ryan's plants. Free the gods, for gods' sake. We can work together."

"Oh, pssh," she violently snapped. "What have the gods done for you lately? Look at you. What quality of life is this? Living in hiding for thousands of years, supposedly protecting your Descendants when you've just been keeping everyone prisoner, punished to live and die on this sad island. You may think my ways are evil, but you're doing the same thing as me: playing god, only on a smaller scale.

"And these gods you worship, who have been absent all this time, how powerful and almighty can they be? I find it deliciously amusing that the twelve of them are so weak, so pathetic they can't break the curse and free themselves and instead are at the mercy of a few demigods and some helpless, pitiful distant mortal relatives." She laughed maniacally, her monsters joining in with her. Studying the Descendants below, she asked, "Have you ever thought that maybe they don't want to come back?"

Nicholas remained cool and collected during the conversation, as if he were having tea with an acquaintance. "I have to give it to you. You excel in massacre as well as manipulation. Seeing as you are loyal only to yourself, you wouldn't understand what it's like to have family, to love one another, to honor a bloodline."

"Is your old age finally catching up to you, Nicholas? It's clear as day that I cherish and protect my family and my children—those who are loyal to me. The Titans and monsters—who are part of Zeus's bloodline, might I add—honor me back. When Zeus was disgusted with these creatures, I took them in. How could you worship a god who could be so cruel to his own brethren? You live by so many double standards, Nicholas. So many of the things you shun about me, your own gods are guilty of."

"Our gods are not infallible, Gaea, but they would never go on a murder spree, on this sick hunt for innocent mortals. Tell me, does it provide you glee to watch your beasts terrorize the poor souls of earth? Do you delight in those who have spent the last moments of their lives terrified as they plunge to their deaths? Do your maternal instincts sing with pride to see the ravaged beg for mercy before drowning? Do you dote on those helpless babies being thrown into the fiery gates of hell? Are they not your children too?"

Nicholas paused, letting his words soak in. "You are the most pathetic excuse of a mother."

He'd clearly struck a chord. "Silence, Nicholas," boomed Gaea, her voice steeped with venom. "I am tired of playing this cat-and-mouse game. It's time to destroy you, once and for all. You obviously haven't learned after our last war and are still more than happy to voluntarily deplete your bloodline. You have sealed the fate of your beloved gods. Your little island that you've so lovingly protected will now become the burial ground of every last Descendant."

"How did you find us?"

Gaea shifted her attention and looked at Ryan. Several Descendants looked with surprise and fear at Ryan's willingness to address Gaea. Ryan herself was surprised, but she didn't have the years of fear and hatred ingrained in her. To her, Gaea was still a peculiarity, and now that she was standing in front of her, she had some questions.

"Ahh," Gaea said, eyebrow arched with interest. "I can't believe that they thought *you* were the Descendant of Artemis." She looked Ryan up and down, tutting. "There is not one extraordinary thing about you, pathetic being."

"Looks can be deceiving," Ryan said, gritting her teeth. "For instance, you cannot possibly be Mother Nature. You see, in grade school, we learned about Mother Nature, and how she is the life-giving nurturer that we revered and honored. Sure, Mother Nature could be cruel, as the circle of life inevitably reveals uncomfortable truths. But you, you are nothing like the kind, caring woman that we learned about. Nothing. You are a stranger."

The Titans and monsters growled around her threateningly.

Gaea smirked at Ryan. "I see that Nicholas has wasted no time indoctrinating you with their foul ideology and false beliefs."

Ryan shook her head. "I've been a human for the past twenty-eight years. It doesn't take a relative to the almighty Greek gods to recognize that you are a terrorist who thrives on annihilation and is devoid of any sort of empathy or love for her own."

With a deep breath, she added, "Also, I am the Descendant of Artemis, and I've made up my own mind on who the real enemy is. And she is standing right before me."

With that, Ryan swished her hands up dramatically. Five Venus fly traps erupted near her own feet, nipping at the ankles around her. It wasn't the grand entrance she'd hoped for, but all the Descendants thrust victorious fists into the air nevertheless.

Gaea and Cyrus exchanged a look of shock, but then Gaea roared with laughter, making the ground shake around them. "Oh, you are adorable," she said, giving Ryan a round of applause. "I know some house flies that are going to succumb to an awful death." As the clapping ceased, she said viciously, "It's going to be especially satisfying to kill you, darling. Tell you what. I'll let you choose whichever flowers you'd like to decorate your tombstone, and while us grown-ups fight, you can work on blooming them until I'm ready to end you."

Nicholas replied icily, "You have made a grave mistake, Gaea, underestimating the Descendant of Artemis."

Gaea didn't respond, simply regarding Ryan idly. Then, without any warning, she flung her arm down in Ryan's direction, and a giant sinkhole exploded, sending dirt and rocks hundreds of feet in the air.

Descendants and mythicals spread out of the way and leapt into combat. The Titans and monsters jumped off their cloud platforms onto the island. Fireballs from both sides shot from every direction. The earth trembled from more blasts, and lightning struck the ground. Ryan crouched behind a big boulder that had landed near her. She couldn't believe the destruction that was already occurring. Descendants and monsters alike littered the ground, not moving. Ryan looked up to see Gaea surveying the destruction below her, floating on her cloud.

She would not allow this. But after her sad show of threatening power, she didn't know how to harness her abilities.

Meanwhile, Kosta shot up from another boulder near Ryan and directed a barrage of fireballs at Gaea. Surprised, Gaea extinguished them just before they hit her. Still hiding, the botanist willed a fireball to come out of her hand, but only a little candlelight came out, burning her pointer finger.

Without skipping a beat, before Gaea had a chance to figure out where it was coming from, Kosta lit a huge fire underneath the cloud platform that she stood on. Within a millisecond, the flames that licked the bottom of the platform turned the cloud into condensation, and Gaea fell the twenty feet to the ground. Still crouched behind the boulder, Ryan furiously tried to decide on a next move.

Just then, the boulder she hid behind exploded around her, cutting her face and hands. She quickly rolled over behind a tree to protect her while she got her bearings and wiped her eyes clear of blood oozing from her forehead.

"Ryan, are you OK?" Kosta had just swung a Titan around by the leg and launched it a half mile into the ocean.

Just as Ryan was about to respond, a bolt of lightning exploded the tree, throwing her back ten feet. She silently chastised herself for becoming distracted by Kosta's strength and beauty in battle.

"Artemis may be the Goddess of the Hunt, but you are my prey, Ryan," shrieked Gaea's voice.

Melina popped up next to Ryan and spun around, creating a mini tornado from the debris around her. She stopped suddenly, and all the debris shot at Gaea. Gaea defended herself with a flick of her wrist: little icicle daggers torpedoed at Melina and Ryan, but they dodged in time. Unfortunately for Gaea, the poorly aimed icicles pierced several heads of a multi-headed monster, who screamed in pain and fury.

While Gaea was momentarily distracted by her howling monster son, Nicholas flung a tidal wave of hot lava from one of the open sinkholes at her and several of her Titans. In the last second, Gaea coated herself with ice, but her Titans were not so quick.

To Ryan's absolute shock, Agalia ran by with Greta in tow, both screaming, "Alala alala alala," brandishing what looked to be decapitated granite-like Titan arms, an army of the kobaloi-ninja-Care-Bear creatures following in their wake. After the two women's Greek battle cry faded, the voice of the Sirens rose, projected from the mouths of three Seers a few feet away. A Titan shouted to one of the Gorgon sisters nearby to plug her ears, but Medusa was already clawing her own eyes out, leaving bloody holes, the product of the lethal Siren song.

OK, Ryan, thought to herself. *It's time to ask for help.* She dodged rainfall of what looked to be bloody body parts and stood at the edge of the arena where the thick forest of trees began.

"Dear trees and living greenery that grace this wonderful island. You have given the Descendants so much for thousands of years.

Shelter. Sustenance. Respite. Beauty. Life. Gaea may have created you, but it is us who appreciate your purpose and respect your sacrifices. We cannot thank you enough. I'd like to ask if you'll stand with us and fight!"

With that, a huge crack resounded around her. When she looked up, all the enormous trees had freed their roots from the soil—they marched toward Ryan in precise army lines, ready for battle. Many of the Descendants and Gaea-followers alike stopped and looked agog. The gargantuan tree at the head of the rows, who seemed to be their leader, approached Ryan, bowed at her with a dangerous crack, whipped its enormous branch at the trees behind it in a "let's go" gesture, and broke into a full sprint.

Ryan watched in awe as the trees flung themselves at the enemy. Many of the Titans lit the trees on fire, trying to destroy them, but this just made them more powerful, as their many branches flung fire everywhere. Ryan couldn't believe how many trees there were . . . some were covered with leaves and others looked like they'd been dead for centuries.

"Ryan, watch out!"

Melina flung herself into Ryan, who just missed getting pierced by a flaming tree branch.

"Thank you," Ryan said breathlessly, resting her hands on her knees.

"You need to get your head in the game. You were nearly killed!" Melina bellowed angrily.

They both blocked the tidal wave of water that had barreled toward them from a nearby Titan. Melina sent an invisible curse at him, and the Titan burst into open sores that spewed greenish pus. He scratched in vain as his cells assaulted him from the inside.

OK, we're overpowered. What can I do about that? I create life with flowers. I also brought the dead trees to life. Dead . . .

"Melina, I need to go back to the cave. I'll be really quick."

Melina glanced briefly at Ryan, then kept her eyes on what was going on around them. "Ryan, we really can't spare you. But I trust you."

A tree in front of them exploded into a million pieces. Melina twisted them up into a cyclone and threw it at a Titan, who was pierced repeatedly with tiny splinters.

Before Ryan could change her mind or be persuaded to stay and help her family, she jumped up and motioned for the nearest tree to come over.

"Please cover me until I get back to the entrance."

The tree nodded and started running toward the mountain. Ryan sprinted ahead of it, hearing her leafy guardian successfully blocking the shots aimed at her.

After a harrowing journey back to the mountain, she turned around and thanked the tree.

"Return to the battle with your brethren. I appreciate your help."

The tree bowed and ran off.

She ran for the crypt.

HELLO, DEARLY DEPARTED. MY NAME is Ryan." She slowly walked along a row of tombs, making her way to the center of the crypt.

For the second time in that same place, she heard footsteps rapidly running down the tunnel and knew from their intonation that they were Kosta's.

"What are you doing here?" they asked each other at the same time.

Ryan spoke first. "I have a hunch."

"What? You abandoned everyone outside because you had a hunch?" Kosta asked wildly.

Ryan became impatient. "We need backup, Kosta. And that's what I'm trying to find."

Kosta gave her a disbelieving look. "Everyone we have is out there now, Ryan."

"Not everyone," she replied. Pure astonishment washed over Kosta's face. She turned half a quarter around, so she didn't have to see his reaction; she was already feeling self-conscious without watching his face.

"I need your help. No one has ever called on you. Gods know that when you were all alive, you fought with the best of them to free the gods. Your ancestors, your family, your bloodline, they're dying out there. They're on their way to joining you."

She caught Kosta's eye as she said this. His were slightly squinting at her, and she couldn't tell if he was dubious or slowly warming up to her harebrained idea. She decided to go with the latter and figured that if the ghosts of Descendants past were listening, they were having the same sort of reaction.

"It's unprecedented, I know. But as the long-lost Descendant of Artemis, I summon you." Ryan didn't remember when her voice had risen louder and louder, but she found that she was bellowing, her powerful voice echoing off the rocky walls. "I've finally found my purpose. Follow me to free the gods!"

With that, Ryan took off in a sprint, rushing past Kosta and into the dark passageway. She didn't know what was going on behind her, didn't know if anyone besides Kosta was following her or whether she'd just spent the last few moments in vain, begging an empty room for help. But instinct told her to keep pushing forward and not to question her actions any further.

She broke out onto the main level, hearing the brutality of the battle much closer than where she'd left it. By this time, Kosta had caught up, and the panicked look on his face confirmed that what they were hearing could not be good.

When they got to the cave entrance, what they saw stopped them in their tracks.

There was complete mayhem—carnage consumed the entire panoramic outside the mountain. The number of Descendants that were fighting had significantly dwindled; Ryan was hoping that there was another battle just beyond the tree line that she couldn't see. The Descendants she could see fighting were injured and bloody, yet they fought as though they'd just entered battle, with relish and determination. The trees were still engaged in the battle, but half of them lay in big piles of twisted, broken branches, immobile.

She spotted Elias in the distance. She gasped when she saw him fling fiery, broken branches at Nicholas.

"What is Elias doing?" Ryan shouted to Kosta.

"What do you mean?" he replied. He had not seen what Ryan had, and she now wondered if she'd imagined it.

"What are you doing? Where have you been?" Melina shrieked at them as she ran by, shooting hail the size of basketballs behind her back. She doubled back, running toward Ryan and Kosta, then stopped dead in her tracks. Her eyes were enormous, looking like they were going to pop clear out of her head. Ryan saw what little color she had in her face drain away.

Just as Ryan was about to ask her what was wrong, she noticed another oddity. The monster Melina had been fighting had also stopped in its tracks and was looking just beyond Ryan and Kosta.

"Dad?"

That was literally the last word Ryan had expected to escape from Melina's mouth. By this time, the fighting around the mouth of the cave had come to an abrupt halt, the same incredulous expressions reflected in every person and monster's face.

Ryan snuck a look at Kosta and realized that it wasn't just the two of them standing there.

She slowly turned around and saw, to her utter disbelief, thousands of ghosts standing behind her. She could pick out the features of some of the living Descendants she knew, especially the kind eyes of Melina on a tall, brute-like warrior.

"Hello, my sweet girl, Melina. We've been called to action by the Descendant of Artemis. In the name of Zeus and all that is holy, it is time we seek our revenge to free the gods at last."

With that, the crowd of spirits erupted in a battle cry, a crescendo of piercing shouts like a drumbeat. The Descendants and demigods joined in, stomping their feet; clanging their spears, knives, and tridents; beating armor with clenched fists until the ground shook and the roars climaxed into a savage charge of warriors. Ryan watched in awe as the Descendant spirits attacked the Titans and monsters, using the powers they hadn't exercised in centuries. Not knowing how to fight the ghosts, many monsters retreated in terror.

Feeling as though she'd spent enough time away from battle, Ryan was ready to participate and obliterate Gaea and her cronies. She raced forward and teamed up with a tiny, scarf-wearing, ancient ghost who resembled a *yia yia*—the Greek version of a granny. Together, they catapulted an eight-headed monster straight up into the atmosphere. Ryan shook the ghost's wrinkled hand afterward, not knowing exactly how much her powers had contributed but feeling more confident.

"Who is the origin of your descendancy?" asked the yia yia.

"Artemis," Ryan responded, out of breath.

A puzzled expression crossed her heavily lined face. She looked Ryan up and down and nodded confidently. "Yes, koukla. You are," she said simply.

Ryan smiled and turned away so that the aged Wonder Woman wouldn't see her blush. As she turned her head, she saw the robes of Nicholas shoot up from the ground and spin rapidly, soaring twenty feet across the field.

"Nicholas!"

She sprinted toward him, and nearly came face-to-face with the hundred-eyed monster who'd tossed Nicholas like an empty pop can.

"NO!" she shouted, her finger pointed like she was disciplining a puppy.

The monster stopped his pursuit, regarding her curiously.

"Get back."

The monster frowned and blinked his countless eyes, his mouth open in confusion as though battling an internal struggle. He looked around and idly walked away.

She reached Nicholas, who lay crumpled on the ground.

"Are you hurt?" She quickly assessed him and thankfully didn't find any limbs missing.

"I'll live, but I'm afraid I am injured."

As he removed his hand from his chest, Ryan saw a gaping wound, crimson liquid pooling on his midnight-black chiton. Nicholas was in danger, and he was getting paler and paler by the second.

"I'm going to carry you into the cave."

"You conjured the Eidolon."

"Huh?" Ryan put pressure on Nicholas's chest and glanced around to make sure they weren't in imminent danger.

"The Eidolon. They are the spirit image of a dead person. Raising the Eidolon from their eternal rest . . . I didn't think it was possible. You genius girl. I'm so proud," Nicholas said in concussed wonder.

"You can thank me when we win the war, Nicholas. Right now, we need to get you to Melina or the Centaurs."

"Ryan, wait. There's something I have to tell you." By this time, his words were sputtering, and Ryan had to bend down to hear what he was saying.

"Nicholas," she said with gentle urgency. "You need medical attention now. Conserve your energy while I get you to safety."

"No!" he urged, insistently. "You must listen. It's Elias. He's turned."

Ryan stopped what she was doing and stared at Nicholas.

"Turned into what?"

"He's a traitor, Ryan. He's working with Gaea."

Ryan felt no pride that her theory was finally confirmed; disgust and hatred seethed through her veins.

"I need to warn everyone," she said between gritted teeth, peering up to see if she could spot Elias. She needed to stop him.

"No, Ryan, you have one final mission."

"Nicholas, there are Descendants out there relying on Elias . . . Kosta is fighting alongside him. We need to expose him now."

"Ryan, listen to me."

To her horror, Ryan saw little droplets of blood spurt every time Nicholas tried to say something. He had laid back and was looking straight up, as though all energy had escaped his body.

"Despite Elias's ultimate deceit, we're close to ending this, thanks to your ingenuity."

A huge explosion ripped ten feet away, and Ryan and Nicholas were showered with rocks and soil. Ryan brushed off Nicholas and saw a gash on his head—his eyes were glazed, as though he were struggling to stay conscious. Her instinct was to pick him up, drag him to safety within the cave, and get her revenge on Elias. But a nagging feeling prevented her from disobeying Nicholas; he had never been wrong since Ryan had known him. If there were any man who had pure faith in what he believed, it was Nicholas. He was the godliest being she'd been closest to, and therefore she needed to do his bidding.

"Nicholas. NICHOLAS." She nudged him awake. He jolted, eyes blinking rapidly in confusion, his face wet from the blood seeping from his head.

"I need you to tell me what to do," she said calmly, her voice not reflecting the string of expletives screaming in her head.

Pure determination blossomed as Nicholas readied his directives.

"There is a door, Ryan, a door to the heavens. It's at the top of the mountain. Past the little outlook where I proposed to Kalliope. It's been sealed for thousands of years by the ancient curse of Gaea. I'm confident that her powers are weakening, even more than she recognizes. You need to open it."

"Open it and do what?"

"Free the gods."

The gravity of his last sentence, of this mission itself, produced paralyzing fear and anxiety within Ryan. This was such a momentous task; surely she hadn't earned the right to do what generations of Descendants have tried to do for over two millennia. And she was embarrassed to admit that, suddenly, she felt shy about meeting the gods.

Then Ryan looked around and saw the dead figures of Alexandros and Leonides. The Muses were wailing, some of them carrying motionless sisters between them. Centaurs were still fighting, limbs missing.

Gaea was evil; this was complete carnage. Nicholas might die, and then the whole magical bloodline would become extinct. She realized she had to free the gods.

"Now, Ryan. Just keep making your way up."

She figured that she could continue this internal battle as she made her way to this door that Nicholas was speaking of, so she nodded curtly at him, arranged leaves and sticks over his body so that he would not be seen, and left him.

"I'm so proud of you, Ryan," she heard him say faintly.

Ryan sprinted back to the cave entrance, where she found Kosta. "Nicholas. He's gravely injured. He's under the brush about two hundred yards away. Go get him some help."

Before he could react or question why she didn't do it herself, she was off.

As she ran up the outer stairs to the mezzanine of the cave, she spotted Melina. Ryan halted, about to call her name and request her company. *No*, she thought firmly, needling herself to continue moving. Despite her earlier feelings of unworthiness, Ryan needed to do this alone. Maybe it wasn't her right, but she was the missing link that had ultimately kept the gods locked on Mount Olympus and made the Descendants prisoners of this godsforsaken island for centuries upon centuries. This was her ultimate gift to them. An apology on behalf of her own god, Artemis.

She continued onward and upward, running down hallways she'd never ventured into, stumbling upon stairways in hidden alcoves and continually making her way up, up, up. She was running full speed down a hallway when she glanced to her left and saw Nicholas's sacred room. Oh, how grateful she was that he hadn't given up on her, when so many in her life had.

Up and up she went, where the sounds of the battle grew fainter, the smell of the sea grew less salty, and the air thinned and cooled. The halls and stairways she trekked had clearly been in disuse for quite some time. Half the walls had crumbled, making it difficult to squeeze her way through some parts. The floor was uneven, making her trip several times as she tried to move as quickly as possible. It started to get windier up there; the walls were sloping more, and there were little holes here and there exposing open air. All she could see was white.

She was getting close. She hadn't stumbled upon any stairs for a while now; the incline had increased, and she was winding around and around toward the top of the mountain. She was certain that there were no other rooms at the end of this path, and that she would find what she was looking for.

And when Ryan turned a corner, there it was: a large slab of rock decorated with engraved icons and inscriptions. There was a bunch of Greek writing she couldn't read, but unmistakably, there were twelve figures in a line from one end of the door to the other. She walked up close to inspect the intricate carvings and felt heat radiating from the door, as if it were a living being.

As she examined each of the gods in front of her, she heard a pebble slide across the floor. She figured that Kosta had followed her as he had down by the crypt.

It wasn't until she spun around, the beginnings of a smile upon her face, that she immediately recognized how wrong she was.

N FRONT OF HER STOOD Gaea. She must have silently stalked Ryan up the mountain. A violent shudder tore through the botanist, her body responding out of both terror and disgust.

Ryan had thought she had a fairly good idea what Gaea looked like when she saw her on the battlefield, but being a mere five feet away from her, Ryan's stomach quivered with nausea. Gaea's skin was cracked and peeling, little flakes raining down with every jagged movement. The perfume of sickly-sweet rot from her hair wafted throughout the little foyer, an invisible force extinguishing any hint of fresh air. Her jaundice-yellow eyes feverishly raked in every detail of Ryan and the situation, curiosity mixed with raw fury.

Ryan wondered if Gaea turning physically foul was a new phenomenon, the side effect of destroying what she had so intricately built around her. She was mildly relieved to note that Gaea looked less powerful than she had at the beginning of the battle; her confidence was fraying at the edges, her actions more noticeably aggravated and erratic. Contempt and violence still oozed from her being, but Ryan was most concerned with a foreboding observation: Gaea was becoming desperate.

"What are you doing up here, little girl?" growled Gaea.

Apparently, there was no need for pleasantries. Ryan felt the breath inside her constrict and her hands start to shake.

"It's over, Gaea. You've lost the war." As soon as Gaea was about to dispute this, Ryan quickly added, "The rest of the Descendants are on their way up, ready to liberate the gods."

Gaea instinctively glanced behind her. Ryan could kick herself for not enlisting the help of Melina. *What the hell was I thinking?* she berated herself. *That I'd simply ring the doorbell and invite the gods down for dinner?*

Gaea's head whipped back to Ryan, a smirk on her vile face. She clasped her hands behind her back, the dagger-sharp nails interweaving, and idly strolled around the botanist to study the long door.

"No one is coming, Ryan. Both you and I know that." Gaea spoke in a light tone, but Ryan detected a jeer underneath. "I'm curious. What was your plan?"

Ryan needed to stall. She naively hoped that Kosta had rescued Nicholas and Nicholas had shared the mission he'd sent her to do. She strained to hear if anyone was sprinting up the mountain.

"I can assure you, my plan is more courageous than yours. It seems awfully reckless to trap yourself up here, alone in our territory, stuck between the gods and the Descendants, while the rest of your side dies pitiful deaths. What kind of leader are you to abandon your army for slaughter?"

Ryan had clearly struck a nerve; Gaea's cheeks flushed a deep crimson, and little inky veins throbbed visibly under her skin, like worms in crisis.

"You're a stupid little girl. And a delusional one. I have been Mother Nature for billions of years. You've been a Descendant for the blink of an eye, and you think you can overpower me? That you can liberate the gods?" Gaea cackled maniacally, the rocky walls shuddering from its force, but the laugh didn't quite reach her eyes.

They steadfastly and hauntingly trained on Ryan, like a predator homing in on its prey.

Ryan realized she needed to defuse Gaea's temper or she'd reach her demise sooner than anticipated.

"You are fighting for the wrong side, Ryan. You may be the missing link for the Descendants, but maybe that's the way it was supposed to be. I've spent millions of years creating life that is optimal for humans like you. When the gods roamed the earth, there was discord between us. I wanted what was best for all living creatures; the gods only wanted what was best for themselves. They are selfish, indulgent, foolish. Their best interests are not for mankind but for the select few who are Descendants of them." Gaea gazed at the door with scorn and then turned to look at Ryan.

"And do you think that they'll care one lick about you? Artemis tried to eliminate your bloodline once. She was ashamed of you. Do you think that behind that door is a goddess who is grateful that her gene pool has survived? Who is ashamed of her decision years and years ago? No. I have known Artemis for an exceptionally long time. There is not one maternal bone in her body.

"If you're expecting that other gods will come to your aid when Artemis ultimately abandons you, think again. You're going to have a real problem with her twin brother, Apollo, who murdered Orion, your distant grandfather, in cold blood. The others are going to be so focused on their own bloodlines that, once again, you'll fall through the cracks.

"But me, Ryan? I'm a mother. To all. Always have been. Always will be. You need someone to nurture and protect you. You clearly have an affinity for nature. I can help you hone your powers for good—be that maternal figure you've always yearned for."

Gaea had struck a chord with some deep-seated anxieties that Ryan was feeling. Her head was spinning, and she needed to focus.

Visions of Nicholas popped into her mind—Ryan realized that the reason she could now fully accept the gods was that she trusted him and all that he represented. That she trusted Melina. That she trusted Kosta. That there wasn't a bad bone in any of their bodies. If these were the relatives of the gods, the apples couldn't have fallen far from the tree. She needed to have faith and continue her mission. A mission she felt deep inside her core.

She couldn't imagine how the initial meeting with Artemis would go, but she'd dealt with rejection all her life. She wouldn't let the potential of Artemis's rejection define her. Ryan was stronger than she believed. Her life as a mortal had shaped the Descendant she was meant to be.

Ryan decided to take a chance and bet on stroking Gaea's vanity. It was her only shot.

"You're right, Gaea. Even from the beginning, when I was unknowingly injecting life into new species, I always felt closest to you. I idolized you. I could never live up to the powers that you have or what you've created the past billion years, but I want to learn from you. I want to be a nurturer like you and be a mother to all that I bring to life. Will you teach me, Gaea?"

Gaea stared hard into her face, trying to determine the level of honesty in her revelation. "If you execute Nicholas and the rest of the demigods, I will allow you to live."

Ryan nodded. "Also, I can't stop thinking about Cyrus," she said, looking coy. "What a babe of a Titan."

With that, Gaea swung her head back and let out a roar of laughter. "Well, we better go check to see if he's still alive. I'm glad you two hit it off. I didn't even want to send him in to investigate you in the first place—it was a complete waste of time—but we agreed, what with the curiosity of your flowers . . ." Gaea trailed off, cleared her throat, and continued, "But with you in my back pocket and Elias already pledging his allegiance to me, the treachery alone will destroy some of your friends. Let's finish off the rest and forever terminate this island."

"Let's go," Ryan said, smiling. Gaea turned around.

Ryan pounced on this millisecond-long opportunity. With Gaea's back toward her, she silently pleaded for the stone walls around her to encapsulate her enemy, making a hugging motion with her arms.

A giant cracking of granite and dust erupted, and Gaea screamed, but she was gone, completely entombed in the wall.

Ryan didn't know if or how long this would hold Gaea, but she had to act fast. She absentmindedly brushed rock and debris off her bloody, raw face as she turned around, now with only two feet to work within to figure out how to open the door.

Body shaking from fear and adrenaline, she furiously pounded on the marble door, her fists blue with bruises. She shot her unpredictable powers at the door—fire, wind, ice, water—to try to break it down, but it didn't budge. She could hear Gaea working to remove the wall, and what alarmed the botanist even more was that she could hear that the two of them would not be alone for much longer; the sound of rock-on-rock footsteps was pounding up toward them. While she had hoped that the Descendants would join her in this battle, it sounded like Gaea was instead getting assistance in reaching Ryan.

She heard a large crack behind her, and when she turned around, she could see that Gaea had created a small opening the size of a watermelon in the layer that separated them. She stood with her back against the door, watching as the hole grew bigger. Cyrus came into view; he took one look at the situation and started pounding the thick walls around Gaea with his massive boulder biceps, decimating the rock to dust and freeing his mother.

Gaea let out another booming laugh as she took in Ryan's surroundings.

"Pathetic girl. Foolish girl. I may have had a momentary lapse of judgment and thought you might join my team, but you clearly have failed in your useless mission. Cyrus, grab her. We'll take her back to the lair, and I'll decide what I want to do with her later."

"No," Ryan said confidently. All the anxiety, terror, and doubt flooded out of her. The angry tears stopped flowing, replaced by sheer determination. She wiped her arm against her forehead, noting it was slick with blood, and held her head high. "I am not coming with you. Despite what you say, I am a Descendant. And I belong on this island, fighting for the freedom of the gods."

She took a deep, steadying breath. "You're going to have to kill me."

A vicious grin spread on Gaea's face. "With pleasure."

Ryan turned around, resting her bloodied forehead and hands against the warm door, closed her eyes, and silently apologized. For failing the gods, for letting down Nicholas, for hurting Kosta. Waiting for the moment that Gaea would certainly end her, eyes squeezed shut, hoping it was quick and that dying didn't hurt.

Suddenly, the mountain shook tremendously. Ryan jerked her head up and steadied herself. Against her better judgment, she peeked behind her to see a puzzled Gaea, eyes wide as she watched the walls shudder. The mountain stilled once more, and the silence was replaced by little clicking noises.

Ryan turned back to the door to witness the icons of the gods, one by one, receding an inch into the solid stone, left to right, of their own volition. Gaea and Cyrus were just as mesmerized, watching the door instead of acting.

As soon as the last icon clicked out, the entire door shifted a foot away from Ryan and slowly slid into the wall. The doorway revealed marble steps that reached high into darkness. As soon as the door halted, Ryan heard heavy footsteps descending quickly toward her.

Cyrus bolted down the mountain without a second glance behind him.

"What? How did . . . ?"

Ryan looked victoriously at a stunned Gaea, but her triumph turned to confusion. Gaea had changed. All the smugness, all the hatred, all the red-hot venom was gone. The transformation was astounding. The murderous empress was replaced by a confounded, scared-looking woman.

"I'm the only one who can open this . . ." sputtered Gaea.

"Clearly not," Ryan said as sassily as she could, although the sudden change in Gaea paralyzed any fight left in her.

They heard footsteps drawing nearer.

Gaea peered hard at Ryan, as if looking at her clearly for the first time. Her gaze stopped at her forehead, and before Ryan could realize what she was doing, Gaea gently touched the gash on her head.

Ryan slapped her hand away. "Don't touch me!"

Ryan watched as Gaea intently studied her bloodied finger, a drop of Ryan's deep red blood lazily descending toward her dirt-stained palm. Gaea slowly raised her knife-sharp nails toward a hole in the mountain wall where light illuminated the small antechamber. She rotated her wrist slightly, until at last, a ray of light reflected off the blood. Gaea gasped while Ryan, forgetting herself completely, grabbed Gaea's hand for a closer look. It was unmistakable: a faint hint of pearlescent green swirled within the sea of scarlet. Shock swept across Gaea's harsh features while Ryan stared back, puzzled.

"Ryan . . . you don't understand. The ancient curse I put on this mountain. Only Gaea can open this door. *I'm* Gaea," she said, frantically hammering her chest with such force, Ryan was certain there'd be bruises.

Heavy steps from above were barreling closer.

Gaea took a step closer to Ryan. "Ryan," Gaea pleaded urgently. "I don't think you're one of them."

"What?" breathed Ryan.

"Ryan, don't you understand? You're not a full Descendant. You can't be if you opened that door. Your blood . . ."

Ryan shook her head in disbelief.

"Your powers . . . they're not like theirs, are they? At least, not completely."

An imposing shadow appeared over them.

With a last look of anguish and awe, Gaea fled. As she disappeared behind the curve of the mountain, Ryan heard her faintly shout, "You're not one of them. Find me, Ryan. Find me."

Stunned, Ryan numbly turned around. The outline of a large figure started to come into focus. As it advanced toward her, the conversation with the Fates inexplicably zapped into her brain.

"Your fate is sealed, but your identity remains fluid." Ryan looked wildly to where Gaea had retreated, then back to the doorway. *"And so does her allegiance."*

At last, the magnificent figure reached the bottom of the stairs and stepped into the light. In all her glory, Artemis stood before her.

Like an animal freed from captivity, her eyes hungrily assessed the scene in front of her, her fists clenching and unclenching as though rigid from disuse, a look of grim determination set on her face.

At last, her eyes rested on Ryan. Unmistakably, her harsh features softened. She tipped her head, her messy hair spilling forward, and said, "Well done, my kin."

EPILOGUE

RYAN WALKED OUT OF THE infirmary after watching Nicholas sleep for a couple hours. He'd been put into a coma for the past few days so that his body could regenerate and heal in peace. As she stroked his long silver hair, she told him everything that had happened since they'd last seen each other.

How she'd watched as all the Olympians followed Artemis down the stairs, and how, last down the mountain, Apollo surveyed her with unmistakable antipathy, then raced to join the battle without a second glance behind him.

How Gaea had managed to escape with some of her Titans and monsters due to the duplicity of Elias, and how a couple of other demigods along with the Furies and harpies had also disappeared without a trace.

How the gods Ares and Dionysus had rounded up the monsters that Gaea had left for dead and confined them within the mountain; and how, in an act of civility and goodwill, they'd asked the Centaurs to heal and mend them instead of executing them.

How Kosta had told Ryan that after she'd inexplicably demanded he find and save Nicholas, he'd found him being watched over by the ghost of his wife, Kalliope, while his brave daughter, Spiras, had stood guard over her parents.

Nicholas lay still and unresponsive during her monologue, but

Ryan felt in her heart that he had understood every word she said. Taking her leave, she walked the quiet, winding halls, hoping that Nicholas would remember that his kin were with him during the battle.

She opened the door to her room, where Kosta was waiting for her. Wordlessly, he picked up Ryan's suitcase. They walked out, and Ryan took one last look at her little haven.

She waved to the few somber Descendants they passed on their way to the rotunda. Gone were the electricity of battle and excitement of freedom. Grief and tension hung in the air like a stifling humidity as the Descendants and mythicals anxiously awaited orders from the gods. The twelve Olympians had decided to stealthily repair the atrocities Gaea had inflicted upon humanity before discussing the future role they'd all play in this new world. Ryan had heard whisperings about feeling like caged animals, and although there was shock and dismay at Elias's betrayal, there was underlying jealousy of his getting to leave the island.

Greta and Agalia were huddled around Melina, crooning soft words of comfort. As Ryan approached, Melina launched herself into her arms, crying hard into her shoulder. Ryan hugged her back fiercely, wishing she could shoulder some of the pain her friend was experiencing. She knew what it was like to lose a mother and to be an orphan.

They parted, and Melina gave Ryan a weak, watery smile. "Thank you for everything, Melina. You truly are my broad from another god," Ryan said.

Melina cackled, shaking her head. "Did someone give you espresso?"

Kosta led the way to the dock by the sea. He helped Greta into the boat—she'd feigned weakness so that he would lift her up like a baby and gently place her inside. Kosta peered into the cat carrier and gave Lester a few chin scratches; Lester begrudgingly accepted the love.

Then he walked back to where Ryan waited for him on the sand. They both looked out at the pale, hazy sky. They couldn't see them, but they knew the gods were out there, exercising their powers and abilities to repair the damage and harm done to humanity.

Ryan turned to Kosta, who had a grim look on his face. She knew he was hiding the hurt he felt.

"I don't know why you have to go," he said gruffly. "This most assuredly is your home now. You're one of us."

She looked around and nodded. "Yes and no, Kosta. I found myself here, and I found a family that has been missing for centuries. But Greta is also my home, and I need to take her back."

Kosta let out a frustrated sigh in response.

Ryan picked up his hand and interlaced his tan fingers with hers. "Kosta, is this your home? You now have the freedom to explore the entire world. To meet people. To enjoy new experiences. To create memories. It's out there waiting for you." She pointed out toward the horizon. "What you have now may not be what you need anymore."

Kosta bristled. "I know exactly what I need, loulouthaki. Nothing could change that."

Ryan squinted up at him. "I never did learn what that word means."

He sighed, looking down at her with those heavenly caramel eyes. "My little flower girl."

Ryan smiled wistfully, her nose stinging and eyes threatening to flood with tears. She knew in her heart that she needed to let him go experience the whole new world in front of him.

Her heart also ached for lying to him. She'd left out a few key details from what had happened atop Mount Olympus, letting the Descendants come to the wrong conclusion about how the ancient curse was broken. They were right in that Ryan was the only one of them who could have opened the door, but for the wrong reason: she'd let them believe that only someone who honored both the god bloodline and the mortal bloodline could break the curse.

She needed time alone to explore her own identity: half Descendant and half Gaea. She loved the Descendants with everything within her—they were the family she'd always wanted—but she wouldn't blindly accept that a world where the gods reigned over humanity was the right thing. She'd only discovered half her story; how Gaea intertwined into her destiny affected her role in protecting humanity. Had Gaea unwittingly birthed a human child with a male heir of Artemis? Or had a Titan impregnated a woman of Artemis's lineage?

Until Ryan uncovered the mystery of her bloodline, she couldn't stay here when her allegiance was in question.

But gods almighty, Ryan thought as she looked at Kosta, *I hope our paths lead to one another in the end.*

"This isn't goodbye, Kosta." She rose on her tippy toes, planted a soft kiss on his lips, and set half of small laurel stick in his hands, the other half tucked safely in her knapsack.

And with that, she departed the island.

☙ ACKNOWLEDGMENTS ☙

Wirmal advice, thorough conversations about my novel characters, and a competitive game of Spitey. I'm so lucky to be your WD. Marcie

RITING IS SUCH A LOVELY solo activity, but the transition from unedited manuscript to published novel truly takes a team of supportive, brilliant people.

To my many friends, whom I bribed with wine/baked goods/my undying affection: thank you for reading and editing draft after draft. Each of you has left your mark on the pages of *All the Blues Come Through*, and more importantly, my life. Equally important is the support and guidance I've received from my tribe. Thank you all for lifting me up! Carly Borchert, I'm OK if we're the only two people who think this book is funny. Your edits and heart have elevated this book tremendously. Jessica Carlson, I can always count on my BFF boss lady to get the job done professionally and flawlessly, whether it be as an editor, lawyer, mom, or SCB. Mary Mehr, you are my editing ninja, always willing to strike out a quick revision. More importantly, you are my pizza toppings soulmate. Brooke Brandenborg, my assistant's assistant is sending your assistant's assistant a personalized thank-you C/O BM Productions.

Mom (I love you more), all I ever want to do is make you proud, bring you joy, and make you laugh until you cry. I hope this book delivers at least one of the three. Dan, I can depend on you for rational advice, thorough conversations about my novel characters, and a competitive game of Spitey. I'm so lucky to be your WD. Marcie

273

Kootsikas, your belief in me means more than you will ever know. I'm one of the few who get to call their mother-in-law a close friend. Nick Kootsikas, I can always count on you to ask me for updates on my book and for a cup of coffee (both are equally appreciated!).

Caitlin Moodie, like you, your edits were thoughtful and no-nonsense; I'm always hopeful your confidence will rub off on me. Amy Walsh/Sandy, my friend, mentor (frentor?), and partner-in-sarcasm: thanks for being my sounding board for all things book, business, and pop culture. Catherine Erickson, whether it be an edit, an adventure with the kids, or a laugh, I can count on you. Cassy Lenz, the eternal optimist, your positive outlook and sunny spirit are the antidote to my self-doubt. Rachel Rosen, I'm constantly in awe of your creativity and unapologetic quirkiness; thanks for always reminding me it's OK to be authentically you. Little Doe, your pursuit for knowledge is so admirable and your unshakable faith in your little cousin is unmatched; I'm so glad I get to be your family. Kathy Higgins and Joany Dauphinee, you are my soul cheerleaders and my sheroes.

Thanks to my Harpo lifelines, Stephanie Sorensen, Gia Anayas, Charlie Biskupic, and Stacey Pacini. I'm so grateful our unbelievable shared experience has solidified a lifelong sisterhood (sorry, Biscuit) to one another—we're gloriously stuck together forever. Emily Hagerman, thank you for the time and effort put forth to edit a very early version of the novel; I hope you're not too traumatized! To my Twitter critique partners—Alexis Nicholson and Jessica Palmer—it was a privilege to receive your thoughtful reviews and profound insights, and an honor to edit your own work.

To the ridiculously talented team at Wise Ink—Alyssa Bluhm, Patrick Maloney, and Abbie Phelps—thank you for your leadership, professionalism, and cheerleading. Introducing me to the wizards of words and design that are Amanda Rutter and Holly Ovendon truly breathed life into my manuscript and cover artwork. Thank you all for lending your gifts to nurture my vision.

I wouldn't have allowed myself the luxury of exploring the depths of my imagination without knowing that the most important people in my life—Miloh, Cooper, and Quincy—were taken care of. You have all lovingly sacrificed so much to allow me the time to carry out my dream. Thank you to my husband, Michael Kootsikas, who always managed to find spurts of time for me to run upstairs and escape to the island. Molly Bartzen, you are a national treasure; I'm delighted you and Len are a part of our family. Nick and Marcie Kootsikas, whose house has become the kids' vacation home, thanks for always welcoming the kids to Gramma and Papou's house for lots of M&Ms and love.

Dan and Doris Higgins, thanks for building our family's little haven on Lake Minnewaska; I'm so proud the kids get to make memories among family like I did. Peter and Tracy Kootsikas, thanks for loving my kids like your own and sharing yours with me. Kevin and Margaret Somers-Higgins, nothing makes me happier than watching our kids develop lifelong friendships together. Armon Walker and Molly Dunham, you keep me young and laughing.

To my husband, Michael: You may not be a bookworm, but you certainly devoured countless versions of this book, took copious notes on the elliptical, spoke of my characters as though they were real people, and pushed me to keep writing. You never once faltered from believing in my dream, or me. We really are the real deal, aren't we?

And to my readers, I am honored that you chose to take this journey with me and Ryan.

ABOUT THE AUTHOR

A UW–Madison school of journalism graduate, Metra Farrari landed her dream job right out of college to become a member of the production team for the final three seasons of *The Oprah Winfrey Show*. Chicago proved to be fruitful; Metra picked up a husband, a big-boned (fat) cat, and lifelong friends, but the draw of family called her home to Minnesota. A self-proclaimed naptime novelist, Metra managed to write her debut novel to the soundtrack of the everyday chaos that comes with raising three small children. When not squirreled away in her writing nook, Metra can be found unapologetically consuming reality shows, jogging to the motivational beat of suspenseful audiobooks, and negotiating with her husband for another cat. Metra resides in Minneapolis with her family.